SEARCHING FOR SODYE

BY

A.M. Mensah

Published by New Generation Publishing in 2013

Copyright © A. M. Mensah 2013

First Edition

The author asserts the moral right under the Copyright, Designs and Patents Act 1988 to be identified as the author of this work.

All Rights reserved. No part of this publication may be reproduced, stored in a retrieval system or transmitted, in any form or by any means without the prior consent of the author, nor be otherwise circulated in any form of binding or cover other than that which it is published and without a similar condition being imposed on the subsequent purchaser.

www.newgeneration-publishing.com

New Generation Publishing

Chapter I

They could never pronounce her name correctly the woman concluded to herself after being informed by the voice at the other end of the telephone that Sue had died. African names were not that familiar when Sue was born in the mid 1950's.

"She fell down the stairs this morning and broke her neck."

At the time the woman was not sure if what she was hearing was correct because the words she heard seemed to echo back on themselves since they persistently rebounded about in her mind, as they endeavoured to find ways of presenting themselves to her with coherent meaning. Their message unremittingly ricocheted around in her head. The predominated thoughts in the woman's mind at that precise moment, despite the shock, were that all through Sue's life no one could pronounce her name correctly; not even Sue. The woman was now annoyed because she had desperately wanted to tell Sue how her name should have been pronounced, particularly since she had only recently discovered the correct pronunciation herself. Sodye the woman was told is pronounced So – dy – ee and the name had a mellifluous ring to its pronunciation. She had so wanted to tell Sue how beautiful her Ghanaian name sounded. Now that Sue was dead, the opportunity to have cleared away the life time ambiguity concerning her name was lost forever. The woman detested lost opportunities and now she mourned this wasted one almost as much as she began to grieve Sue's death. Several memories began to formulate in her mind as she began to recall the continuous mis-pronouncement of Sue's name, which meant that the name, Sodye inevitably became shortened to Sue. Perhaps this had resulted in Sue having no knowledge of her own cultural heritage. As a consequence, Sue had abhorred anyone who tried to call her by her African name, because ultimately she possessed no sense of who she was, what she was or where she had come from. Now the woman tried to struggle in that pregnant moment of understanding and pain, to manoeuvre her comprehension around the exact meaning all the words, that were trying to deliver themselves to her. Her mind was still resistant to their full meaning, in its feeble attempt to aggregate the words formidably. She simply did not or could not accept the brevity of the message the words finally conveyed.

"Hello, hello, are you still there?" she thought she heard the voice say from a faraway place. The young woman who was about thirty five years old could not be sure whether she heard the voice or not anymore since a great part of her had disengaged, and closed down as nausea and disbelief wasted no time in wrapping themselves around her in a mummified fashion.

"Yes, yes, I am still here," responded a small sad voice inside her. This voice would have thrown her at any other time because it had been such a long time since she had identified herself with this disconsolate voice, but now invariably it sought to vocalize her feelings. By now and more determinedly, the words had rearranged themselves into an assemblance of logical meaning, in which her comprehension appeared to assimilate in a more manageable way, the full realization that Sue had died that morning. The words had finally, irrevocably negotiated themselves into a coherent enough manner for her to feel the stone cold shiver of death. The eventuality of the words undoubtedly sanctioned what she had tried so hard to deny herself from hearing. Oh how the woman wished that she were anywhere but where the woman was at that précised moment but where else could she be she asked herself. There was no place to hide from the reality of what the woman had heard or indeed felt, so she forced herself to accept the bitter truth, but for a split second, which seemed to encapsulate infinity, she pretended that what she heard did not fit into her everyday reality and therefore could for a few minutes longer not possibly be true.

"The police broke into her flat after I telephoned them, informing them that Sue had not popped around for her dinner yesterday."

"I'll be right over," the young woman found herself saying in her I can always cope voice.

Somehow her numb legs escorted her to the nearest chair where the tears released themselves freely. Time refused to tell the woman how long she sat there as she cried into the well of her own despair and betrayal of life's expectations. When she did finally look at the clock on the wall, as much as she tried to will the hands of the clock to turn backwards to yesterday, they declined. After all Sue had been through, the woman admitted to herself; it had finally come to this. She was stunned; never in her wildest dreams did she think Sue's life would end so suddenly, so cruelly. Death was swift and ruthless in its embrace. There had been no time to say goodbye, only time for remembrance and the one thing the woman did not want to do was to remember but in not wanting to forget Sue, she allowed herself the process of remembering Sue' childhood and that of her sister's.

The sisters childhood came flooding back to her like a huge tidal wave washing over her as the torrent of memories welled up inside her like an overflowing fountain, so she conceded to them. One of her first memories of Sue and her sister was when they were jumping up and down on their parents' dilapidated large double bed which dominated the bed sitting room, the family lived in until they moved on to another one. The bed represented comfort and security to the children and was where they both slept with their parents each night. Besides, during the day there was not much else to do apart from playing and fighting together in the small dreary room. Sue and her sister lived in a solitary protective space carved out of life's mundane routine by their mother who the children perceived as their primary guardian. There were times when Sue longed once again to sit on her mother's lap as she had done so as a baby. At two and a half years old she still felt that her mother's attention should be exclusively her own. But deep down inside her she knew that the chance to be cuddled at leisure again had escaped her prematurely.

"Mummy, mummy, I want to sit on your lap now,' demanded the child as she quickly climbed on to her mother's lap whenever her mother had dozed off for five minutes between her chores.

"Not now Sue," her mother always replied when jostling herself from sleep. "I've got the washing to do and the dinner to make for your father." Sue's mother struggled to get her small daughter off her lap. Sue always cried inconsolably and would go and sit in a corner of the room.

"Don't cry Sue, I must wash the clothes and put them on the washing line before it rains," said her mother sadly. When her girls were babies their mother sought consolation of her plight, knowing that her babies' nappies were some of the whitest and cleanest nappies on the washing line in the yard outside of one of the previous bedsitter the family had lived in; of the entire neighbourhood, and this gave her much pride.

Sue's crying often woke up her father who usually slept during the day because of his irregular night work and nightly social gatherings. Once her father had immediately identified the cause of his interrupted sleep, he proceeded to smack Sue without hesitation. His actions made her cry even more. Her father found the noise and the demands of his young children tiresome and usually projected his anger and frustrations at the world onto his wife and children. This was due to the constant discrimination he faced when trying to find a stable and satisfactory job. The constant rejections in a hostile world, which was not the world he was familiar with because it was not the place of his birth, but rather a world he was forced to endure despite his indignations of the harsh reality of his circumstances.

To the children the shabby bed sitter was marginally warm and cosy despite the constant bitter chill that permeated the room during the winter months. The paraffin heater's attempts to warm up the wintry cold room had been designated by the children's mother as a rather poor one. The heater's challenging task to be the hub of warmth failed miserably due to the cold air constantly seeping through the old window frames. The cold air managed to squash the heater's thin heat back onto itself so the room remained unbearably cold. To counter this, Sue and her sister huddled closer to the paraffin heater, their bodies undoubtedly blocking out the mediocre heat to the rest of the room.

"How many times have I told you children not to sit so close to the heater?"

Their mother found herself scolding her dependents. "If you are not careful it will burn you one day, anyway move away from the heater this very minute, so that I can put these clothes on it now its raining outside."

The rest of the house was similarly as cold and

remote during the winter months. The Victorian house was large and foreboding with its high ceilings that Sue often wondered if she would ever be able to reach when she grew up. The child preferred not to venture outside the bed sitting room because the sharp cold draft went though her thin clothes on too many occasions. Even her shoes seemed not to tolerate as the toddler stepped out in them onto the cold worn lino floor covering. It was the daily ritual of all the occupants in the house to use the communal toilet located outside and about a metre away from the communal kitchen back door. Sue similarly to everyone else in the house, had to make her way down the hallway, through the kitchen and out of the kitchen back door. Most times though both girls were accompanied by their mother. The child found the toilet even colder than the house in those winter months, especially since the door did not reach the top or bottom of the cubicle, which meant the cold wind invariably curled itself around the child's socks, and then wound its way up through her thin clothes into her young body. Invariably both children braced themselves when going to the toilet and more often than not Sue wet herself before she ever got there. It was not that her daughter wet herself which added to her mother's frustrations, she was used to that, it was rather the nightly bedwetting which greeted everyone each morning with its particularly odious smell and the wet patch which left a stain on the family mattress. Someone, the next morning, unceasingly found themselves lying in the wet patch as Sue had managed successfully during the night to negotiate herself towards a drier spot in the bed.

Despite the hardship brought on by the cold and damp and the little money, which was stretched deftly around by the children's mother to buy food, pay bills and sometimes cover other bare necessities, the children felt unassumingly secure. Other times though the children experienced bewilderment; these were times when they accompanied their mother walking the streets with Sue often tagging along behind, when looking for alternative accommodation. The family had been left homeless on a number of occasions prior to their current accommodation due to rent arrears. The children frequently glanced up at their mother when she looked at the notices in the front bay windows of houses, for the ones that did not have placards on them stating; *"No coloureds, no Irish and no dogs welcomed here."* Every so often the children observed their mother knocking on a door. They watched as the landlord or in some cases landlady opened the door to peer at their mother and then at them before closing the door in their mother's face. The children's mother would turn away from the closed doors in despair and persistently sought for less expensive temporary accommodation. The little girls especially resented walking the streets in winter as they were once again reminded of the bitter wind through their thin coats.

"Why do we have to walk the streets?" one of the little girls moaned to their mother on more than one occasion, "can't we just go inside one of the houses and be warm?"

"There are only certain houses that will take us and if we don't keep up the rent payments we will be evicted again just like the last time," the children's mother answered unemotionally.

The summer months brought some relief for the sisters because the warmer weather suited them, what with the deepening of their pale brown complexions to richer ones. Neither child understood why grown ups discarded their dull heavy winter clothes for lighter ones in the unpredictable summer days. The girls observed that women changed into thin flowery dresses and their children were dressed in similar fashion. By contrast the sisters were always determined to keep their cardigans on for as long as possible as they convinced themselves that the majority of summer days were usually just as cold as winter days, and the children's chronic anxieties about feeling cold depressed them tremendously. This affected them obsessively in their reluctance to remove their cardigans unless they absolutely had to, as one child copied the behaviour of the other. The youngsters without exception treated the cooler summer breezes with suspicion since they were convinced autumnal weather lurked immediately around the corner at every possible moment, apart from on the hottest days of summer. The little girls were only ever finally convinced that summer was truly hanging around for longer than a few days when their bed sitting room became humid to the extent, that sharing the sleeping arrangements with their parents became overbearingly suffocating. At these times Sue particularly, did not mind her mother leaving the window slightly open and after a few days of humid temperatures in the low eighties, the children became brave enough to expose their bare arms to the elements. As much as the children adored the continuously long hot summer days, it seemed no time at all when the rich myriad of blossoms and the textured array of summer green leaves that had busied themselves enticingly displaying their glorious splendour to the children; promptly curtseyed away to make way for the more intense colours of copper browns, acute reds and exquisite golden allure of autumn. The hot rich summer's days were replaced by the cooler, colder weather that autumn brought and the children were far wearier off. The sisters seemingly contemplated the fallen leaves sweeping around the edges of their hot summer world that eventually took them back once again to their cold, bitter one.

Sue's greatest joy was going shopping with her mother and her older sister. The little girl was very fond of her big sister whom she felt was very protective towards her. The child had been given for the Christmas before her third birthday a surprised present of a doll from her father who managed to scrape together enough money from the odd jobs that he did intermittedly. Sue had marvelled at the doll's blue eyes and blond curly hair that sprung out from its head as if from a colander because its scalp had tiny holes in it where the wiry hair was threaded. She did not quite understand how she had broken the doll when the child had wanted to see inside the doll's head to establish how its hair grew. Her curiosity had also been aroused because while her own hair was black, the doll's hair was blond and she found this fascinating. The doll was not an inexpensive toy so her father became angry at his daughter for breaking it and as a consequence had smacked his little daughter. Sue, in turn smacked the doll even though it now lay on the carpet with its head broken off. She did this to see if despite being broken it would cry tears like her mother did whenever her father assaulted her mother. At the time her father had shouted to her, "What do you think, that money grows on trees?"

Sue instantly imagined money growing on trees but then remembered, to her disappointment, that she had never seen any money growing on trees. After that episode her curiosity had extended to her elder sister's doll. The doll her sister was given had also commanded huge fascination for her, since it could walk and talk whilst its head turned from right and left. Neither she nor her sister had ever seen such a mechanical toy before, never mind owned one. They found themselves both delighted and fearful of something which was, animated enough to be very much out of their control. Sue's curiosity got the better of her again and within a couple of hours her sister's doll lay on the bed sitting room floor with its arms and legs spluttered about by the bed. Her eldest sister cried at her loss because she understood with her five year old wisdom that this novelty doll was irreplaceable. She lamented to her mother that she had hardly had any time to enjoy her new doll before Sue had destroyed the evidence of her having ever own such a beautiful toy, even though the doll looked more like their mother than themselves.

Many evenings, fellow Ghanaians and several Nigerian friends visited the girls' father. On these evenings highlife music was played as loud as possible. Their father also loved blues music and the sisters could sing most of the words to Harry Belafonte's *"Little Island in the Sun."* They were captivated by the gramophone player and watched as the dog on the record label spun around as the music played while almost making them dizzy.

The children's parents were attractive in their difference. Their father being small framed with a certain finesse about him. His black skin was silky smooth and unblemished; the children's father had arrived in Britain from Ghana a few years earlier. The children's mother had long black hair worn in a plait that hung down her back. Her pale alabaster skin and blue eyes were distinctively typical of her Irish appearance. The children assumed that their parents' skin tones were irrelevant as was theirs.

Sue and her sister always accompanied their mother to the local shops to buy groceries. They never tired of leaving their home when the weather was conducive to such outings. Each time their mother went shopping she struggled with the shopping bags especially when climbing the steps to their front door. These times Sue when following her mother up the steps could barely climb such steps herself, particularly if she was given the responsibility of carrying a bag for her mother as well. On the whole the little girls viewed the shopping trips to the local corner shop as an adventurous outing. At such times the sisters were so eager in their desire for the few pennies' worth of sweets that their mother sometimes bought them, they did not always have the patience to observe the activities in the street they lived on. The corner shop held great interest to the children as they endeavoured to clarify in their mind, the role of the shopkeeper and the significance of the numerous tins of products that were displayed on the countless shelves, never mind the jars of sweets. Every so often the children could not help but notice the shopkeeper getting angry with their mother and the children could not comprehend the reason.

"Look madam, why do you have to bring your children with you to the shop?" he repeated many times. "I do not allow children into my shop."

"Well, I cannot leave them at home on their own," the children's mother replied hopelessly.

"But they are always touching things and are quite unruly," snapped the shopkeeper.

"It seems like there is no pleasing you, is there?" the children's mother responded in a tired, exasperated voice,"they are simply lively children!"

"If you cannot control your youngsters, then don't come here again," the shopkeeper retorted, uncompromisingly.

They both knew that this was the nearest corner shop within walking distance.

"Oh stop whingeing, you two!" the mother told the girls, as she turned her attention towards her children who were by now bored with the opaque discussions adults seem to have, especially since they had not been given any sweets yet. Both the sisters knew that some of the conversation referred to themselves in some manner but their need for entertainment and immediate self-satisfaction that only sweets could give them, was the only pre-occupation on their young minds at the time. The self-preservation of their mother saw her leave the shop as soon as she has paid for her shopping after apologising to the shopkeeper for her young daughters' behaviour.

Sue, similarly to her sister was given her one-penny lollypop which she habitually sucked for as long as possible. This was the competitive game the sisters played together to keep themselves entertained. The one who managed not to finish eating her lollypop before the other was considered the winner. Invariably Sue always discovered that her lollypop was the first to be devoured since she was left with the lollypop stick before her sister. This usually made her very cross especially since her sister refused adamantly to give her a lick of her half finished lollypop, no matter how much she begged or bribed her.

It was not unusual for the children's mother to stop for a chat and a gossip with her neighbours and friends on the way home. Similar to the children's background, the local neighbourhood in northwest London consisted of many immigrant families. These were mainly families from Africa, the Caribbean, Ireland and Southern Europe. Sue and her sister were two of the very few mixed race children in the neighbourhood and, so were sometimes considered to be of another nationality. Frequently Sue was mistaken to be from a Maltese background while her sister was considered to be from a Caribbean one.

The children adored their mother who they perceived as kind and loving and whom they felt was their only true ally. Their mother represented a sense of stability, compassion and with purpose while the children's father on the other hand represented complexity. The children were ambiguous about their father because of his argumentative and violent behavior towards their mother which, frightened them and consequentially left an indelible mark on them. Apart from the episodes of anger, frustration and violence towards their mother, the children's life was without incident until one night, when the shouting and screaming the children heard outside the bed sitter door woke them up. Sue shook with fright and sought solace from her older sister because her mother was not in the room. Their mother's lack of presence in the room left an empty void which scared her children. At some point during the confusion the sisters were able to distinguish their mother's screams which was coming from the kitchen. Both children crouched in one corner of the bed hugging each other as they tried to protect themselves from hearing the screams of their mother. The girls' eyes were full of panic as they desperately tried to cope with the confusion of that terrible night. These episodes were to become more frequent as time went on. That night their father came back into the room with the children's mother sobbing uncontrollably.

"I have told you time and time again that is not how you cook Ghanaian food. Do you expect me to eat that rubbish?" he shouted raising his hand again.

"No, no please, not in front of the children, think of the children Emanuel, think of the children," their mother said, struggling for breathe. After what seemed like an eternity for the children, their father left the room; a few moments afterwards the front door slammed shut. The young mother immediately ran crying towards the bed while the two little girls instantly climbed all over their mother as she lay there sobbing as they tried to comfort her as well as themselves.

Many times the young sisters played out in the streets or went to the local park to play. When the two little girls came home for lunch, usually the older sister fed them both because it was not unusual for their mother to be out. There were times when the bruises on their mother's face and arms were visible enough for the children to make a comment.

"Mummy, what's that red mark on your face?" Sue asked.

"Oh that's where I bumped into a lamp post when I wasn't looking properly, I must need glasses," was her mother's reply.

The children were taken to church every Sunday by their mother but the girls found church a strange place since they were not allowed to play or make any kind of noise whatsoever. Sitting on the benches motionless proved impossible for the children. The three and five year olds could neither sit still nor keep quiet as they scrambled up and down the pews chasing each other.

"Can't you control your darkies?" the sisters heard a man whisper harshly to their mother one time. Each child had a faint suspicion that the man was referring to them but since he had used the word 'darkies' and they both knew their own names, neither sister was sure whom he was referring to.

"Now children, please keep quiet because you are making too much noise," the children's mother had told them in a strained voice. The Mass seemed endless as the priest's Latin dialogue and the congregational responses went over the heads of the young children which meant that their attention span became even more diminished as boredom gave way to more pranks. Outside the church, each child resumed clutching the hand of their mother's as the two of them walked beside her.

"I wish you children would behave in church!" scolded their mother endlessly,"it's the only place I can get away from everything and seek peace of mind."

"It's not our fault mummy," protested the oldest child defensively,"we can't understand what the priest was saying."

"He's saying the Mass in Latin that's why," replied their mother.

"So how are we supposed to understand him then?" asked her eldest daughter as she looked up admiringly at her mother who was wearing an elegant 1950's suit, with its tight waistline and pencil straight skirt. Both children loved playing with their mother's long black hair, pulling it over their own short afro hair and pretending it was their own hair. The children's mother always dressed smartly for church and ensured her children did by dressing them as best she could.

One day Sue was playing with her sister in the bed sitter while their mother washed their clothes in the communal kitchen.

"Now, you are coming with us?" Sue heard a very stern, authoritative voice shout.

"No, I am not coming with you." Sue distinctly heard her father reply.

"Come on let's handcuff him now," an unknown voice said. The commotion outside the bed sitter when on for quite some time before they heard their father shout;

"I'll be coming back for you girls!"

With that the front door slammed shut while the bed sitter door opened and three people in uniform entered the room. These were two policemen and a policewoman.

"Come on you children you are coming with us to

the police-station."

The sisters were even more terrified but could not articulate their fear other than by holding one another tightly, yet each sister was alone in her own thoughts watching the traumatic events unfolding before their eyes. A wet patch spread under the legs of the sisters but it did not matter who had wet themselves that was the least of their concerns. One of the policemen lifted Sue up as she looked over his shoulder at her sister who was being led out of the room by the policewoman. Both girls cried hopelessly as they were put in the back of a Black Maria car.

It was completely and utterly incomprehensible to the oldest child's five year old mind that her mother was dead. Even though she tried to push her imagination to its furthest point in her mind, the youngster's mind still could not bring itself to a place where it could understand what death was or meant since the child had no concept of death at all. Her limited years in the world had so far no references to which she could imagine or understand the notion of death.

"Your mother is dead," the child heard the young policewoman say to her again when the girls had been at the police station for the best part of the afternoon and evening. The word death seemed to have an atmosphere, an identity of its own which was all consuming. Death seemed to take up a place in the room and settle there so in her mind the child intuitively knew that it must be something final.

"What is death?" Sue had asked her sister who stood there silently when the policewoman, suddenly left the room after being summoned.

"I don't know."

"Do you understand what I am saying?" the policewoman asked the children when she returned to the room. "Please try not to cry."

"But I am hungry," replied the elder child.

"So am I," said Sue with tears running down her face.

"When did you last eat?" enquired the policewoman.

"I don't remember," answered the eldest child timidly.

"You don't remember when you last ate?"

"No."

"I've get you something to eat quickly then, do you like spaghetti?"

"What is that?" asked Sue.

"You don't know what spaghetti is?" queried the policewoman sounding astonished.

"No!" the children replied together.

"Never mind, I will get you some and I promise you will like it," said the policewoman gently as she hurried away again.

"I didn't understand it when the police lady says mummy's gone to her death, where is that?" enquired Sue.

"I think it's a place where someone never comes back from again," her older sister whispered after a long silence.

Sue looked at her sister's hazel brown eyes and saw the isolation and loneliness in them but failed to see the fearful pain of abandonment in her own smoky brown ones, although the reflection of each child's pain left them with a shared burden. The little girls watched the only world they knew break up before them like a jigsaw puzzle whose pieces had been thrown up into the air by an unknown hand, promptly sending pieces in complete disarray. Both girls found themselves hoping that the day could start again and end like it always did with their mother kissing each one of her small daughters' goodnight. They wished the day might rearrange itself in a nice safe orderly fashion similar to all the other days, but it did not so both girls had to accept that they were in a strange place the local police station without either one of their parents. The police station was as impersonal and empty as the new world around them, now that it was devoid of their mother.

Sue and her sister sat in a room on their own for what seemed like an eternity. They said nothing to each other because there was nothing to say, each lost in their own mental prison of incomprehension about what death implied. The loss of their mother meant that they had no one to look out for them. Life ahead seemed unfathomable and confronting this reality was overwhelming. They focused their attention at the peeling wallpaper on the ceiling which seemed to nosedive straight down at them They appeared to take on a life of its own by bubbling up all knobbly and uneven which grated against their teeth forcing them to grid them uncontrollably as they wanted desperately to scratch off the uneven wallpaper so that it could be made nice and smooth again.

The two children did not know where the Policewoman went, but a timeless period of disorientation preoccupied them until she returned to the room with two bowls of spaghetti. All the children remember was eating strings of pasta which tasted very good. Eventually a social worker came and took Sue away. The older child did not say goodbye to Sue because in the confusion and in their lack of understanding of the unfolding events, all the two sisters heard was: "We will have to separate them because the care homes only have a place for one child in each." Each child cried softly to themselves on their way to their separate institutions.

Chapter II

Sue's eldest sister experienced several temporary placements before she arrived at North Mount Place which was the largest of the care homes she had been admitted to so far. Arriving at North Mount Place also meant that she was to start another primary school again and she wondered how Sue had fared. Had her little sister been moved about as much as she had been? Sometimes she did not complete one term before she was moved to another school. The child did not know the whereabouts of her sister although she was now six and a half years old.

The first night the little girl was admitted at North Mount Place she was reprimanded. The child was caught talking to another little girl in the bed beside her after the dormitory lights were switched off. She had arrived quite late in the evening and had only time to eat a little supper before the staring eyes of hostile adults when she was ordered to bed, and all she had wanted to know from the other little girl was what North Mount Place was like since, she found herself sleeping in a dormitory with more unfamiliar children. It was the social contact she wanted with another child in order to reassure her because she still was not accustomed to sharing a dormitory, and missed her little sister and her parents tremendously. Being shifted from one place to another meant that she felt extremely demoralised although the child could not describe adequately how she felt so could not begin to share her distress with anyone else, not even the other children who all seemed very strange to her. Out of desperation she had tried talking to the little girl about her situation but the other little girl did not understand so they talked for a little while about North Mount Place.

"Shut up, you new child," barked the rather

matronly looking woman who sat at a table in the hall outside the dormitory double doors. Sue's sister did not help but notice that the light in the hall made scary shadows on the walls of the now dimly light dormitory as she looked over the white starch sheet at the sleeping children. The child was undoubtedly afraid of the care assistant who appeared indifferent and rude.

"I hate night duty," the other residential care worker stated. "I'd much rather be at home with my husband and cats. If it wasn't for the money I have to work for to pay for our holiday this year, I wouldn't bother doing these shifts and quite frankly I much prefer doing night duty at the old people's home across town. I can't stand children at the best of times!"

"Oh I don't mind covering on night duty at children's homes as long as they are seen and not heard and I get well paid!" replied the matron.

"I've never wanted children and I haven't got them thank goodness. They are more trouble than they are worth and look, the parents of these children couldn't even look after their own children," said her colleague.

"Well the Irish women have so many of them anyway," remarked the matron.

"If you don't shut up you new girl, yes you the dark one, I will make you stand outside the dormitory doors all night if you continual whispering."

Sue's sister could not help herself but continued to talk quietly in the hope that she could whisper away her anxieties and fears. However in no time at all she found herself standing against the wall of the hall opposite the matron's table.

"You can stand where I can see you and if you make any noise I will give you a hard smack on your legs again," the matron had informed the little girl.

The child stood still in the dark lonely corridor in her bare feet and night dress staring blankly at the magnolia wall in front of her. She was petrified that she would be smacked again if she so much as made a noise of any description. The psychological fear of being smacked a second time was far greater than the smack itself to the little girl. To combat the boredom and the fear the child fantasized about her family. She wondered what had happened to her father and younger sister and wondered why her father had not come for his daughters like he had promised. Her feelings of utter rejection and abandonment were indescribable as was the overall loss of her family. The hostile environment the child was placed in forced her to repress the distress she acutely felt because there was simply no one to share it with. When she was given permission to go back to bed she took her insurmountable grief with her. Undoubtedly the child was traumatized by the prolonged stress she had experienced since she had been forcibly separated from her family and although she had no frame of reference she felt similar to an inmate who had entered a prison for a crime she had no recollection of committing. Every day Sue's sister earnestly tried to make sense of the bizarre circumstances she found herself in, but she could not because she yearn to go home and resume her normal family life again. Each night the little girl cried herself to sleep inconsolably because she missed so much her mother's love and kisses and her sibling's affections. During the days as much as she could, the girl shrunk away from the care assistants; avoiding contact with them as much as possible because she was so terrified of them. She saw them as hostile and scary since she was not used to dealing directly with the hostility her mother had daily contact with, whenever the family had stepped out of their bedsitter. Her mother had been the constant buffer, the persistent defender of her children. The care assistants were indifferent to the little girl and surprisedly quickly she became used to their indifference towards her. The child assumed that it was the normal attitude of all adults to behave in such a manner.

"Right you get out of your bed and go and stand at the dormitory door, now," bellowed the matron on the second night. Fright made Sue's sister jump out of bed immediately as she had done the previous night. She thought that she would be slapped on the legs as she had been the first night but mercifully she was not this time.

The only place that gave the child joy was the large playroom. It had the biggest dolls' house imaginable and although she was shy and taciturn, nonetheless she scrabbled to play with the tiny dolls' and with the furniture whenever she could get past the bigger children. The dolls' house allowed the child to drift off once more to her favourite place of day dreams and fantasies that filled the vacuum within her for another brief moment; so much so that she was able to forget the depressing circumstances she now existed in. Playing her imaginary games was her way of gaining some peace of mind and semblance of her broken life especially when the bigger children chided and bullied her. The child was able to recreate the family life she had lost by playing with the dolls, house. The little girl was able to recreate her family life with the toys in an idealistic fashion. She incessantly fantasized that the policewoman had made a mistake and that her mother was still alive. Sue's sister on numerous occasions waited cautiously near the front door of North Mount Place hoping that somehow she could be rescued from her predicament by her mother. The child's nightly dreams were of her home life not of the care homes.

"Where do you come from?" the other children asked her initially and always new arrivals were curious to the child's background.

"How come most of your hair is frizzy and coarse but some of it is silky and of the tiniest curls?" they asked inquistively. The six year old stumbled over her words to explain to the other children where she had lived before North Mount Place.

"I am from London," the child told them.

"But you are not white," the children responded.

"But my mother is white," stated the youngster trying to afford herself some validity in this new world. In time some of the children did not appear to mind her skin colour while others were more obsessive as they continued with their hostility and intimidation. Sue's sister never sort support or comfort from the care assistants since their initial reaction to her had been so negative, although one she remembered had read her bedtime stories whenever he had been on the night shift but after a while he was replaced by someone else.

"Your mother isn't white because if she is why aren't you?" some of the children kept coming at the six year old with their accusations that she was a fraud. The little girl wished with all her might that she could magically conjure up her mother to speak on her behalf. Just like in the fairy tale books when the fairy godmother appeared suddenly and came to the rescue of the child in need. If only, she thought, her mother was to appear as her fairy godmother now so that she too could be rescued from her tormentors. But then she remembered that her mother was dead.

"And where is your dad from?" the children's demanding questions were relentless.

"My dad is from Ghana," the six year old answered in a small frighten voice. "Why doesn't he come and visit you?" one of the older children asked the child. "He will come and take me home one day when he's collected my little sister first," the child replied hoping that her wish would become her reality.

She missed her father's food enormously and the social evenings when her father's friends arrived and talked well into the night, when Sue and herself fell asleep with the light on night after night either to the murmurs of the voices as they spoke *tri;* a language neither children was familiar with or to the sounds of Fats Waller's *"I left my freedom on blueberry hill....."* His daughters learnt not to touch their father's records because they could so easily be broken. Their father treated his records like precious diamonds polishing them repeatedly. She was nostalgic for all that had been good in her brief life so far and she longed for the warmth, security and love, which were now denied her.

The little girl endured the unexplained first day at another new school where she found herself in a room with children's pictures on the walls. Something she did not remember noticing at the previous schools, perhaps it was because she was not at these schools long enough to feel remotely settled to assimilate the little children's scrawled pictures which hung on all the walls, amongst the huge colourful letters of the alphabet. The times she fell over in the playground and one or both of her knees had bled, while she looked frantically around for someone to run to for comfort and realising very quickly that no one was there for her. Instead, she watched the cuts on her knees heal themselves in their own time and nursed and comforted herself the best she could. She was one child amongst many whether at school or at North Mount Place so she quickly adapted by losing her single identity to the group. The child was not bothered or interested in her lessons because her primary need was to be reassured and her disorientation minimised, but this over riding need was not met. A loving familiar face was so much what the little girl wanted to greet her from school each day, similarly to the other children whose parents waited for them every day, as they hugged and kissed them while taking an interest in their daily school activities. The youngster rehearsed over and over in her young mind what she would do if her mother were waiting. She would run into her arms and kiss and cuddle her and never let her go. But no matter how much she day dreamed that her mother was waiting at the school gates with Sue, it was not to be. At the end of the school day one of the care assistants waited to take her back to North Mount Place.

"Hey, do you want to see a dead rat this evening because if you do come to the fields with us tonight; some have been left partially eaten."

Sue's sister followed the other children with trepidation to the playing fields at the back of the care home that night, to see for herself the partially eaten rodents. The faired haired boy who had initially invited her was with a group of older children who had lined up for tea that evening. This proposition seemed really exciting to the child who wanted more than anything to be accepted by the older children.

Despite North Mount Place regimented routine, along with the rest of the children, Sue's sister experienced great freedom when out playing in the massive grounds of the large institutional care home. Although the freedom of the outdoors was not quite the same as the repetitious jumping on her parents bed or the make believe games she used to play with her little sister or, the trips to the local park, the grounds made her feel safe and secure because she could run around with some of the other children, without the care assistants haranguing her with their constant scolding or derogatory remarks. By now the child had identified the children who were friendly and those who were bullies. The children she felt comfortable with, she spent many evenings playing conker games and examining dead mice left by overfed owls. The winter evenings were dark and cold but this added to the excitement and the child loved bonfire night when baked potatoes were passed around and fire works set off. Often before the evening meal groups of children chatted about all sorts of things while outside in the grounds.

"You know I saw a witch lurking up the chimney in my house where I used to live with my mum and dad," one of the children told the rest of the group that had formed a semi circle made up of about ten children of varying ages.

"Oh don't be silly Keith," replied an eleven-year-old girl called Jean.

"There are no such things as witches; they are only in fairytale books,"

affirmed Sandra.

"Oh yes there are," Keith insisted, "They are horribly black and nasty, just like everything else that is black and evil."

"Hm, you're not such a big boy if you still believe in witches and fairytales, that's girls stuff anyway," declared Alan who was roughly the same age as Sandra.

Both Sandra and Alan seemed so grown up and mature compared to the other children. They fascinated the young child because she had never interacted with ten year olds before and they seemed to know everything even the gossip of the care staff. They also appeared to accept their parentless situation even though Alan was regularly back and forth to North Mount Place which seemed like every other month.

"I don't care if my mother cannot look after me anymore," Alan said defensively each time he came back to North Mount Place, as he tried very hard not to cry. At these time Sue' sister felt the tears swell up in her own eyes but she wasn't sure whether it was in empathy for Alan or because of her own motherless situation. Sometimes she eavesdropped on the gossip of the bigger children. The child was curious as to what all the whispering was about between some of the older children and some of the care staff. Whenever one of the younger children tried to find out what the gossiping was about, they were told, "Oh you are far too young to know about the birds and the bees."

The child's curiosity tried to ascertain what the secret of the birds and the bees were but this was met with complete opposition and a wall of silence.

Anyway in time she decided that whatever the birds and bees did apart from making honey or singing, was probably boring which reaffirmed to her, that when children grew up they eventually became boring adults. There was no desire then on her part to grow up and remaining a child for as long as was possible seemed a better option.

For the sake of self-preservation Sue' sister assimilated into the institutionalised life that all the children at North Mouth Place had to unwittingly subscribe to. The meals were dull and bland and school dinners more appealing. The child queued up in line with the other noisy children and learnt to accept what was given to her and appreciate it. It was during her time at North Mount Place that the child started to get headaches regularly which the care assistants dismissed as insignificant. At seven years old the child was left to battle against the overpowering piecing head pains. Whenever the headaches started she tried in vain to alert one of the care assistants to help her particularly before the headache became full blown. "Oh it's only a headache so I don't know why you are making such a fuss child," she was repeatedly informed by one of the many non-descript care staff. They all seemed a blur of faces to her in their indifference and callousness, "so run along and stop bothering me."

The headaches got worse and she became physically sick with nausea and cried with the pain.

"Miss, miss can I go to the dormitory and lie down," she begged the care assistants who was on shift at the time of her all consuming migraine.

"You know the rules, no lying on the beds after they have been made in the mornings that is the rules."

"Please then can I sit on my chair beside my bed."

The care staff only relented after the child had vomited on the floor one time too many.

"Clean that mess up and then go and sit on your chair in the dormitory, and how many times have I told you to go to the toilet if you are feeling sick."

"Sorry miss, I won't do it again, I promise."

"Go to the dormitory where it is quiet and the little headache will go away in no time," said another in her unwise statement. No child was ever allowed to lie on their bed once they had been made during the day. The child fathomed out that her headaches' must be bad enough for the care assistants' to finally let her sit on her chair in the dormitory whenever the headaches started. Sue's sister learnt to endure the migraines that became more and more regular and more and more violent. The child in her anguish struggled mentally to tolerate the throbbing pain in her head and the more she dreaded the pain, the more the migraines raged.

"Miss, miss." she called out to the care staff on duty one day, when she could no longer tolerate the on coming migraine. "My head is hurting again," she told her. "Well you know what to do then, go and sit quietly in the dormitory until the headache has gone." was always the reply. The reply was sometimes said in a more kindly tone than other times, but by the time the child had alerted the staff to her plight, she no longer cared how the permission to go to the dormitory sounded or was granted, because her only concern by then was that she only hoped that she could make the nearest toilet before she was sick. The toilet bowel was the child's reassurance that she would not have to clean up her own vomit because she had made it to the toilet bowl rather than the floor. The bile sometimes came instead of the vomit. Loads of it and she had to separate the bile which hang from her mouth all the way down to the toilet basin with her fingers. When her young mind satisfied itself that all the bile had expelled itself she washed her face and hands and then went and sat quietly in the dormitory; drawing the curtains to block out the daylight as she sat there watching the blinding shadows dancing in front of her eyes. The little girl never knew how many hours she sat on the chair because the nausea overwhelmed her so much. During the day she refused all meals and she sat reclusively alone keeping her perplexing thoughts to herself. Counting the beds over and over again was one of her past times that were a means of distracting herself from the pain. When it was time for bed, she crawled into it and slept off the migraine.

"Now you, your social worker is visiting you today," the youngster was informed every so often. The child was not sure why social workers came to see her or what role they played in her young life. All she knew was that a very posh lady arrived once in a while and talked to her about how she was doing in a matter of fact voice. The child always told them that she was fine because there was nothing else to say and she was afraid to say anything negative just in case the care staff bullied her after the social worker had left. She viewed the social worker as the harbinger of news about her little sister because sometimes they informed her how Sue was doing. On this occasion her social worker told her: "You will be moving from here shortly because we have found you a foster family in Dover which will be near your sister.

You do want to be near your little sister don't you?"

"Yes."

The child had mixed feelings about moving again because she had become so used to the routine at North Mount Place but she desperately wanted to be reunited with her sister. The child was very frightened to disclose her fear of upheaval and being moved to another unfamiliar place again. "Well then, in March you will leave here."

Sue's sister was not so bothered then as March seemed in the long distant future. The child had recently enjoyed Christmas at North Mount Place with all its paraphernalia, which she had never quite known before. She had quickly discovered that the care staff had their favourite children. These tended to be the pretty blond blue-eyed girls in particular. The 'favourites' as they were called, received special privileges these included, lots of praise, hugs and kisses that Sue's sister never received.

Christmas time was an infectious time for all the children especially on Christmas Eve when they were each given a Christmas stocking.

"What's this for?" the child had enquired to one of the older children.

"The stocking is where Father Christmas puts your presents in when he climb's down chimney at midnight silly!" was the reply.

Christmas morning ensured all the children were up early even those who had tried to stay awake for as long as possible on Christmas Eve.

"If you don't go to sleep now," the night duty care staff had warned the excited children, "Father

Christmas will not bring you any toys tomorrow."

By then all the children who had jumped out of bed to hurriedly go to the toilet, got back into bed as soon as possible and those who has tried to stay awake in the hope that they would at least hear Father Christmas were fast asleep long before midnight.

The child discovered on Christmas morning a variety of parcels in all shapes and sizes at the bottom of her bed . Tearing off the paper, she found beauty accessories for the dolls she was given; pink hairbrushes, combs and dainty pink mirrors. There were also hairbrushes for her too but brushing or combing her own hair presented a problem which no one could sort out. She was told that her hair was far too difficult to brush or comb because the child was told that her hair was coarse compared to the other girls' hair. "Oh why can't your hair be like the other girls' hair which is completely soft and silky", she heard them say accusingly, as they used soft bristle hairbrushes and very fine thin hair combs which constantly broke when used on her hair. The child always suffered the pain of her hair being pulled and tugged at. "Your hair is so course and tough that it is difficult to do anything with it." The little girl was fed up being told off about her hair type in, 'and it's your fault' tone of voice by every one of the care staff who happened to be on duty at the time.

In order to resolve the aggravation of looking after the little girl's hair, it was unanimously decided by the care staff, to cut the child's hair close to her scalp similarly to a boys' haircut and that style remained. Subsequently the child was teased by the other children including the schoolchildren who told her that she looked more like a boy.

One day during the Christmas holidays, a huge coach arrived. "Now hurry up children the coach has arrived and none of you are ready yet," one of the care staff could be heard to say.

"Now stop mucking around and get ready for the pantomime," instructed another. Sue's sister did what she was told and went to get her coat on. Following the other children she climbed the huge steps into the coach and was told where to sit. It seemed Christmas has brought with it a relaxed mood to all those in the coach because the child could not help but notice that even the care staff seemed friendlier. Some of them joked and laughed with the children while a couple of the women even flirted with the coach driver and his co driver and this she was amazed by. The child managed at some point to drag her attention away from this interaction least of all she might be accused of staring although, she wondered as she looked out of the window again as to whether flirting had anything to do with the birds and the bees. The youngster could not believe to what extent the care staff was fooling around and this equally surprised her.

The pantomime was fun and although the group were about half way down the middle rows in the stalls, Sue's sister had an excellent view of the show.

"Come dear, come and sit on my lap so I can cuddle you," one of the care staff said jovially to one of the smaller children with blond wavy hair. How Sue's sister wished she could shrink and become small enough so that she too could sit on one of the care assistants' lap. The child also wished she had blond wavy hair because she could not help but feel a mixture of jealously, hurt and envy at the rejection and denial of a cuddle. Although most of her attention was on the show, she often found herself staring at the other children sitting comfortably on the lap of one of the care staff.

"We now have some special children here for this

afternoon's matinee from North Mount Place care home," the child was surprised to hear one of the actors up on the stage mention her care home. "A well known national newspaper has given free tickets for this show to the children whose parents cannot look after them, so all the children from North Mount Place, wave your hands so we can see you," the actor continued. All the children put their arms up and waved to the actors and actresses on stage. For a brief moment they felt special in their quasi-celebratory status.

It was dark when the care group emerged from the theatre. The multi coloured bright lights gave out a magical hue to the night. "If you all hurry up and get back into the coach quickly, the coach driver said he would drive us to the

West End so that we can see the Christmas lights in Regent Street because we are very close by," a care assistant announced happily.

Another care assistant starting checking the names of all the children as they boarded the coach again. Sweets and chocolates were handed around by the national newspaper representatives of whom some had accompanied the children on the coach trip.

"Here you are angel have some of these sweets," one of them said to her gently.

The child also visited the cinema with her placement at North Mount Place. Along with the other children she had waited in the cinema's reception until the usherette led the group of children into the darkened auditorium. The child sat in one of the seats in the numerous rows facing a huge red curtain while wondering what was behind it. The interior design of the cinema was moderate in its decoration compared to the elaborate curtains. Eventually the curtains' were pulled back and an image of a cock announced Pathe news to those watching the screen. Sue's sister was intrigued. The film was, *'The Wizard of Oz'* and the child were fascinated by the huge black and white images on screen that later gave way to colour ones. She sat in her seat completely transfixed, so much so that the wicked witch of the West appeared absolutely real to her more so than the other characters. After the film the child left the cinema afraid to go out into the evening air because she was sure that the wicked witch of the West was following her. All the way back to North Mount Place she was haunted by the witch and felt far too afraid the tell anyone of her fear of witches that she took this unshared fear with her to bed. Immediately her nightmares claimed her as their hostage because all night the child hardly slept for fear that the witch would swoop down and do unimaginable things to her. The child fretfully observed the night shadows present all their gory images to her seven-year-old mind as she tossed and turned. She was relieved when she saw the wintry morning sun begin to creep in through the curtains and cast its bright light against the dark shadows exposing them back to their original harmless states, which were pieces of furniture in the sparse dormitory. The nightmares finally relented when the daytime migraines made it impossible for the child to stay awake at night. In time the child outgrew her nightmares as well as her belief in fairies.

"Right you," the care assistant pointed at the child one Friday afternoon, "your social worker is coming tomorrow to take you to Dover."

Her social worker arrived after breakfast the following morning. The child continued to have mixed feelings about leaving the large home because despite the indifference of the care assistants, it had nevertheless been home and she was now so used to its particular routines that she feared another change.

The child did not remember much of the car journey

to Dover only that she had been persistently car sick, which meant that the social worker had to keep stopping the car to get another brown paper bag for the child to be vomit in.

"Look, look," said the social worker, trying to distract the little girl as they arrived in Dover, "look at the white cliffs, over there." By now she could smell the clear sea air and this was refreshing compared to the petrol fumes and it was only then that the child's pessimistic mood began to lift to one of more optimism.

The car pulled up at a row of terrace houses, a few streets away from the seafront. The child was struck by the narrowness of the houses and how close in proximity they were to each other in comparison to the vast grounds of North Mount. Her social worker knocked on the door of one of the houses which was opened by a rather plumpish middle-aged lady who stood looking down at the child. The lady wore a pinafore over her dress and had a scarf tied in a front knot covering her rather untidy hair.

"Hello," said the social worker, "you must be Mrs. Gregory?"

"Oh yes I am dear," replied Mrs. Gregory, looking at the social worker.

"Oh isn't she simply adorable," Mrs. Gregory exclaimed looking back at the little girl.

The child instantly looked around wondering whom the lady was referring to but since she could not see any other little girl she was confused because it never occurred her that Mrs. Gregory might be referring to herself.

They entered into the small cosy house where an open fire dominated the sitting room, which was decorated with two floral armchairs and a settee.

The little girl's shyness became even more pronounced because Mrs. Gregory appeared so extroverted and demonstrative.

"Now you little one, this is going to be your new home, so run along and explore the house." Mrs. Gregory told her new foster child. The little girl got up slowly and left the sitting room not really knowing what to do.

Living with Mrs. Gregory and her family released a feeling of carefree freedom for the child, which she hungrily embraced.

"Now you lovely thing, we are going out shopping today to buy you some nice clothes", Mrs. Gregory told the child a week afterward she had arrived. "These clothes you have with you are shabby and ordinary for such a pretty little girl."

The child could not help but giggled to herself as she looked up into Mrs. Gregory kind eyes and as the days went by she became less shy and more comfortable particularly as Mrs. Gregory's behaviour revealed that she was rather laid back and quite eccentric. The child was astounded by some of the things her new foster mother did or said.

"I don't know what kind of place you were in before you came here," she commented, "but you are so withdrawn and timid as if you are frightened to say boo to a goose which is not natural for a child in my view, and I didn't particularly care for that social worker. She's a stuck up middle class nitwit with no idea whatsoever about children dear. What you need is love and lots of it and I sure know that you haven't had a lot of that where you were before." So the child found herself in a children's clothes shop, which had the most exquisite clothes she had ever seen. Mrs. Gregory dressed her foster child in the most gorgeous colours and people stopped them in the streets to comment on her appearance.

"Oh she does look lovely," a passer-by would say when the child went out with Mrs. Gregory, who was more than happy to show her off which she did at every opportunity.

"Such a pretty coloured child," another passer -by commented.

"Where is she from?" the child heard almost daily.

"Oh she was abandoned by her mother and father, her mother being Irish and her father was from somewhere in Africa." Mrs. Gregory always replied

"She looks just like a little doll," someone else said.

With all this attention and comments the little girl did not know quite what to make off them. She became instantly shy again as she hung her head and stared at the ground. This stance she had learnt at North Mount Place whenever she was told off for something she did not know she had done or for things that confused her.

Mrs. Gregory's family consisted of her husband who was a chimneysweeper and so was their son Trevor who lived with his parents as his wife Sylvia did. It was not long before the child thrived at Mrs. Gregory's home because the family teased her endlessly and played with her at every opportunity. The little girl loved the attention she was given and Trevor being over six foot four often threw the little girl high up in the air which was an activity she enjoyed.

"Trevor looks very nice?" the little girl told Mrs Gregory one evening when her son had arrived downstairs from the two up two down house on a Saturday evening. It was a new experience for the child to feel confident enough to speak to an adult without twitching her face. By now she had grown attached to Mrs. Gregory who in her unconditional regard for the child had made life seem quite surreal, in fact the whole family engaged meaningfully with the little girl who continued to blossom as a result.

"I am dressed in these clothes because I am going to a rock and roll party. Do you like the jacket and my blue suede shoes?" asked Trevor to the little girl, overhearing her remark.

To be asked for her opinion saw the child reply shyly "I don't know."

Trevor came home at different times in the evening, all dirty from sweeping local chimneys and headed straight for the outdoor metal bath tub which his wife had prepared for his usual bath. Trevor always turned down his mother's offer of a cup of tea until he had bathed and changed into his clean clothes. Saturdays nights saw Sylvia and Trevor either off to a club or party to dance the rock and roll. His wife dressed in her full skirts with their wide net petticoats, which the child admired so much so, she could not wait to grow up to wear one of her own. Sylvia's stiletto high heels similarly did not go unnoticed by the little girl admiration although she was not sure if her skinny legs would be able to balance on them, never mind walk in such glamorous footwear. The child wondered if she would be like Bambi, in the Walt Disney film that Mrs. Gregory had taken her to see during the Easter holidays. This had been her first animated film and she imagined that her young legs would never grow into slim elegant grown up ones. However this did not stop her sneaking into the young couple's bedroom when they were out working to try on the shoes whenever the thought occurred to her. The little girl found the pointed toes comical and often giggled to herself at adults' fashion.

The Gregory's house was always full of activity of one sort or another. Neighbours regularly dropped by for cups of tea and a chat around the black and white television set. Trevor lived for his weekends when he and his wife could go out socialising to the local pub with their mates on Fridays and subsequent dancing nights every Saturday. His passion for rock and roll meant that most of his wages went on the latest 78 records. Bill Hayley and the Comets "Rock around the Clock" was all the rage then so were Elvis Presley, Little Richard and Chuck Berry and Trevor played his records as often as he could.

Every Friday and Saturday night the child witnessed Trevor undergo a complete transformation. He seemed almost unrecognisable when he donned his latest weekend clothes. No more the local chimneysweeper but the elegant and sophisticated Mr. Trevor Gregory husband of Sylvia Gregory, who worked in the local hairdresser's. To the little girl they looked like the movie stars she seen on television. Trevor's hair was swept back in a huge quiff and Sylvia wore her strawberry blond hair in a ponytail. She either wore little white ankle socks with pumps or stockings with the seam at the back to complete her outfit.

"Oh mum is the seam in my stockings straight?" she asked her mother in law whenever she was not satisfied that she looked the business.

"You look fine and the seams in your stockings are perfect," Mrs. Gregory reassured her daughter in law while taking a puff on her cigarette.

"Here have a cigarette to calm you down because you are getting too excited as usual," Mrs. Gregory told Sylvia.

"I can't help it, I can't wait to try out my new dance steps tonight with Trevor," Sylvia replied taking the cigarette from Mrs. Gregory with her freshly painted fingernails. She put the cigarette into her bright pink lipstick mouth and inhaled. The smoke circled her cigarette for a moment before it disappeared leaving its distinctive smell in the room.

"I don't know why you are nervous; you and Trevor have been practising those new steps all week," Mrs. Gregory encouraged.

So off the couple went to dance the night away to the latest rock and roll sounds from the States.

To get to school the child walked along the cliffs accompanied by her foster mother each day glancing over at the sea. The sense of liberation was indescribable. The unhappy memories of North Mount Place were replaced gradually by the happier ones, she experienced when she looked out at the sea. There were days when the blue skies with their billowing clouds drifted slowly across the horizon greeting the school child as she walked to and from school. The school walk was long and often her tired legs complained, but the child never questioned the long walk because the pay off was that she felt happier than she had been since the separation from her family.

School was not easy although Sue's sister felt less bullied or intimidated than at her previous school. Mainly, perhaps because her clothes no longer reeked of the odour of a care institution, which she imagined screamed out at everyone when she attended the local primary school. But she still felt ill equipped to deal with the cruel questions and curiosities about her colour and where her origins.

"Why are your parents white and you are coloured?" the children asked constantly in the playground.

"Because Mrs. Gregory is my foster mother," the child replied exasperatedly; the frustration she felt finally replacing her patience.

"I don't like coloureds," said another schoolchild.

"Oh I don't care," exclaimed another.

For all the pretty clothes and special attention the child received from Mrs. Gregory and her family, because the she was the only 'coloured' child in the neighbourhood, it was not enough to provide her with the support and nurturing her innately carved for, so she remained shy and grateful for any niceties that were offered to her.

About five months' after the child had been placed to Dover, Mrs. Gregory informed her one morning;

"I have something to tell to you so come into the sitting room and sit down little one." The child knew that it was important because of the serious tone in Mrs. Gregory voice.

"Next weekend you are going to spend the time with a very nice couple who are looking to adopt a child."

Sue's sister did not know what adoption meant but trusted Mrs. Gregory enough to think that she would not come to any harm if she spent a weekend away from her with strangers. The child was collected by her social worker who she now associated with travelling from one care home to another. After a relatively short drive she found herself outside a beautiful house covered in ivy. A very elegant blond haired lady met them at the front door as her husband stood behind her. They followed the couple into the house, which was beautifully decorated.

"Would you like to go and play on the swing in the garden?" the lady kindly asked the child.

"There are several apple and pear trees in the garden; you might like to pick some," the man softly said. That was all the permission the child needed to excuse her from the discussions of the adults. She went and sat on the swing in the garden and swung herself high enough, almost to the tops of the pear trees, in her exulted state. The garden reminded her of the idyllic gardens she had seen in the storybooks at school. As her feet left the ground when, she swung herself backwards and forwards, the little girl thought to herself how she had never been on a swing in a private garden before. In fact she had not quite believed the lady when she said she had a swing in her garden. Later on the blond lady came out to the garden followed by her husband to speak to the child who was struck by their gently kindness towards her.

"What do you like to do at Mrs. Gregory's?" the lady asked her as she gently began to push the swing backwards and forwards. They listened intensely to the child as she whispered what she did at the Gregory's family home. They did not seem to mind her shyness and accepted it as being part of her.

In due course the couple informed the child that it was tea time and that there was home made apple pie if the child would like to come inside and have some.

During tea time the couple asked the little girl if she would like to be come and live with them rather than at Mrs. Gregory's. The child replied shyly that she did not know. After the weekend the child returned to her foster home.

"Did you like staying with the young couple?" Mrs. Gregory asked the little girl when she had returned.

"Oh yes I did," the child answered.

"Well let's see if the adoption goes ahead then," Mrs. Gregory said, "because you deserve a descent home and social services have told me that I am too old to adopt you and that has made me feel very sad because I'd loved to have adopted you."

The child thought no more of the weekend visit only that it had been another one of the best weekends she had ever had in her life. One day Mrs. Gregory said that the child's mother had refused to have the child adopted because she wanted her home in the future. The little girl was completely confused about what she was told because she immediately remembered the policewoman words when she had been forced from her family home that her mother had died. It appeared that Mrs. Gregory had not been made aware of this information and the child was now not sure if her mother was alive. Shortly afterwards, the child's false sense of security was dashed by Mrs. Gregory's announcement. "Your social worker is coming in a few days time to take you to another foster home where you will be reunited with your younger sister." The child noticed that Mrs. Gregory was weeping. "Oh it's such a shame," her foster mother continued, "I love you so much and have grown so attached to you and so have all my family, you are such a lovely girl. I don't know what will become of you and you have been doing so well at school, settling in and all."

The child was stunned because she was happy and settled at Mrs. Gregory's, more settled than she had ever felt before. School had become a lot less disoriented because she had made friends. This meant that she did not have to walk around at playtime on her own. Besides the other children had begun to accept her and did not seem so curious about her background anymore and she had acquired two best friends who were called Charlotte and Elizabeth.

"Why do you always play with that coloured girl," she overheard a boy ask Charlotte one day.

"Leave my friend alone," Charlotte had retorted angrily.

"Yes you leave our friend alone," Elizabeth had chipped in, "She can't help being coloured."

Having such loyal friends at primary school made the news that the child was on the move again even more distressing.

It seemed no time at all that the child watched Mrs. Gregory pack her bags ready for the next care home.

"I didn't want to tell you before now," said Mrs. Gregory, "I didn't want you to be upset anymore than necessary."

"Oh mum you should have told her sooner so that she could say goodbye to everyone." Mrs. Gregory's daughter in law reprimanded her mother in law.

"Well I did tell the social worker that she couldn't take the child until the end of the school term but the social worker informed me that the child had to be placed at her new foster home immediately, or else the placement would go to another child."

Mrs. Gregory began to sob openly and so did her daughter. By teatime everyone was crying including the child who went to her bedroom for a while. She sat on her bed while remembering the first and last Christmas she had spent at Mrs. Gregory's. The little girl remembered Mrs. Gregory and her neighbours doing the oke-koke in the street outside the terrace houses at midnight on New Year's Day, and Mr. Gregory had sat in his tin bath in the middle of the road with a wooden spoon in his hand pretending to row down the river. This was a forfeit he had to pay for a question he had not answered correctly to a quiz the adults had played that evening. Trevor had to drop his trousers and show his bottom as his forfeit, which the child had found both embarrassing and funny, particularly because she had never seen a man's bottom before which he had exposed publicly to every one at the New Year's Eve party. She had been allowed to stay up for the party and had mingled with the grown ups who were enjoying themselves immensely. Next year thought the child they would do the same again and she looked forward to celebrating Christmas and the New Year as part of the Gregory family, but now she realised that there would never be a next time and that made her sadder since the little girl's future seemed blank, empty and unknown and that frightened her insurmountably.

"But I don't want to go, "the child declared to Mrs. Gregory at bath time.

"I know poppet, I don't want you to go either and I told the social worker that, but she would have none of it," Mrs. Gregory replied.

"I do love my sister Sue but I want to stay here with you," the little girl lamented in earnest.

"I know, I know and I had a really argy bargy with the social worker on the telephone yesterday," Mrs. Gregory went on. "I gave her a piece of my mind I did, I told her that it's not right keep chopping and changing your foster homes and carting you off here and there."

"Why won't they listen to you?" the child enquired.

"Well she kept on saying that you are a Roman Catholic and that you should therefore be in a Catholic foster home. That's what your mother wants and you should be in a home together with your sister so that you can get to know each other and grow up together." Mrs. Gregory replied.

The child took her confusion and her incomprehension to bed with her. She had not suffered a single migraine since she had been at Mrs. Gregory's so she wondered if they had left her forever.

The Gregory family's tears were wasted on the social worker who looked embarrassed as she came and collected the eight year old.

"We will come and see you and we will write," affirmed Mrs. Gregory as she hugged and kissed the child. All the Gregory family followed and hugged and kissed the child too and then the tearful youngster climbed into the car, which immediately did a three point turn in the street and headed towards Dymchurch.

"Why couldn't I have stayed with Mrs. Gregory," asked the child accusingly through her tears to the social worker.

"Because you are a Catholic and you need to be brought up a Catholic home along with your sister," the social worker answered in a calm matter of fact voice.

"The walk to school was also very long for a little girl such as you," the social worker added in a somewhat concerned voice.

"No, it wasn't," challenged the child.

"Well it was rather a journey for such a young child," the social worker confirmed, "and besides it has come to the attention of social services that Mrs. Gregory's health is not a robust at it needs to be."

"What does that mean?"

"Oh never mind."

The child did not understand what all the fuss was about. She did not know what to do with this information so she kept it buried deep down inside her where all her other hurts were and in burying all her hurts, she repressed her true feelings.

"Mrs. Gregory should not have been making so much fuss by crying when you were leaving," the social worker voice interrupted the child's confused thoughts.

"Why?" Sue's sister asked as she continued to cry quietly to herself.

"Well you were only placed with the Gregory family until Social Services could find a foster home which would take the two of you," the social worker answered the child defensively. The little girl did not say anymore because she now resented her younger sister since she had never felt as happy as she did when living with the Gregory family. The youngster felt it was now her sister's fault that she was forced to leave what she perceived as a loving home, however a part of her was unquestionably looking forward to seeing her sister.

"I wanted to stay at the Gregory's house forever," she finally said.

"The Gregory family was a short stay foster home, until a placement could be found for you and your sister," the social worker replied coolly, "you do want to be with your sister don't you and besides Mrs. Gregory became far too close to you which she should not have done. You know its not easy trying to place coloured children together and most foster homes do not have the room," the social worker said as if expecting the child to be grateful for such an achievement with regard to placing the two sisters with one foster family.

The child listened for a while to the social worker's explanation, which seemed meaningless to her. She then succumbed to her silent place, the place where she withdrew within herself when her anguish became unbearable; from that detached place she observed the passing May scenery.

The car eventually turned into a wide gravelled road where detached red brick houses stood in the cul de sac. On one side of the road was a high wall. The car stopped at the largest detached house which was almost opposite from where the car had entered the gravelled road. The front garden was well maintained with a borderline of flowers around the edge of the lawn. The car stopped and the child climbed out, immediately she became agitated as her anxieties began to play havoc with her. What would Sue be like now she wondered? What had her little sister's care homes been like the child thought, had they been better than North Mount Place or the Gregory's foster home? Had Sue coped well; had she been happy? These thoughts raced around in the child's head. She wondered too if this new home with its new foster carer would make her as happy as the Gregory's home had made her, or would it be awful like North Mount Place which had not met the child's expectations.

The child accompanied the social worker to the front door of the child's new foster home, where the front door opened and a lady who was possibly in her late fifties greeted the little girl and her social worker.

"Hello dear, do come in," invited the lady.

The child was struck by the authoritativeness of the lady's voice.

"Come in and I have a pot of tea ready and some fairy cakes, I'm Miss Breen by the way, your new foster mother," the lady said introducing herself, "and you must be…………..? Your sister will be arriving tomorrow so we thought we had better settle you in first because you are the elder sister aren't you, and you will be able to greet your little sister tomorrow," Miss Breen chatted on.

Miss Breen's welcome was friendly and after tea the child was introduced to Miss Breen's assistant whose name was Estelle. The little girl noticed Estelle wore a similar style of dress as Sylvia which was the full mid carved skirts with their full net petticoats underneath. Estelle later told the child that she was twenty two and that she was passionate about looking after children as it was something that she had always wanted to do.

"Are there any other children or are these the only ones staying here?" the child had instantaneously inquired of Estelle as she was being shown around her new foster home.

"When your little sister arrives tomorrow there will be eight children all together," replied Estelle, "and that is the quota here because there isn't anymore room."

"I can't wait to see my sister tomorrow," responded the child excitedly, "at least we will be in the same care home at last."

"Oh don't call this *a care home,*" insisted Miss Breen as she came up behind the child.

"This house has a name, it is called Dunraven's," she continued as her two Chihuahua dogs yelped around her legs. The child was surprised that the house had a name because she thought only large care institutions like North Mount Place were allowed their own names. The hall was furnished with Victorian furniture with a carved mirror frame on one of the walls with the bevelled mirror encased inside it.

"I like this seat," she found herself saying to Miss Breen approvingly as the little girl sat down on the exquisite bench in the hall.

"That's a Victorian ottoman seat which belonged to my mother," Miss Breen replied in a pleased tone. Beside it were several ornate chairs.

The child joined the other children for tea that evening where they ate from stainless steel cutlery and from plastic plates, along with the other children the little girl drunk from a plastic beaker that she had grown unused to since living with the Mrs. Gregory who always used china crockery. The plastic cookery reminded her of North Mount Place but she knew this home was different, after all the furniture was ornate and she appreciated that. The little girl also liked the fact that although she was now with a group of children again, there was not so many of them as there had been at North Mount Place. The children ages varied; Anne and Steven were four and five years old respectively. Tom was six-years-old and Maureen thirteen. The children seemed friendly enough and Estelle appeared to enjoy playing mostly with the children rather than attending to the household duties. Miss Breen expected all children to help with the clearing up of the table after each meal.

"I don't use china here because the children will break it and cut themselves," the child's new foster mother has informed the child when she had asked her why she did not use china crockery.

The little girl woke up very excited the following

morning, her predominate thoughts were the reunion with her little sister at this new foster home.

"When will my sister arrive?" the child asked Miss Breen at the breakfast table as she picked up her spoon to eat her cornflakes.

"Not until after lunch," was the reply, "after breakfast you can play in the back garden and at the weekend we can all go for a walk along the beach."

"Where is the beach?" the child inquired.

"It's just behind that wall over there," answered Miss Breen pointing her finger in the direction of the front door. "Do you remember seeing a big wall when you arrived yesterday?"

"Yes, I do" replied the young girl.

"Well behind that wall is the sea so we live very close to it," disclosed Miss Breen.

The morning came and went and by lunchtime the child's anticipation and excitement grew even more. All the child could think about was to be reunited with her younger sister because it seemed like a lifetime ago that she had last seen her sibling. She and Sue would be a little family together and she wanted that more than anything else in the world. After impatiently looking out the front window in the sitting room, which faced onto the drive way and towards the seawall, the time arrived for the child to meet her little sister. A blue car could be seen turning into the driveway of the cul du sac just like the red car that had brought the child the day before to Dunraven's. Sue's sister instinctively knew it was the car that was finally bringing Sue to her new foster home.

"Now come along," Miss Breen said, "let's go outside to the front garden so that we can welcome your little sister."

The child hesitated a little bit because she had mixed feelings now and felt a bit panicky but she did not know why. She followed the other children into the front garden and watched as Sue's social worker helped her out of the car. Her six year old sister walked into the front garden her body huddled over a teddy bear, the baby fat no longer visible on her face and hands. It seemed as if Sue was clinging on to her teddy bear for dear life as she placed a protective hand over the toy while squeezing it. She looked around about her until her haunted confused eyes looked out in terror as they glanced out at the sea of unrecognised faces until they rested on mine. She nervously half smiled at me as her face twitched involuntarily. I looked at my younger sister and wondered what torment she had endured that made her actions resemble the mannerisms of a frightened animal. The indelible moment Sue and I were reunited was undeniably the most indescribable moment of my life. I was the witness to my sister's bewildered broken spirit since she was the living reminder of how unjust our predicament was. She walked towards me but it was all too much for me to bear. I burst out crying uncontrollably, embarrassed in front of the other children around me. Sue's lopsided smile immediately crumbled into a flood of tears too. I rushed towards Sue and hugged her until our pain merged into one. When we were able to draw sufficient strength from one another we instinctively took each other's hand and bravely walked towards our new foster home together. In that poignant and tragic moment I felt as if the sun had eclipsed in the sky as the dark imposing clouds began to weigh down heavily on my young shoulders like a boulder. I felt overwhelming guilty at my sister's demise because she was not the resourceful sister I had remembered.

My observations of my sister brought back the traumatic night when we were at the police station when we had suffered the news of our mother's death and consequently our separation. The memories of the peeling plaster hanging off the ceiling that I desperately wanted to scratch it off but the ceiling was far too high and therefore out of reach, in the same way that my mother was out of reach. I wanted desperately to scratch off the hanging wallpaper in my feeble attempt to make the ceiling smooth again, to make my shattered world smooth again; I was mentally tithing over the edge at the time because I was beside myself with grief at my loss. I was almost twenty year's old before I could go into a room and look up at a ceiling, which had hanging uneven wallpaper or plastering on it without walking out in a state of neurosis. I had to physically and mentally force myself to stand and look at ceilings in this state of disrepair and fuller relive the anxiety and trauma in order to let go of the phobia. Before then, anything uneven, such as warts, or uneven pavements' brought on a panic attack where I broke out in a sweat, which left me feeling breathless and shaky. I fanatically wanted to scratch off the unevenness until the surface was nice and smooth again.

Sue's confusion and disorientation did not go away and when I asked her what had happened when she and I were separated at the Police station and taken into care my sister remained even more confused and just shivered. Sue was now six years old and had been three when she was separated from her family. Empathy for her suffering finally stopped me asking her. I imagined years later that perhaps she was left in her bed to cry alone unattended in her fearful state until she was so exhausted she eventually fell asleep. Perhaps the love and nurturing she had grown used to from our mother had stopped far too abruptly and her new care assistants were unable or unwilling to comfort an extremely vulnerable toddler. The sudden and ruthless withdrawal of her mother's love before its allotted time hung like a heavy burden over her. Perhaps the few suitable foster parents who would take in 'coloured' children were not available. Whatever happened Sue's emotionally scars were like gaping wounds. It hurt to know that I could not wipe away Sue's earlier traumatic experiences but in wanting to make it up to her I became not just her big sister but her little mother as well.

Sue settled down at a fashion in Dunraven's foster home. She was different to the rest of the children even different from me. She did not seem to conform to any of the rules and was soon labelled by Miss Breen as 'maladjusted'. I did not know what that meant but sensed that it was something bad and irreparable. Sue's challenging behaviour often resulted in her being kicked and slapped by Miss Breen's who sometimes used hairbrushes to punish my sister. Sue wiggled and withered around on the landing floor near the bedrooms to avoid the beatings. I despaired the times I witnessed this because it did not seem to resolve anything. Sue tried Miss Breen's patience to the extent that Miss Breen would explode, lose her temper and kick and slap my sister until Sue fell to the floor. The other children also witnessed Sue's treatment silently and incomprehensively. I was ambiguous about whether this treatment was justifiable but I was deemed insignificant because I grew to accept that children did not have a voice to challenge adults who fostered them.

Chapter III

Sue broke her heart with her tears. She broke mine too since I was powerless to stop the cycle of beatings which were mainly to do with her constantly wetting the bed. At other times my sister's punishments were attempts by our foster mother to address her wilful behaviour. The punishments metered out to Sue were that she was sent to bed earlier than the normal time. Other times, Sue was depraved of special treats or puddings after her dinner. When my sister cried I often cried in sympathy because her treatment was just as upsetting for me to behold. Sue's smoky brown grey eyes were always swollen and red for sometime after her ordeal and many times when she was sent to bed early, I discovered my sister had cried herself to sleep when I came up to bed later that evening. If something had upset me it was not unusual for Sue to shed emphatic tears in solidarity as we cried together to comfort ourselves in our lack of understanding of our motherless situation.

"You don't need to cry Sue just because I got punched this afternoon by a boy at school," I told her one day after a boy had punched me in the face because he did not like 'darkies'.

"I can't help it Mandy," she replied.

"Now children, Sue will not be coming down for tea this evening," Miss Breen informed us yet again. We all knew what that meant my sister had wet the bed again. In fact Sue wet the bed most nights.

"Not only did she wet the bed again, the child has also stolen some money from my purse to buy sweets," Miss Breen told us in an infuriated tone at the tea table that evening, "so this time she has her tea upstairs in her bedroom for the rest of the week."

We all sat in silence when this statement was announced because despite Sue being labelled as 'maladjusted,' the other children loved her as much as I did. We knew that she would give a child her last sweet if they were upset and crying. Nevertheless, she always seemed to pay a price for her 'maladjusted' behaviour At the time I believed that Sue's behaviour was her fault and if her behaviour was her fault I told myself that it was somehow my fault as well since we were sisters.

"Sue, are you alright?" I asked her the moment I managed to cleverly sneak upstairs to find my sister crouched up in the foetal position on top of her bed.

"I'm alright Mandy," she told me on many an occasion in that resigned tearful voice of hers.

Reluctantly after a few moments I left her alone in the bedroom, as I remembered the rules were that no one was to talk to Sue when she was naughty.

"Why can't we talk to Sue?" one or other of the little children frequently asked. Their young minds failed to comprehend what 'being naughty' meant.

"Because she needs time to think about why she stole some money from my purse and then lied to me about what she had done, never mind the persistent bedwetting," Miss Breen pompously informed the children.

I felt tremendously guilty every time my younger sister was being punished and yet resented her when she disrupted a game I was playing, or broke a cherished toy I played with.

"I am always getting smacked by Miss Breen," Sue told me with tears running down her face.

"If you do as you are told and not misbehave then Miss Breen will not punish you," Maureen informed Sue for the umpteenth time. I nodded my head in agreement.

"Why don't you try and stop wetting the bed. Miss Been does try and help you by making sure that you don't have anything to drink after tea time," I reminded my sister several times.

"I try very hard not to wet the bed but I can't help it," Sue repeatedly stressed. She was now seven and I was nine but her bedwetting never wavered.

"Oh don't upset yourself little Sue," consoled Estelle.

There was an understanding between Sue and Estelle which made Dunraven bearable for my sister. Estelle rescued Sue from all sorts of situations even if it meant lying to save Sue from a fate worse than death. The wrath of Miss Breen whenever she lost her temper was not to be underestimated.

Despite Sue's unhappiness at the foster home she was very popular at primary school; although she was not outstanding academically her PE skills were extraordinary. Miss Smith the PE teacher also had a special affection for Sue and encouraged Sue's talent for gymnastics at every opportunity. Her attention span at any other subject was limited so it was not unheard of for my sister to be punished at school for misbehaving during a lesson.

"But the history lesson was so boring Mandy and the teacher's voice drone on and on and besides I was not the only one talking in class!"

"Sue that is not the point and now your end of year report will not be very good because your school results will be poor and Miss Breen will be angry with you again."

"Miss Smith said I can have tea with her this afternoon," Sue told me happily changing the subject.

"What about the bus home, you will miss it," I informed her.

"Oh that's alright, Miss Smith said that she will

telephone Miss Breen to inform her that she will bring me home in her car afterwards," replied Sue looking extremely pleased with herself. I was secretly envious of the special attention Sue managed to create for herself amongst an individual teacher who genuinely seemed to like her. Similarly to Estelle, Sue formed a special relationship with Miss Smith who also tried to protect my sister from punishment.

"Miss Breen," I detected Estelle's voice calling Miss Breen one morning when they were upstairs after Sue had got another beating with the hairbrush from her foster mother, for her bedwetting.

"What is it now Estelle?" replied a frustrated Miss Breen.

"Look Sue cannot help wetting the bed and the more you hit her the more she *will* wet the bed," responded an exasperated Estelle.

"Now since when have I asked you to do my job?" Miss Breen questioned her employee.

"I am not asking to do your job but I just feel that it's not right to keep hitting her as if she is wetting her bed on purpose," replied Estelle.

"Of course she is doing it on purpose, she has been wetting the bed since she was six and she is almost eight now and the child is still wetting the bed, there is no excuse for her to wet the bed at her age; of course she is wetting the bed on purpose. Don't be so naive Estelle; after all she has all she needs here, what with a roof over her head and plenty of food. The fact is the child is just simply far too lazy to get out of bed at night," assumed Miss Breen," next time she wets the bed, I've a good mind to rub her nose in the wet sheet."

"But she's not drinking anything late at night since you've stopped all her evening drinks including her hot cocoa." continued Estelle.

"Your blooming right I have, she's a lazy, lazy good

for nothing child that is what she is," remonstrated Miss Breen, "now Estelle let me get on with my chores."

It was the afternoon of the annual village green summer festival, which was organised by our local Catholic Church. My initial weekly attendance at Sunday Mass was strangely unfamiliar because Mrs. Gregory was not religious and therefore did not attend Church. The Mass ceremony had recently changed from Latin to English so along with the other foster children I was less distracted.

However Miss Breen was a staunch Roman Catholic and often quoted a parable to make a point. That particular afternoon there were various stalls that displayed goods on the village green and I vividly remember being fascinated by a game, which was played by the children whereby we had to drop a coin in a bucket of water to cover the existing coin at the bottom of the bucket. The little pocket money I had earned at Miss Breen's ensured that I was dubious about gambling it away. Needless to say I decided to have a go, after a few unsuccessful attempts Sue came bounded up to me with a handful of coins she was holding.

"Oh Mandy you will never get anywhere by doing it that way," Sue laughingly declared.

"But Father Murphy showed me how to play the game and he said I must drop my own coin into the water first to see whether it floats down to cover

the half a crown in the middle of the bucket," I informed her somewhat peeved by my previously unsuccessful attempts.

"Is Father Murphy looking?" asked Sue quickly her back to the priest.

"No," I replied." He is talking to the lady who prepares the floral arrangements for the Sunday service."

"This is how you do it," demonstrated Sue, who in a flash had taken my penny and put it manually over the half a crown.

"Now tell Father Murphy that you have won," instructed my younger sister.

"I can't Sue, that would be a lie and besides it's cheating," I protested timidly.

"Father Murphy, Father Murphy," I heard Sue shouting as she turned her head towards the priest.

"Mandy's won, look she had covered the half a crown," illustrated Sue unscrupulously as Father Murphy looked at me and then at Sue before walking over and peering into the bucket.

"If you had said that you had won again Susan, I would have been suspicious," Father Murphy cautioned, "but seeing it is your big sister Mandy who is always such a good girl, I know that she has won the half a crown decorously."

"Can I take the half a crown out of the bucket then and give it to her," Sue offered eagerly.

"Yes you can," responded Father Murphy putting his hand in his pocket of his robes and taking out a handful of coins as he looked amongst them for another half a crown to replace the previous one.

"Oh Sue you shouldn't have done that!" I verified immediately I had the half a crown safely in the pocket of my pinafore dress. I was feeling secretly pleased that my sister had tricked the priest rather than me. I discovered that Sue had a knack for stealing or playing tricks on others particularly adults, in the attempt to get something for herself, or for me or indeed for any one of the children. Consequently Sue took the blame for many things in which some cases were not her fault.

"Here you are Mandy, here are some sweets for you."

"Where did you get these Sue?" I knew full well that she had stolen the sweets from the local sweet shop.

"Do you want them or not?" Sue asked.

"Yes, please."

Father Murphy was familiar with all Miss Breen's foster children because he sat on the board of governors at our school and assisted Miss Breen to place each child at St Augustine's, the local Primary school when they arrived at her foster home. Miss Breen and the priest always made a habit of speaking to each other after Sunday Mass while we chatted to our school friends. We used to travel to school by bus since the school in Hythe was some distance away from our foster home. Each morning we all clamoured upstairs of the double decker bus, some of the children screaming and shouting until the bus conductor came upstairs to tell us to be quiet. I felt a sense of accomplishment travelling to school by bus without adult supervision since Miss Breen had instructed me to supervise the younger children to and from school and I did this as best I could. The bus stopped conveniently right outside the school gates. It was apparent to me that one of my teacher's whose name was Miss Dean was very fond of me because she spent time explaining to me my homework and always greeted me with a pleasant smile each morning. She was also very highly thought of by Miss Breen and they exchanged Christmas and Easter greeting cards which she signed Miss Margaret Dean.

"You are a very good Catholic girl," Miss Dean informed me on numerous occasions. "Perhaps you will be a nun when you grow up," she mentioned to me a few times.

"Yes Miss Dean," I had replied, somewhat warming to the idea at the time.

I remember being very happy at the school and because it was not a large school, subsequently there was a tremendous community spirit attached to it. One year the school organised a day trip to London that was a grand event because the metropolis seemed so beguiling to all of us being from the country.

"All the children in this class will be going on a trip to London next week to see the Houses of Parliament, Big Ben and Buckingham Palace," Miss Peggy Berber announced one day when we had just finished our English class.

"I've never been to London before," said Clare the girl who sat at the desk behind me.

"Oh I have," I replied proudly.

"Have you, what's it like?" asked Clare wide eyed.

"I used to live there and it's quite nice, "I said trying hard to remember what the city of London was like since I had only lived in one of its neighbourhoods where I had been born. The following week I travelled to London along with my classmates on the school coach. I sat next to Clare but I felt very much alone with my memories of the London I had left behind almost five years ago. The trip had been organised before the end of the summer term and on the day of the outing the weather had been moderate. We admired the tourist sights of London and I recall that as we were walking around Westminster sometime during the afternoon I felt as if I was being watched. I looked around me and eventually looked up and noticed three adults staring at me; the observers were a man who was with two women. I was momentarily struck by their skin tones because their complexions were similar to mine and Sue's and because of this I was instantly reminded that it had been a long time since I had seen or been amongst people of my own skin tone. The black eyes of the three adults I noted complimented their rich black and brown skins complexions as I similarly observed them, curiously looking at me. Intuitively I became aware that they had in their possession something that I did not have but innately desired. I was not sure what those three people had in their custody but whatever it was; those adults appeared sagacious in such a manner in which I could only aspire to whilst they continued looking at me with their benevolent, pensive eyes. There was a huge almost uncontrollable urge within me to follow these people so that I could discover what they had in their possession that I did not.

"Oh don't look at those colored people," Clare remarked as she caught me watching them,"they are nothing to do with you anyway your mother is white so you are not like them. Besides, your sister Sue looks even more like she's from somewhere in Southern Europe such as Malta because she appears almost white in winter and gets a suntan in summer and, she doesn't have such frizzy hair as you!"

"Come on you two what are you staring at, you are going to get left behind if you don't hurry up," I heard Miss Berber shout out to us.

I reluctantly walked with Clare towards our group of schoolchildren, looking behind me at the three people who continued to stare at me until I was out of sight.

"What's the matter Mandy?" asked Clare when the coach was entering the school gates after we had returned from our trip to London,"you haven't said a word since we got on the coach!"

"Nothing is the matter!" I replied as I looked out of the window and noticed the wind gently teasing the branches of an oak tree until they finally succumbed and started to sway and dance to the rhythms the wind forced upon them.

As often as possible, Miss Breen took us all out for

Sunday walks, sometimes along the beach or for walks in the Romney Marshes; or to the woods. Other times we went on these outings during the school holidays. Usually Miss Breen enlisted her best friend and neighbour Miss Trellis to help look after the children. As Miss Breen's hatchback car could not take everyone Miss Trellis took the remaining children since Sunday was one of the days Estelle did not work. We clamoured into one of the two cars and along with the older children I sat in the boot of the hatchback. Since I was still susceptible to car sickness I made sure that I sat as far back in the car so that I could minimise the smell the petrol fumes.

On one of the first outings Miss Breen took us for a walk in the local woods.

"What Mandy, is this your first time walking in woods?" stated Miss Breen, amazed that a few of the children in her care had never walked through woods before.

"No I haven't," I replied resentful because I had to get out of the car and go for a walk when the weather was rather unsettled. "It's cold and I want to get back into the car to keep warm."

"You London children don't know what's good for you," Miss Breen inferred. "This clean crisp air will do you a world of good Mandy; you don't want to be coped up in a stuffy car or a stuffy house for that matter!"

I was obliged to walk through the woods in my wellington boots along with the other children, some of whom were dwindling behind. I stayed close to Miss Breen because as one of the older children I was keen to ask her questions about herself as well as her view of the world.

"What did you do before you was a foster mother?" I questioned her on one of these walks.

"I was a teacher until I retired at fifty," Miss Breen replied.

"How long were you a teacher? " Mark asked who was a tall thin boy.

"Oh for most of my working life," responded Miss Breen.

"How old are you then?" asked Peter who was the eldest boy at Dunraven.

"I'm almost sixty three," answered Miss Breen.

"Why did you not get married?" I asked her.

"Oh I had a beau but he was killed in the First World War," informed Miss Breen reflectively.

"Did you not meet anyone else?" queried Sandra another child who had straight brown should length hair and who was the same age as Sue.

"No, a lot of men died in the war," confirmed Miss Breen.

"What about Miss Trellis did her beau die in the war too?" I asked her.

"I don't think Miss Trellis ever had a beau," our foster mother replied.

"How long have you and Miss Trellis been friends?" Peter inquired.

"About thirty years now," stated Miss Breen.

"Why did you decide to foster children?" Sandra asked.

"Because I always wanted too and I felt that as a retired teacher I could offer something more to children who had been placed in care," Miss Breen affirmed.

"Have you got any brother or sisters?" I continued questioning my foster mother.

"I've got a cousin who is famous because he is an inventor," Miss Breen told us.

"What did he invent?" asked Peter his curiosity getting the better of the fostered child.

"Oh he designed some of the railways," answered

Miss Breen elusively.

"You have all met my mother too and I have several uncles and aunts as well."

"Are they happy that you fostered children?" Peter carried on probing his foster mother.

"No, unfortunately they cannot understand why I foster 'orphans'
which is the term they persist on using for foster children," Miss Breen replied.

"Are they Catholics like you?" I asked her.

"Yes, in fact I come from one of the oldest Catholic families in England who are part of the aristocracy!" Miss Breen commented.

"If they are Catholics why don't they like you fostering children, after all we are Catholics as well," Sue remarked slightly peeved; she had just run up to join our little group.

"Well not all people are the same and not everyone thinks like me," Miss Breen explained.

"I wished there were more mixed raced children around!" I found myself disclosing to her.

"You might be in the minority now Mandy," said Miss Breen, "but by the time you two grow up, mark my words, the world will be very different because more white people will marry black people and vice versa, that will be the trend you wait and see!"

"How can you be sure of that?" I said exquisitely.

"Because that will be the way of the world," attested Miss Breen.

I felt relieved that this might be a possibility, that there might be more children similar to Sue and me in the world, but as I was nine years old at the time and the possibility of a multi-racial and multi-cultural society seemed beyond my imagination.

"What are the names of these flowers?" Sue asked as she stooped down to pick the blue flowers.

"They are bluebells and the little yellow ones over there are buttercups," Miss Breen pointed out to my younger sister.

"Are you feeling warmer now Mandy?" Miss Breen inquired glancing over at me.

"Yes, I am a lot warmer now thank you. I like the bluebells but they seem a bit lonely though growing in the shade of those tall trees, they don't seem to have much sunlight," I answered.

"That does not stop them from growing or for that matter blossoming and because they are spring flowers they blossom before the leaves of the trees block out the sunlight completely," noted Miss Breen.

"They look a bit sad with their bells hanging down."

"Yes almost in shame."

"It seems that some flowers need a lot of sun light to blossom while others hardly need any sunlight at all."

"Bluebells are known to be one of the sturdiest of flowers."

"There are so many of them and I can see even more of them ahead of us."

"They make the wood look so much more appealing because they make the ground appear as if it is covered in a blue subliminal carpet from a distance."

"They almost seem as if they are hiding in the woods!"

"Now Mandy you are old enough to join the local library."

"Where is the library and how do I get there?"

"The library is in the village and you can walk along the sea promenade to reach it. Saturday mornings will be an excellent time to walk there, after you have had breakfast." concluded Miss Been.

"When will I join, next Saturday?"

"That's a good idea, in fact I will drive you there myself next Saturday so that you can register, and of course you can also loan library books during the school holidays!"

"I don't know if I will like reading books."

"Of course you will Mandy because you are a bright little girl so you will enjoy reading once you have got into the habit of reading books, besides you and Sue are going to have to work hard all your lives for a living, so you will need to have an education."

"Why will we have to work hard for a living?"

"Well because you have no other relatives apart from your mother and she will not be in a position to help you or support you financially, so you are going to have to work very hard to make a living for yourselves."

"Is our mother alive?" Sue asked our foster mother in astonishment.

"Your mother is very much alive. In fact she sent you both a letter this morning which I intended to bring with me on this outing so that I could read it to you two girls but unfortunately, come to think of it, I must have left it on my office desk this morning. I will read it to you as soon as we get home."

When we arrived home sure enough Miss Breen read Sue and I a letter from our mother.

"Your mother hopes you are both well and wants you to know that you have another baby sister, isn't that lovely?"

"That's nice."

Although the walk along the sea promenade to the local library was a fair distance, I enjoyed the walk immensely especially in the summer months because I could walk along the beach and paddle in the sea when the tide was out. I collected seashells and often picked up the black or green seaweed to pop the buds. In winter I was more mindful when walking along the promenade, because the waves often reached a tremendous height as they came crashing down over the sea wall and into the front gardens of the houses nearest the beach. At every opportunity we played on the beach and swam in the sea and I was always keen to swim as far out to sea as possible.

"Now Mandy don't swim too far," Miss Breen constantly reminded me, "there are undercurrents that are very strong and a man was swept out to sea yesterday."

"Was he drowned?" asked one of the children.

"I don't know," replied Miss Breen.

"I think so," confirmed Estelle,"because the lady who lives at no8 was saying so in the baker's this morning when I was buying the bread."

"Now don't be frightening the younger children Estelle," warned Miss Breen, lowering her voice.

I dare not mention that while I was walking on the beach yesterday, I witnessed a man being rescued by the lifeguards who had wrapped him in a blanket and carried him to the waiting ambulance on a stretcher. I could not help but notice that although the man was completely wrapped up his feet were exposed, since they had fallen away from the blanket. I had never seen such yellow feet before and stared and stared at them in a mixture of disbelief and shock. That night I had the most horrendous nightmares about dead yellow feet, so from then on I heeded Miss Beacon's warning and never swam too far out to sea again for fear that I might end up with the same scary yellow feet.

The winter months in Kent did not agree with me for along with the occasional migraines I was plagued with chilblains, which persistently itched and irritated me unremittingly.

"Mandy what are you doing bending down to the floor?" my maths teacher enquired one morning during my lesson.

"It's my chilblains Miss," I distinctly remember replying.

"Well you probably have poor blood circulation and sitting too near the radiator will not help either," advised the teacher.

"I can't help it Miss, I try not to sit too near the radiator but if I don't then I get very cold," I replied clearly distressed.

"When you go out to play in the playground after this lesson you must run around more in order to improve your circulation," instructed the teacher.

"Yes Miss," I replied resuming the scratching of my toes and fingers.

Every Wednesday afternoon Miss Breen was off duty until the following morning. She always stayed overnight at Miss Trellis's house, who lived in a detached cottage in the next village. Miss Breen also spent one weekend a month at Miss Trellis's house so Estelle was left in charge of us along with another carer, although Miss Breen rang several times to ensure that her foster children were fine. Pixie and Trixie accompanied their mistress wherever she went. Pixie unfortunately limped due to being run over by a car some years earlier and Trixie sustained an infected right eye, which wept interminably. So on the first Friday of every month Miss Breen packed her overnight bag and drove off to her best friend's house with her dogs barking in the back of her car. Miss Breen spent her annual holidays with her companion as well, when they travelled abroad in Miss Breen camper van. Their favourite destinations by far were Spain and Italy.

"Do you always go to Italy or Spain?" I decided to ask my foster mother one day.

"Oh I go to France occasionally," answered Miss Breen.

"Do you go to any other countries? " Peter asked joining in the conversation.

"Not really, I prefer to visit Catholic countries only so that I can celebrate Mass on Sundays; the Churches abroad are also admirable because their architecture are so magnificent." added Miss Breen.

"Where are you going to go this year?" I inquired.

"Miss Trellis and I are going return to Spain in the camper van," Miss Breen replied.

The camper van was ideal for travelling since whenever our foster mother took us out for day trips during the summer holidays; we stopped for refreshments or a picnic whenever she thought appropriate. We visited Canterbury Cathedral, Hastings and various other towns where we stopped in nearby country lanes for walks and to have our picnics. We ate an assortment of sandwiches such as: egg mayonnaise, sandwich spread, peanut butter, jam and marmite sandwiches. The gingham tablecloth was laid out in all its glory as were the plastic cutlery and salad bowls.

"Pass the egg and salad cream sandwiches as I don't care much for the jam sandwiches?" Maureen asked Sue as she sat sunning herself in the lukewarm sunshine.

"Now you young ones are to eat your sandwiches first before you have some of my homemade fruit cake," instructed Miss Breen.

Sue and I often helped with the baking on Saturdays.

"You two sisters will need to learn how to bake bread and cakes," Miss Breen told us the first year we lived at Dunraven.

"Why do you use this flour?" I asked her the first time I had watched her bake bread.

"Because wholemeal flour it much better for you that the ordinary white flour," was her reply. "I also always read the labels of the tinned products I buy to establish which ones have the least preservatives and additives."

Miss Breen placed great emphasis on the outdoor life whatever the season, we embarked on our long walks most Sundays except if it were raining heavily.

"Now you children you are all getting far too raucous," she regularly stated on Sunday afternoons, "its time to get your cardigans and pullovers on and we will go to the marshes for the rest of the afternoon."

"But Miss Breen its cold," I as usual protested because of the overcast day, "it looks like it might rain again."

"A little bit of rain won't hurt you Mandy and it will probably clear up later." was her standard reply.

On hearing her response my usual behavior was to go as slowly as I could upstairs to the bedroom to find my cardigan as a means of delaying the outing. I then sulked in the car throughout the entire journey to the marshes. Once however I had acclimatised myself to the dreary weather I nevertheless forgot my resentments and joined the other foster children who were strolling across the marshes listening to Miss Breen pointing out the name of one tree or another. I was always amazed that my foster mother's prediction of the weather, the majority of the times, she was uncannily accurate.

"Since it is your first summer holiday here," announced Miss Breen in the summer of 1961, "I am arranging to take you two girls for a weekend in my caravan."

Hence, it was in mid August that Sue and I set of with Miss Breen in her car to the caravan site. I had never seen a caravan before so I had no idea what to expect. I was astounded when I initially followed Miss Breen inside her one especially when my foster mother starting pulling down the beds from the walls. I was shown the little kitchenette at the front of the caravan and a little seating area at the back.

"Miss Breen I want to go to the toilet, where it is?" I inquired no sooner had I discovered the secret hiding places of the furniture.

"The toilets will be over by the entrance where we drove in and there is a sign marked *'toilets'* so you can't miss it," she replied.

The idea of outside toilets brought back unhappy memories to me immediately.

"I don't want to go on my own," I told her apprehensively.

"Well I need to unpack the clothes so I cannot go with you," replied Miss Breen.

"I will go with you," volunteered Sue excitedly.

"Now Mandy you are a big girl so you are perfectly capable of going those few yards to the toilets by yourself besides Sue needs to help me unpack," said Miss Breen who was having none of it.

I walked up to the communal toilets with my head down hoping that no one would see me. I did not know why I felt so self conscious and vulnerable but I did. For most part of that weekend, I undertook the trek to the toilet most of the time on my own, which I simply detested. Several times however Sue accompanied me and I found this extremely reassuring.

"Now Mandy and Sue," Miss Breen told us while holidaying at the caravan, "I am going to make an omelette for each of you for breakfast."

"What is an omelette?" Sue and I asked our foster mother in unison.

"What you two do not know what an omelette is at your ages, well I never!" exclaimed Miss Breen in shock at such a revelation.

"No," we both answered in chorus. Any initiation

into the workings of a kitchen and any insight into the preparation of food in general were beyond us.

"Well let's get on with it then, one of you pass me those eggs over by the fridge and I will show you," Miss Breen notified us, "and pass me that bowl as well."

"This one?"

"Yes, that glass one, now I want you to crack a couple of eggs on the edge of the bowl making sure that both the egg yolks and egg whites fall into the bowl, you try first Mandy."

"Like this? "I said rather nervously as I watched some of the white of the egg slide over the outer edge of the glass bowl.

"Quick get the eggshell to scope up the egg white and put it back in the bowl," Miss Breen said in her attempt to rescue the egg white.

Luckily I managed to retrieve most of the egg white.

"Here you are Mandy, here is the fork and now I want you to whisk the eggs."

I did this relatively successfully as I tried to control my erratic hand movements.

"That's fine;" said Miss Breen patiently and encouragingly, "let's put the mixture into the frying pan now that the butter has melted. It was Sue's turn after me and we were both dumbfounded by the end result since the eggs were transformed into what closely resembled pancakes.

When Miss Breen embarked on her annual holidays abroad she liaised with social services who organised a Matron to come and look after us. The

Matron seemed to be rather insignificant similarly to the weekend carer; compared to our foster mother because Dunraven had Miss Breen's indelible stamp written all over the eight bed roomed house, likewise Estelle stayed over night during this period as well.

"There a postcard for each of you children from Miss Breen and here is yours Mandy," proclaimed Estelle one morning as she handed out the individual postcards to the children. I had just helped to clear the breakfast table when I took the beautifully embroidered postcard from Estelle. Upon closer observation I noticed that the image on the postcard was of a Spanish Flamenco dancer wearing a red embroidery dress. I was thrilled because not only had I never received a postcard addressed to me solely. Similarly I had never seen a postcard such as this one before. The only other postcards I was familiar with were the ones of the English seaside, which were displayed in the tourist shops near the beach or in the amusement arcades, where Alma Cogan songs seemed to be played consistently. There were times when we hung around these arcades usually with Estelle who took the older children out with her. It was normally Sue, Maureen and I.

"Here Mandy have one of these," Estelle offered one day while we were walking along the seafront.

"Urg", I responded," what are those awful things?"

"These are cockles and the others are whelks," Estelle replied amused at my reaction.

"They look so vile, so awful."

"They are very good for you," said Estelle somewhat defensively.

"I don't care; I'd rather have an ice-cream any day!" I retorted unconvinced.

"Mandy and Maureen, look after Sue for a moment."

Estelle was not averse to saying at times, "I've arrange to meet my new boyfriend by the dodgems cars over there so here's some money to play the slot machines while you are waiting for me."

Undoubtedly it was enormous fun whenever we

were out with Estelle. In fact we viewed Estelle as rather like our older sister, what with her updates on her love life and on fashion.

"The boy from the local greengrocery shop asked me out last Tuesday when I was in there buying the vegetables for dinner," she informed us, and we were intrigued as a result of Estelle's willingness to share her personal life with us.

"But I told him that I already have a boyfriend," the care assistant continued.

"Are you still seeing Nigel then?" enquired Sue.

"Yes I am, but he likes heavy petting and now he wants me to go all the way!" Estelle informed her audience, "but I won't let him."

"What's heavy petting?" Sue asked.

"You know, when boyfriends' try and do well rude things."

"I don't think you should let him then," I said knowing that this meant more than kissing.

"I definitely don't want to get pregnant without being married."

"Well get him to stop it then," I said.

"Oh, I don't mind a little petting because that's what girlfriend's and boyfriend's do and if I don't let Nigel have a bit of a grope then I will lose him to someone else."

I was not sure about that reply so I remained quiet.

Estelle went off to meet the boy from the greengrocery shop and in the meantime we played the slot machines until she returned. We walked back to our foster home along the beach while Estelle discussed her complicated love life. All the way home she could not decide whether she should pack in Nigel and we were too young to advise her any which way. Sue was extremely fond of Estelle and the fondness was mutual to the extent that Sue became Estelle's confidante although my sister was by now only eight years old.

"Estelle," commanded Miss Breen one afternoon.
"Yes Miss Breen."
"I am fed up with you always sticking up for Sue Mensan whenever she is defiant and troublesome."
"Oh Miss Breen it wasn't Sue's fault, it was Peter who broke your chair."
"How do you know, did you see it happen?"
"No I didn't but Sue never lies to me."
"Oh, so you think she would not lie to you, why are you so special, anyway that is precisely the sort of thing she would do, believe me it is!"
"She may be a bit of a tomboy and is naughty but that does not mean that she should get blamed for everything that gets broken, and I know she'd never lie to me."
"That chair was my mother's and cannot be replaced," continued Miss Breen pointing to the broken Victorian chair in the corner of the hall.
"Just because it was your mother's chair does not mean that Sue should get blamed for breaking it especially since it was Peter who broke your valuable chair!"
"Come here Peter," said Miss Breen turning immediately to Peter who happened to be standing in the hall close to the staircase. The ten year old boy came up to his foster mother tentatively.
"Did you break that chair?"
"No Miss Breen," said Peter looking at the floor.
"There I told you Sue broke the chair and blamed it on Peter," stated Miss Breen rather triumphantly.
"Of course he'd say that, because he is afraid that you will punish him," responded Estelle despondently.
"Oh stop it Estelle, it's extremely infuriatingly enough having the children answer me back, never

mind a staff member, if you want to stay in this job I suggest you go back to your duties."

"Yes Miss Breen."

"Go and tell Sue that she is to stay in her room for the rest of the day and she is only to come down for her meals."

"Never mind Sue," I heard Estelle saying to my sister after she had given Sue Miss Breen's message, "when I have finished my duties I'll pop upstairs to see you and I'll get you some of your favourites sweets while we have a chat about my family and the new clothes I am going to buy for the dance next Friday night."

"I don't know why Estelle is so close to that child I will have to have another chat with her if she wants to stay on here. She is getting far too close to some of the children and its not right," I heard Miss Breen telling to Miss Trellis during her usual evening telephone conversation to her friend when we were all upstairs in bed.

One day Miss Breen took us to visit her mother. We entered a small house, it had barely any light in the front room because the heavy velvet curtains were drawn blocking out the early afternoon sunshine.

"Now children you will need to speak up a bit because my mother is rather deaf," Miss Breen told us as she began ushering us into the small parlour, where her mother was sitting in a rocking chair, dressed in a white lace blouse and cream skirt with a shawl covering her lap. Miss Breen informed us that her mother was in her nineties.

"All my family have longevity of life," she said as she started to prepare the china cups for tea and cakes. I had never seen someone so old and I was struck at her mother's fragility. She smiled a bright smile at us and held out a long elegant but delicate bony hand from which the blue veins protruded. There was hardly any hair on her head but what was there had been styled in such a skilful manner that her head was covered in soft waves. I felt privileged to have visited Miss Breen's elderly mother because I felt as if I was seeing someone acutely historical because her mother had been born in another time and another era.

"My mother was born in the last century, in the Victoria times," confirmed Miss Breen proudly, "and as you know I visit my mother frequently to make sure the housekeeper is attending to her properly."

We knew when Miss Breen visited her mother because at times she just popped out of our foster home and left Estelle to look after us. Sometimes she went to visit her mother in the evenings after we went to bed. Bedtime was at seven o'clock and eight o'clock at the weekends for the older children; Miss Trellis then looked after us. Other times she left us to play in the playroom. This was an extra room that had been built as an extension to the house. It was big and airy with lots of windows and at these times either Estelle or Miss Trellis kept an eye on us. Miss Trellis was younger than Miss Breen, possibly in her early fifties and compared to Miss Breen, she looked rather glamorous with her dyed black hair and make up. Miss Breen never wore make up and always worn her hair in a grey plait which stopped just past her shoulders.

"I used to wear my hair longer when I was younger because it was so much thicker then but age has made it thinner," we were told.

Miss Trellis also owned a dog; she also used a walking stick to assist her mobility. Miss Breen's companion was a quiet lady who did not say very much, usually only to agree to whatever Miss Breen stated. Several months after the visit to Miss Breen's mother she died.

I was very attached to Maureen who I discovered was an orphan. We spent hours together doing what we considered big girls activities which were reading girls comics and experimenting with nail polish. Maureen became my mentor because she had breasts and wore a bra. I desperately wanted to grow breasts too but being so skinny I was pretty undeveloped.

"Mandy, why are you turning your back as you are changing out of your wet bathing costume, I can understand Maureen doing so but not you?" Miss Breen said one day when she caught me imitating Maureen. I blushed knowing that I had been caught out in front of the younger children and did not respond to my foster mother's question. It was as such that I so desperately wanted to be a teenager so that I could have some status.

One Saturday morning during breakfast when we were all reasonably quiet Miss Breen announced, "Children I have something to say to you all so I want you to listen very carefully."

I remembered that her tone of voice sounded distinctly more serious than normal because of this I felt an old familiar feeling in the pit of my stomach, which I had not felt for a long time. I could feel my body brace itself and prepare me for something, which at that time was unknown to me.

"I've put Dunraven on the market," Miss Breen announced, "I am selling the house. You must not worry children because all of you will be fine since most of you will be going back to London and Mandy and Sue will be going to live in a Convent which will be near your mother," I heard Miss Breen say reassuringly to us, "the Convent is in South London and it sounds very nice."

"But I don't want to go to some silly Convent," said Sue sounding affronted.

"Now Sue, I expected that from you, do you realise how difficult it has been to find a Catholic home who will take two children which is so near to your mother, and it was her wish that you go to a Convent. You are very lucky children," continued Miss Breen, "and I have spoken to the Reverent Mother on the telephone who sounds extremely pleasant."

"Why are you selling Dunraven?" my sensible understanding voice asked as I tried desperately not to cry in front of Sue.

"I am getting on now and apart from the fact that my mother has died there is nothing to stop me from fulfilling my life long dream which is to travel for a whole year to visit all of Europe in my camper van with Miss Trellis before we are both far too old to do so."

"Oh that makes sense," I admitted to myself since I had learnt very early on to embrace and advocate on behave of other people's needs at the detriment of my own.

"I knew I could relay on you Mandy to be circumspective about the subject," said Miss Breen sounding somewhat relieved, "and Sue you need not worry, your big sister Mandy will look after you."

"You are so sensible Mandy and you do watch out for me, in fact most times I think of you as taking the place of mummy!" Sue acknowledged to me afterwards while we were in the garden. It was evening and the weather had become rather unsettled after a warm early June day, "I am glad that I have a big sister like you but I am scared to move again especially to move to a Convent."

"Miss Breen never lies to us, does she?" I replied assuredly.

"Perhaps she doesn't lie but what does she know about living in a Convent?" alleged Sue.

"She knows a lot more about these matters than you

or I and you know as well that she had numerous conversations with Father Murphy after Sunday Mass, and sometimes she goes on a day's retreat to a Convent." I continued judiciously.

"Trust Miss Breen to get us into a Convent," Sue concluded not taking much notice of my advice.

"Oh I trust Miss Breen completely and I am sure the Convent won't be so terrible."

"Come up Mandy you know nothing about living in a Convent."

"What can we do, we have to trust Miss Breen as she has been involved in our next placement," I stated rather smugly.

"Hmm, I know that I will not be happy there. I am not happy here so why should I be happy there; anyway you are one of Miss Breen's favourites especially because you are always such a good girl and always do as you are told, because you are so afraid of getting into trouble in front of Miss Breen, just in case she will not like you anymore."

"That's not true" I retorted intractably.

"Anyway she doesn't love me but I think Estelle does," said Sue pulling one of her usual funny face, which made us both fall about laughing.

"I don't think we are supposed to be loved because we are in care," I told my sister since I was equally ambiguous about the concept of love.

"No, I don't think so either," agreed Sue.

"Well let's try and make the best of it," I said hiding my own fears and anxieties.

"I suppose so anyway we don't have any choice!"

For the rest of the time I spent at Dunraven's I had a few panic attacks along the way where I woke up at night in a cold sweat. I seemed fine in the day but at night I woke up with thoughts going around and around in my head about whether I would make new friends at the secondary modern school, which Miss Breen had said, was adjacent to the Convent. I had nightmares where Sue and I were running away from the devil who was trying to catch us. He always managed to catch Sue but because I was the fastest runner in my primary school, I always got away in the reoccurring nightmare. Although I was not caught, I returned to find my sister, knowing that I could never leave her. I used myself as a decoy so that Sue could get away. At that point in the nightmare I always woke up utterly terrified.

"What's the matter Mandy?" asked Miss Breen, the few times when she had caught me awake sitting up in bed when she conducted her routine nightly checks.

"I can't sleep," I told her fretfully.

"Try counting sheep up to a hundred that will send you to sleep again," she told me.

Other times I struggled with my inner thoughts as I tried to reason with God as to why we had to leave Dunraven. I always concluded that I had not been a good enough girl since I construed good girls always deserved more in life and always got what they wanted. I assumed that they were very happy living at home with their parents unlike Sue and I whose personal circumstances were so very different to other children's. No amount of care homes could prevent the insatiable longing of wanting to go home to our own family and the empty void left which we carried around internally could not be easily mollified. Invariably, my inner struggles with God left me feeling guilty about the next placement in London. After all, I told myself, Miss Breen was right she was nearly fifty-nine and many times she had reminded us, that she was far too old to look after children. So I endeavoured to gather all my inner strength and inner resources in order to prepare for the move to the new care home. However two years at Dunraven seemed no time at all to become settled into yet another placement which I had assumed was permanent before, Sue and I was on the move again. It was the end of July 1964 when my sister was nearly nine years old and I was almost eleven.

"But what about if I don't do well at school?" I told Miss Breen one morning.

"There's a parable in the Bible that says something like this Mandy, the man who has a multitude of talents but uses none of them will not be successful in the same way that a man, who has only one talent but nurtures it and develops it so that it grows, will be!"

I wanted so much to share my fears and anxieties with Miss Breen in greater depth but she was always preoccupied with the other foster children so I kept them to myself. Her manner of reciting parables from the Bible as a means of trying to allay my worries did not always help because I did not often understand their meanings. I had no concept of what my talents were and even less of a sense of how to develop them even if I could identify what they were. In the end as always I reprimanded myself for having asked for reassurance in the first instance. Besides I had to put on a brave face for Sue because who else did she have apart from me to comfort her.

"We all have our cross to bear," Miss Breen told all of us at the tea table a few weeks before we went our separate ways, when yet again we started to express doubts about yet another overwhelming move.

"Now you're the eldest Mandy so you need to set an example to your sister especially since you will be starting your secondary school in September while you are at the Convent," Miss Breen told me on the morning we left Dunraven.

"Goodbye you two," shouted Estelle as she wavered us off in Miss Breen's car.

"I will miss you Sue," I heard Estelle tell my sister

" and I will be thinking of you and don't you mind those nuns, do your hear me!"

"Don't worry Estelle," answered Sue "I can take care of myself besides at least I will be near my mummy at last so I can go and visit her."

The drive to London was sad and long as gradually the impartial countryside made way for the crowded London buildings. It was nearly six years since Sue and I had been separated from our mother. Now we were going back to London to be resettled into another care home. Undoubtedly it was another new and bewildering experience. I had come to associate London with my mother so the thought of travelling back to London but not to be reconciled with her was one of numerous emotional setbacks for both of us. To be told that we had to go to another care home because our foster mother that I had grown to love and respect, had a need to travel before her life was over seemed like fate had slapped its cruel hand across my face yet again. My hopes of being reunited with my mother before my childhood was over, seemed as remote as ever. I wanted the journey to be endless and for the car never to arrive at its destination. To make matters worse my car sickness did not help either. The nausea only broke up the monotony of the journey, since Miss Breen had to stop the car several times because the fumes from the petrol were more bilious than usual due to the long travelling distance.

"We are nearly there," reassured Miss Breen optimistically after we had travelled in silence for most of the journey.

"Where?" enquired my sister from the back seat of the car as we continued the journey up a winding hill.

"Look there in front of us, can you see the white walls, they are the Convent walls!" replied Miss Breen, as I looked up and saw huge white walls disappear around a corner way up ahead of us.

"Is the Convent behind those walls?" queried Sue aghast.

I said nothing as I withdrew further into myself as I sunk back into the passenger's seat and even further into a heavy depression. I preoccupied myself by staring at the cracks in the car upholstery as an uncontrollable feeling of needing to scratch away the cracks so that I could make the surface of the upholstery material smooth again engulfed me.

"Yes it must be," replied Miss Breen to Sue's question. I could not help but notice the element of surprise in her voice.

"It looks like prison walls," continued Sue in dismay.

"I don't know where the entrance is," said Miss Breen as she drove around the full length of the high white walls.

"Why has the Convent got such high walls?" asked Sue.

"Probably to protect the Convent from intruders I suspect," replied Miss Breen, "remember this is London now, not Kent!"

"It stills looks like a prison," moaned Sue "especially since we can't even find the entrance."

"I think I am going to turn the car around because we have clearly missed the entrance, we need to go back and look carefully for the drive in."

"We didn't see an entrance at the beginning of the wall, did we?" I exclaimed half hoping that we could turn around and go back to Dunraven.

"We've certainly missed it," said Miss Breen "it must have been amongst those hedgerows that can be the only explanation."

We drove back down part of the hill to the beginning of the semi circular wall.

"Look!" Miss Breen declared, "there's the sign which says the Sacred Heart Convent; the plaque is hidden partially by those overgrown brushes."

Silence accompanied anticipation as Miss Breen manoeuvred the car so that the bonnet was now pointed towards the narrow wrought iron entrance gates. Miss Breen got out of the car and opened the gates, we then drove up the gravel driveway with the rows of thick hedges on either side. The late July weather was hot and glorious and the rich green leaves surrounding us gave a Mediterranean mood to the afternoon. The vibrant shades of trees and hedges contributed to the almost grotto appearance we were heading towards.

"Oh what lovely rose brushes," exclaimed a delighted Miss Breen admiring the red flowers, and what a long drive way! "

"I wonder what the Convent looks like at the end of it," said Sue inquiringly.

"It must be quite grand," I answered her.

We were met at the end of the driveway by a huge white mansion.

"Oh part of the Convent must be Georgian," declared Miss Beacon immediately, "just look at those columns, what a magnificent piece of architecture, no doubt some rich aristocrat must have once own this building."

We got out of the car and walked towards a very ornate wooden door, which had a brass handle. Roman flowers urns stood to attention displaying their flowers almost combatively on each side of the pathway which had led us to the door. Miss Breen pressed the door bell as I looked around the front lawn and observed the splendour of the flower beds which bordered the huge lawns. After what seemed like ages, the door opened and a nun greeted Miss Breen. I was astonished when the nun appeared at the front door because she wore a traditional long black dress with a long pinafore or tunic over the top of it. On her head the nun wore a veil which completely hid her hair so that no strand of hair was visible, it was therefore hard to determine the age of the nun although she had a somewhat ruddy complexion.

"You must be Miss Breen and those must be the children, do come in," invited the nun smiling, "I am the Reverent Mother or Mother Superior, Maria Paul as she addressed herself to Miss Breen.

I noticed that she was tall and perhaps not as old as Miss Breen because she seemed more agile and her face unwrinkled. Since I had little understanding of the differentials of age I could only guess that she was between thirty and forty years of age. I was impressed by her height because I had never seen a woman who was quite so tall.

"How tall do you think she is?" I whispered to Sue.

"She's got to be close to six foot," replied Sue airily as she seemed more preoccupied with the reception hall that we had just entered, which was outstandingly opulent with its noticeably cool marble floor and grand spiral staircase located at the far end of the hall.

"I'm scared," I admitted to Sue squeezing her hand gently.

"She won't hurt you," Sue asserted being the strong one, "but she does look a bit like a penguin?"

"Shush," I murmured, regaining my sensibilities.

"I wouldn't like to wear those clothes all the time," remarked Sue during what appeared to be a lengthy conversation Miss Breen and the Reverent Mother were having as we stood in the reception hall.

"That's what all nuns wear," I acknowledged.

"I wonder if she sleeps in those clothes," proclaimed Sue.

"Don't be silly of course she doesn't wear those

clothes to bed," I said wondering if this assertion could be possible.

Neither one of us was exactly sure if the nuns wore their habits to bed.

On a closer look at the ornate spiral staircase, the balustrade's design was a delicate gold leaf and porcelain effect amidst the wrought iron features. The Reverent Mother led us away from the hall to the corridor on our immediate right.

"This is the library," she said opening the first door to show us a room full of books in impressively decorative bookcases. I noticed that the furniture in the room which had a large square table and six chairs were similar to Miss Breen's in style.

"The next room adjacent to this one is used as one of the two interview rooms where tea is usually served for any visitors. The rooms on the left are private and for the nuns exclusive use only," the Reverent Mother informed us.

"At the very end of this corridor is the chapel, let me show it to you because this is where all the children come to Mass on Sundays and on all the other holy days during the year. Now you children must be very quiet, especially when we enter the chapel; noise will not be tolerated," she said fervently.

We followed the Reverent Mother to the far end of the corridor where she opened the chapel door so that we could peep inside.

"This chapel looks like a fairytale palace!" whispered Sue.

"I know," I agreed, "it's very pretty."

"The chapel is so charming, quite exquisite." Miss Breen uttered in agreement.

"Yes it is delightful," acknowledged the Reverent Mother "we are very proud of it."

"Is the house Georgian?" enquired Miss Breen.

"Yes some parts of it are while some of the house was built during the Reformation however the annexes are more modern. The rest of the house was redeveloped in Victorian times," answered the Reverent Mother. "It originally belonged to a Lord who was a staunch Catholic and he left it to the Sacred Heart Order after the 2nd world war."

"No doubt a listed building then," stated Miss Breen.

"Only the mansion." replied the Reverent Mother, "the new building extensions are divided into three family units where the children are accommodated and each flat has a house mother to look after them with an employed assistant."

I noticed few solitary figures bent in prayer kneeling on some of the pews in the chapel. They appeared oblivious to us since they did not move at all. I wondered if they were breathing because they were so motionless, like statutes because of their trance like states. I guessed these were perhaps local people. After visiting the on site chapel, we followed the Reverent Mother back to one of the interview rooms for tea. This was served by a domestic while another Sister of the Sacred Heart Order entered to greet us and then began to instruct the assistant in the serving of the refreshments. I discovered later that this nun was known as Sister Margarita. She was rotund in stature was a quick smile. Tea was served in china cups while Sue and I drunk diluted orange squash from glass beakers.

"Your new housemother will be coming in to see you shortly," announced the Reverent Mother after we had finished our refreshments. I assumed that she had forgotten about us because she had ignored us for the majority of the time since she spent most of the time engaged in animated conversation with Miss Breen, as

Miss Breen discussed in great detail our recent Holy Communion ceremony.

"Her name is Sister Therese Marie and you probably would not have noticed her but she was in the chapel praying when we were visiting it earlier," continued the Reverent Mother. I instantly remembered that I had noticed a reclusive nun in the chapel but she had not aroused my curiosity enough to pay her much attention. I recollected that she was kneeling in one of the front rows of the pews, a small slight figure who was devoutly praying while keeping her eyes tightly shut. We ate the fairy cakes offered to us in silence because we were both overwhelmed by our new environment.

"I don't want to live in a Church," I heard Sue whisper to me remorsefully as she leaned over to me, when she thought the Reverent Mother could not hear her.

"Shush Sue, this building doesn't entirely comprise of a Church!"

After what seemed like an eternity there was a small sharp forceful knock on the door.

"Come in," requested the Reverent Mother.

The door handle turned and the nun the Reverent Mother had referred to earlier entered the room. Sister Therese Marie was a seemingly diminutive figure who was about five foot two inches in height and of slight build; furthermore it was difficult to estimate her age because similarly to the Reverent Mother, the nun could have been any age between thirty two and fifty such was the impossibility to determine their ages. On closer observation I noticed a strand of grey hair showing from under her veil which made me realise that she must be in her late forties or early fifties.

"Sister Therese Marie, do come in," invited the Reverent Mother standing up.

"This is Miss Breen and here are the two sisters you

will be looking after."

The three of us looked up at Sister Therese Marie who cordially introduced herself.

"Sister Therese Marie is a very experienced housemother and has looked after children who have been placed in our care for a good number of years' now." proclaimed the Reverent Mother.

"Pleased to meet you Sister Therese Marie," Miss Breen greeted our new housemother as she stood up to greet the nun.

"I am pleased to meet you Miss Breen, would you like me to show you where the children will be living?" asked Sister Therese Marie nonchalantly. Miss Breen arose from her chair and Sue and I did the same as we followed Sister Therese Marie who walked a little way ahead of us. We retraced our steps back into the reception hall passing another nun on her way to chapel. The nun bowed her head in acknowledgement as she passed us, making the sign of the cross. We all responded in the same manner continuing to walk across the marble floor towards the corridor opposite. Another nun had her back to us as she ascended the spiral staircase.

"Is that nun going up to heaven," Sue muttered sarcastically.

"Very funny, that must be where they sleep though."

"I don't like Sister Therese Marie or whatever her name is," said Sue sulkily.

"Hmm, well let's see what she's like," I told my sister.

"I can see what she is like already," Sue replied," She looks horrid!"

Miss Breen gave Sue a reproachful look that seemed to say do not dare make any more comments like that. At the end of the marble floor we continued to follow Sister Therese Marie through to the next corridor, which was dimly lit since there was no natural light. The corridor relied to some extent of the natural light that manifested from the two five foot windows at either side of the main front door. The remaining light came from the two small wall lamps on either side of the corridor that eventually took us out into a small open planned area; the floor covering was worn almost threadbare lino which was in stark contrast to the pristine polished wooden floors of the previous corridors, although the area was light and airy. I noticed that the natural light was coming from the fire door immediately to the right of us. Directly ahead of us was another set of stairs, approximately ten in number and they led to a magnolia door.

"Now that is Sister Joan's flat," the Reverent Mother informed us, "she is responsible for twelve children of all ages as well!"

"Is this where we are going to stay," Sue enquired.

"No dear, you will all be looked after by Sister Therese Marie," replied the Reverent Mother "so we need to follow her down these stairs which are to the left."

We proceeded to descend the fifteen steps, which lead us away from the natural light once more. Sister Therese Marie still led the way, followed by the Reverent Mother, while Miss Breen and Sue followed close behind them with me at the back. By the time I reached the last step an electric light had been switched on and the group had entered the lower ground floor.

"Now this is Sister Vincent's group home and she is responsible for fourteen children at the moment because we seemed to have had a influx of children to look after recently," stated the Reverent Mother to Miss Breen," Sister Therese Marie, Sister Therese Marie stop for one second won't you, I want to introduce Miss Breen and the children to Sister Vincent because she will be back from chapel now!"

Sister Therese Marie stopped and began to retrace her steps slowly as the Reverent Mother knocked on a door, which was slightly hidden when we had descended from the staircase due to a partitioning wall that had immediately confronted the staircase at first glance. The Reverent Mother went behind the partitioning wall and knocked on the secluded door.

"Is Sister Vincent there?"

"Sister Vincent, Sister Vincent, Reverent Mother wants to see you," I heard a young voice say amidst a noisy background of children's voices.

After a while Sister Vincent appeared, although she was slightly smaller that Sister Therese Marie she displayed a fuller figure. "Hello Reverent Mother and hello children," she said ardently, looking past the Reverent Mother to greet us.

"This is Miss Breen, who has been the children's foster mother for over two years."

"I am pleased to meet you."

"And you too," replied Miss Breen "the children have been a little bit anxious about the move naturally but I have told them that they do not need to worry because they are in safe hands."

"Yes I was hoping that they would be staying in my care but I simply did not have the room for the two of them," answered Sister Vincent.

"They will be fine with me," said Sister Therese Marie brushing a speck of fluff from the pinafore of her habit, "my children are as good as gold and are not as unruly as some………well I mean children in care can be very difficult at times."

I instantly noticed that Sister Vincent gave Sister Therese Marie a rather disconcerting sideward glance. I could not help but wonder what that meant.

Miss Breen and Sister Vincent conversed for

sometime while Sister Therese Marie entered into a separate discussion with the Reverent Mother.

"Well we best be going now because I know you will be off to the chapel shortly," the Reverent Mother concluded her conversation with our new house mother after what seemed like hours of adult discourse.

"Goodbye Miss Breen it was nice to speak to you and thank you for recommending that particular book to me, I will certainly see if I can get a copy from the Archbishop's library," said Sister Vincent in her softly spoken voice.

"Yes we will need to hurry along a little bit because I do need to return to the chapel this evening," said Sister Therese Marie briskly glancing at her watch that she took out from behind her pinafore. We were led past Sister Vincent's care home to another fire door, which Sister Therese Marie opened and which we went through. I found myself outside the Convent again as we walked in single file along a narrow path where on the right hand side was a school playground, which had a tarmac finish and had a twelve-foot green wire fence. On the left hand side was the Convent wall. In a few moments Sister Therese Marie stopped at another door along the wall.

"Here we are at last!" she declared undoubtedly sounding relieved as she opened the unlocked door.

We entered inside a small hallway as Sister Therese Marie walked over to sliding doors, which she promptly pulled open as the shuffling and whispering behind the partition quickly ceased into quietness and respectfulness.

"Hello Sister Therese Marie," a chorus of children's voices greeted her.

"Hello children," replied Therese Marie, "I hope that you have all been good children while I have been away and that you have been behaving yourselves?"

"Yes, Sister Therese Marie, of course we have Sister Therese Marie," replied the children again in chorus.

"Yes my children are very well behaved," remarked Sister Therese Marie proudly.

"I am sure they are," said Miss Breen approvingly.

I looked at the other children whose ages seemed to range from four upwards.

"This is Caithleen O'Sullivan," said Sister Therese Marie introducing a teenage girl who wore cat's eyes glasses and short white ankle socks, "she is fourteen and is my oldest most senior girl here. Caithleen has been with me since she was four years old. She helps with looking after the younger ones along with my daily help, Bridget O'Riley."

Caithleen, go and get Bridget O'Riley please, so that I can introduce her," ordered Sister Therese Marie.

"I'm here," said a voice from behind a room located to the left of the room.

A rather stout lady came down three steps from a room that had no door. I could partially see a very large table that was set ready for a meal because part of the dinning room was divided by a wall. She immediately began to rub her able hands in Sue's hair as she greeted the Reverent Mother and Miss Breen.

"You've got a good strong head of hair if ever I say so," she told my nine year old little sister.

I caught Sue's giggle out of the corner of my eyes as I tried not to look at her.

"Bridget does a lot of the domestic duties such as making the beds for the young ones, washing the floors and bringing the meals down from the communal kitchen which is on the first floor landing towards the children's bedrooms. I also expect the older children to help as well," Sister Therese Maria said looking directly at me.

As I looked around the room I could not help but

notice the contrast in the furniture from that of Miss Breen's which was of quality compared to the old threadbare and broken furniture, in the communal sitting in which I was now standing in. The settee at the opposite end of the room was not only sporting a broken arm rest but the upholstery was also torn and badly stained. In fact the ninety sixties furniture appeared cheap and of sub standard.

"We are very lucky here you know," I could not help but overhear Sister Therese Marie mention to Miss Breen, "we get a lot of donations of furniture and clothes for the children from the local Catholic charities, which we are so grateful for because if we did not, we simply could not provide for the children adequately enough."

I looked at the children's clothes and was not impressed because their clothes seemed extremely ill fitting. Some of their garments were either too small or too large and some of the clothes I observed to be very old fashioned.

"I always ensure that the children are dressed sensibly," continued Sister Therese Marie, "even the teenagers like Caithleen are dressed decently; none of those indecent mini skirts which are suddenly becoming fashionable; the children are not allowed to wear those sorts of clothes here. Honestly, I do not know what the world is coming to with all this new pop music blaring out from the radio every five minutes."

"Well there are a lot of heathens out there if you ask me," interrupted Hannah O'Riley who I determined with in her early fifties.

"She looks like she's just come over from the Irish bog," mumbled Sue to me a short while afterwards, "she's still probably got cow's shit under her shoes and some straw still left in her hair."

"Oh stop it Sue," I said trying to conceal a secret

smile to myself.

"Well children," declared Miss Breen "it is time for me to go now. I will ring Sister Therese Marie and the Reverent Mother regularly to see how you are getting on and of course I will write to you both too."

In no time our foster mother was gone.

"Follow me and I will show you to your bedroom," the nun instructed, turning around quickly so that her habit flared out like a dancer's dress as we followed her up two sets of staircases to the room at the end of the corridor upstairs to unpack our small suitcases.

The bedroom was furnished with a Formica dressing table top, a wardrobe and two small bedside cabinets, which were on each side of the single beds. I noticed that a bible was laid on each of the bedside cabinets. One pink and one blue rosary were placed on top of each pillow and two wooden crucifixes were pinned to the wall above each headboard.

"Now chose which bed you want to sleep in, then unpack your suitcases and then come down stairs for tea." directed Sister Therese Marie," all the older children have duties to do such as washing the younger children in the mornings and before they go to bed. Mandy you will be starting secondary school soon so you must set the example to the others by washing and dressing the little ones each day, and particularly when I am at chapel praying for you all. Your sister is too young to help you but she can help polish the stairs lending up to the bedrooms on Saturdays along with the other children of her age group!"

We dare not say anything or to even think of answering back the nun.

It was made very clear that we had to do what we were told and to get on with what was expected of us.

"I definitely don't like her," Sue told me after Sister Therese Marie had left the bedroom.

"Oh she's alright," I said not wanting to pursue the matter.

"She's a dragon," continued Sue.

"Don't start Sue I'm tired. It's been a very long day, "I told my sister as I suddenly felt devastatingly tired as I tried to placate her, "and besides I am starting secondary school in September which is a big step for me so let's just make the best of it while we are here."

"That's typical of you Mandy isn't it," replied Sue angrily, "well let me tell you she's no Estelle you know."

"What does that mean?" I said trying not to sound cross.

"It means that she's a nun and a very strict one I'm sure," responded Sue.

"Well you always said that Miss Breen was strict so that's nothing new," I replied.

"Yes I know but at least Estelle knew everything about the outside world, this place is like a prison." muttered Sue indignantly.

"Come on Sue let's go down to tea and meet the other children," I said changing the subject.

We met four boys on the way down to tea; they introduced themselves as Daniel, Bernard, David and Patrick.

"What's your room like?" Daniel immediately asked us.

"Nothing to write home about," Sue replied indifferently.

"I don't like it here sometimes," said Patrick instinctively taking Sue's hand and looking apprehensively up at her. He was a little boy who was perhaps five or six years old. Daniel described to us the layout of the other bedrooms. There were six bedrooms in all; three of the rooms were designated to the girls and the other bedrooms to the boys. As we started to descend the staircase Patrick held on to Sue's hand as if he had just found a new trusted friend.

"Come on Patrick let's go and have our tea," reassured my sister to the little boy.

"Where are your parents from Patrick?" Sue asked the child as Daniel and Harry seemed to have gone on ahead of us, passing the kitchen on the way down to the communal dinning room.

"From Nigeria," replied Patrick sounding slightly unsure. We carried on talking to Patrick for a while until we were interrupted.

"Hey you two new children it's teatime so hurry up, we are waiting for you, we can't say prayers until we are all at the dining table, and Patrick you can hurry along as well!" shouted a voice from the bottom of the stairs. We descended the staircases quickly to the bottom. The first staircase led to an area with a door opposite and a door to the immediate left. The door to the left was open and as I looked inside I saw a huge kitchen with a nun and two domestic ladies helping Sister Margarita, with the cooking. One of the domestics was peeling potatoes taken from a huge sack on the floor which was prompt up against one of the steel frames where one of the two sinks was located. The other domestic was insouciantly prodding peas. The second door I later ascertained was the refectory. We continued down the second stairwell and at the bottom we entered through an open doorway which was facing us and turned immediately left to follow the winding corridor. The corridor on the right seemed to lead to another door at the far end but the corridor was poorly lit and seemed uninviting. We arrived back to the communal living room area where we had said our goodbyes to Miss Breen earlier.

"Hello again," said Caithleen who was waiting for us in the corridor," As Sister Therese Marie mentioned earlier, I am the senior girl here and I expect you will be one as well!"

"Well I don't know," I answered her hesitatingly because I was reluctant to take up the role of a senior child since I was fearful of being allocated more responsibilities than I had just been assigned to already.

"Oh I think so, how old are you?" queried Caithleen.

"She's only eleven," Sue said in my defence.

"You look older although you haven't developed any breasts yet, you are very tall though, aren't you?" observed Caithleen.

"Yes I was one of the tallest girls in my class," I affirmed relieved that Caithleen appeared to be so friendly. "What's it like here?"

"It's not bad, in fact I like it here," Caithleen informed me.

"How long have you been here then?" asked Sue.

"I've been here since I was four years old," answered Caithleen.

"Four years old, that's a long time, it's one year older than when I went into care," acknowledged Sue sounding dismayed.

"If it wasn't for the nuns I don't know what would have happened to me," Caithleen impressed upon us in a grateful tone of voice.

"What happened to your parents?" Sue asked the teenager.

"I don't know, what I do know it that I was left on the steps of the Convent by my mother," explained Caithleen jauntily.

"Why would your mother want to do that?" I inquired.

"Sister Therese Marie said that my mother couldn't cope with me because she wasn't married at the time she gave birth to me," replied Caithleen, "and she had come from a small village in Ireland but came to England to have me. Sister Therese Marie said that her parents more than likely told her that she would not be welcomed back to Ireland if she did not have the baby adopted over here."

By this time we had reached the communal dinner room to take our place behind our allocated chairs I suddenly became extremely shy since all the children were watching 'the new children' as Sue and I were referred to until the next new child arrived at the group home. Sister Therese Marie stood like a sergeant major at the head of the table, in front of the window and Bridget O'Riley stood to her left. Behind Bridget, I could see a sink and kitchen units.

"Now you new children come and stand behind the vacant dining chairs, like good children, so that we can all say our prayers together," Sister Therese Marie commanded. "That's right, now you other children are to set a good example to these new girls so that they can settle in quickly, so stand up straight every one and show the new girls how to behave. There is to be no mumbling at prayers and no slouching at the tea table; and of course there are not to be any elbows on the table. As usual I want you all to speak up clearly and loudly so that you can show God how grateful you are for this lovely meal before you."

I looked down at the meal on the table, it was toad in the hole and it was dried up. There were soggy boiled potatoes beside it and also white bread in the middle of the table, covered in thin margarine that was hardly noticeable. Sister Therese Marie led the woefully extended prayers and if the food was not already cold it certainly was be by the time we finished our prayers, I could not help thinking to myself as I stood behind my chair trying desperately to assimilate into my new, strange home. Goodness knows what was going through the mind of my little sister at that precise moment.

"In the name of the Father and of the Son and of the Holy Ghost'…Sister Therese Marie recited the Lord's Prayer which was followed by the Hail Mary; we then prayed for the holy souls in purgatory before finally sitting down to eat.

"Now children that Amen was not very loud and Bernadette you were playing with your hair the whole time I was saying the Lord's prayer, no pudding for you tonight."

"I wasn't Sister Therese Marie," said a timid voice from the other side of the table. I looked up and saw Bernadette who must have been about five years old. Her blond hair was in two ponytails and I noticed that her pink glasses were lopsided on her face.

"Yes you were, now don't you dare answer me back. Don't you dare tell lies in front of the Lord," scolded Sister Therese Marie stamping her foot and pointing her figure at the little girl.

"No Sister Therese Marie," replied Bernadette in a frightened, resonated voice.

"You know I am always right, don't you child?" stated Sister Therese Marie

"Y,Yes," stuttered Bernadette.

The twelve of us dutifully sat down at the table to eat.

"Now shush children don't scrape the chairs against the floor, pick them up when you sit down," insisted Sister Therese Marie sitting down in her chair.

"Yes Sister Therese Marie," the children's voices were heard, once again in chorus.

"And you two new girl, you are to learn to do what you are told, because there will be no exceptions to the rules here," Sister Therese Marie informed Sue and I.

"See I told you that she was a dragon!" whispered

Sue to me.

"And that new girl, what is your name; I said what is your name, child?" asked Sister Therese Marie; raising her voice and looking in Sue's direction.

"Which one are you talking to Sister?" enquired Bridget O'Riley peering down the table to identify which of us had whispered.

"That one with the blue dress on," responded Sister Therese Marie gesticulating to where Sue was sitting.

"Oh do you mean me," I heard Sue say, knowing full well that Sister Therese Marie indeed meant my sister.

"Yes you, do not whisper or talk when I am speaking, do you hear,"

Sister Therese Marie stated, "I must simply be obeyed consistently and furthermore rudeness will not be tolerated."

"Yes," answered Sue rather skittishly.

"You call me Sister Therese Marie at all times do you hear me, you are to show me respect at all times because I am a Sister of the Sacred Heart Order and I am answerable to God, and to the Lord only."

"Yes Sister Therese Marie," replied Sue in a drawn out tone as she raised her eyes at me.

"Now eat your tea and not another word from any of you," said Sister Therese Marie.

We all eat in silence watched by Sister Therese Marie who was reading her bible but every so often glanced up at us from behind her spectacles.

"Can you pass the bread please?" asked Sue of Daniel.

I watched Daniel lift up the plastic plate with the bread on it and pass it to Sue. Sue and I watched the other children's table manners and took our cue from them. It seemed the only time we could talk was when we were asked to pass some food around to each other.

"Daniel you know that you are not to put your elbows on the table you must set the new children a good example and backs and shoulders straight please, so all of you sit up straight and stop slouching, how many times do I have to tell you, *Jesus, Mary and Joseph*. Mandy help to pass around the teapot because it is far too heavy for the younger children to pass around," reproached Sister Therese Marie.

"Jane can you pass me the orange squash," Sue asked another girl with short red hair.

"I'll pass it to you," I offered reaching out across the table to pick up the rather shoddy plastic jug.

"This isn't proper orange squash, this tastes mainly of water," declared Sue after taking a sip from the beaker in front of her. I could not help but notice the disappointment and hurt in her voice as she spoke. I knew that one thing she always liked and enjoyed at Miss Breen's was her orange squash and barley water drinks because they seemed to be mixed just right and as a result they were very refreshing. Sue drank the watery squash in a sullen silence, which left a solemn mood on all of us.

I did not particularly care for the watchful eye of Sister Therese Marie because she made me feel uncomfortable.

"Now you children are to ensure that you eat with the correct table manners and to always sit up straight, and that means you also, you new girl," said the nun looking over at me. I immediately felt embarrassed and put on the spot. I felt I had been named and shamed on that first meal so I think that I consciously resolved to be as good and as submissive as I possible could be since it seemed to be my only means of self preservation.

"A big girl like you should not be slouching; you should be setting an example to the little ones and especially to your sister, Mandy!"

Sister Therese Marie continued as she stared at me with her icy blue eyes.

"I'm sorry Sister Therese Marie, I won't do it again," I found myself saying in an apologetic voice, which I did not know had existed until then.

"And don't hang you head down like that, look how silly you are!"

"I'm sorry Sister Therese Marie, I will try not to do it again," I said as I noticed that my head sunk further and further into my chest as if it had a mind of its own. I felt humiliated even more so as I was aware that Sue was seeing a side of me that she had never seen before and I felt powerless. The more I wanted to raise my head, the more I could not.

With everyone staring at me, I thought I heard a few giggles. I wished at that moment the floor would open up and consume me. I felt excruciatingly ashamed for no doubt a few minutes but the experience for me was psychologically so traumatic that those minutes seemed like an eternity. Invariably the floor never swallowed me up and those torturous moments only ceased when my new housemother took it upon herself to make her way to the chapel. I was reprieved, by the blessed chapel bells, ringing out across the Convent grounds and into my group home.

"The chapel bells are ringing for the six o'clock Mass so I must be off to chapel shortly otherwise I will be late joining the other Sisters of the Sacred Heart for prayers, so hurry up and finish your tea so that we can all say our prayers at the end of the meal," proclaimed Sister Therese Marie. We had more or less finished our evening meal so when the last child had put down their cutlery Sister Therese Marie led the final prayers of thanks.

"Thank you Father, for this lovely meal, that you

have so generously provided for us today. The children are trying very hard to be good and they are sorry for all the bad things, which they have done today. With your help and blessing they will learn the good ways of the Lord and be forever grateful for your mercy and love for them. Amen. "

With the conclusion of the evening prayers she gathered up her bible and with her rosary jingling from her robes she hurriedly left the dining room; leaving all of us to help with the clearing up of the table and the washing and drying up.

"Mandy you can dry the crockery and Caithleen you can wash up as usual and Lucy you can put all the left over food in that plastic bowl and take it around to the pig's bins around the back. Gordon you can help her. " Bridget O'Riley ordered.

"Do I have to go and empty the slops in the pig's bin," Gordon protested as if it was beneath him.

"Yes you do," said Bridget O'Riley.

After the dining room was cleaned and set again by the younger children for the following morning's breakfast we sat in the sitting room.

"Where have you two come from?" asked one of the other boys who I guessed to be about ten years old.

"We've come from Kent," answered Sue.

"I don't want to eat anymore sausages, not at breakfast time or at tea time when we have 'toad in the hole'," declared Anne who had mousy brown short hair.

"Well you must eat your food because you hardly ate anything," Bridget told her, "you must eat something or you won't grow up to be big and strong and you are lucky Sister Therese Marie did not notice or else she would have made you eat everything on your plate."

"I'm not eating those fatty sausages again either;

they had so many fatty bits inside them," noted Sue in disgust.

"They are not like the sausages Miss Breen used to buy us," I observed.

"Who is Miss Breen?" asked Hilary who had sat opposite Gordon at the tea table.

"She's the lady who used to look after us and she's the one who brought us here today," I replied.

"She used to make her own nut and vegetables burgers," emphasized Sue to the group of children, remembering that instance, one of the things she appreciated about Miss Breen.

"Yes that was your favourite food wasn't it Sue?"

"I am so glad Sister Therese Marie has gone to chapel," said a boy with a pronounced Irish accent which sounding similar to Bridget O'Riley's accent.

"Why?" I asked in astonishment.

"Oh that dragon, Sister Therese Marie and by the way my name is Kieran, what are your names again?" replied the boy.

"Now don't you dare call Sister Therese Marie names behind her back!" proclaimed Bridget who I established was appallingly loyal to her employer.

"Well she is!" replied Kieran defiantly.

"See, "said Sue triumphantly "I told you she was a dragon the first moment I saw her but the Reverent Mother seems quite nice."

"The Reverent Mother is very nice," confirmed Caithleen.

"Yes but we never see her," said Anne.

"How old are you?" asked Sue.

"Seven," answered the girl, "and this is my sister Bernadette."

A younger version of Anne who was sitting beside her on the dilapidated settee gave a shy smile before she looked down at her gingham frock and pulled obsessively at the thread of her hem as it quickly unravelled. I remembered Bernadette being the child who Sister Therese Marie had told off earlier at the tea table. I began to relax a little after noting that the atmosphere had changed entirely now that Sister Therese Marie had made her exit. I noted that Sue also appeared less morose.

"This seems such a strange place," noted Sue, "and does Sister Therese Marie always go to the chapel every evening?"

"Oh yes," replied Kieran" she is so much in love with God, and the Lord Jesus; and the Virgin Mary that she can't bear to tear herself away from the chapel for a single moment longer than she has too!"

"Now, now Kieran, stop teaching the new children bad ways," reprimanded Bridget O'Riley who had a matronly manner about her as she feebly attempted to control the conversation away from Sister Therese Marie.

"Well it's what she does every day and she's always telling me off, nothing is good enough for her," stated Kieran who was sitting at the small table in the living room mindlessly swinging his legs two and fro from underneath it.

"That's because she only likes the younger ones," said an intelligent voice that up until now had been sitting quietly beside Sue on one of the other chairs in the living that was part of a set of three.

"Why is that then?" enquired Sue turning towards the boy who has just spoken.

"Well I suppose they do exactly what they are told," said Bernard who had been one of the boys we had met on the upstairs landing before teatime.

"What is your name, again?" I asked a boy who was sitting on one of the arms of the settee.

"Gordon Smith," he replied in a matter of fact

manner.

"You mean book head," said Bridget O'Riley.

"Oh just because you can't read or write properly," replied Gordon unconcerned.

"Now you children can watch the children's programmes until seven o'clock and then it is bedtime for the younger children." informed Bridget O'Riley.

"Why is Gordon so clever?" I asked plucking up the courage to speak directly to Bridget, after deciding that she no longer intimidated me anymore.

"I don't know if he is clever but he is certainly lazy, he never helps although he is twelve, and all he ever does is put his head in books and comics as an excuse not to help.

"So what, who do you come to when you can't read something in the Irish newspaper." said Gordon.

"Well it's not my fault I had to stop going to school at ten to help out on my father's farm after my mother died," said Bridget O'Riley crossly.

"If you want me to read your letters or newspapers then leave me alone," said Gordon annoyed.

"Is all the food as bad as it was tonight?" I asked Bridget O'Riley.

"Yes, it is," replied Gordon, and we have to eat it."

"I never eat the vegetables," said Kieran.

"Yes you do," said Bridget O'Riley.

"No I don't Bridget O'Riley but you are so unobservant and far too busy trying to impress Sister Therese Marie that you haven't noticed that all I do it mix them all up and then play around with them on my plate to give the impression that I have eaten some of them and that I was given far too much food in the first place."

"But you eat it them when Sister Therese Marie tells you to," said Bridget O'Riley trying unsuccessfully to conceal her confusion.

"You mean that is the times when I stuff especially the greens in my mouth and hold them there until I go to the toilet where I spit them out afterwards. Sister Therese Marie is always insistent that we eat everything on our plates because she says we must think of the starving kids in Africa who have no food, but I do get away with not eating the vegetables sometimes, but not as much as I would like too,"

"I like the food here," stated Anne, "don't we Bernadette?"

"Yes," replied Bernadette, nodding her head in agreement.

"I don't know how you can eat that bubble and squeak; I simply hate any kind of greens,"

"I want my mummy," cried Bernadette now breaking down in tears.

"We will see mummy one day," Anne reassured her little sister protectively who was clearly confused and distressed.

"How old are you both," I asked surprised at my own tone of authority.

"Bernadette is three and I am eight," answered Anne maturely.

"What happened to your mummy?" enquired Sue.

"She's sick and cannot look after us and daddy went away," answered Anne.

"Do you remember you mummy and daddy?" asked Patrick.

"Of course we do, silly!" the sisters replied.

"I don't remember my mummy or my daddy," disclosed Patrick. We were all silent for a while because we did not know what to say.

"We've only been here since Easter," continued Anne, "how long is that now Bridget?"

"That's about let's see, its August now and you both came here last April so it's about five months," replied

Caithleen before Bridget could work out the number of months in question.

"What about you Gordon?" I enquired.

"My parents where killed in a car crash in Scotland and I was the only one to survive. My Auntie and Uncle couldn't look after me so they put me in care and I came here," replied Gordon with a bravado tone to his rather anguished voice.

That night as I lay in my new bed in the same room I shared with Sue while numerous thoughts were going around in my head. I was not sure I could tolerate the food especially after being told by Gordon that most of it was cooked the day before we ate it. What kept going around in my head were Gordon words and you should taste the fried eggs, bacon and sausages, if your taste buds can get passed the thick congealed lard that smothers the eggs you know that you are going to survive here." I felt myself retching then and there so I had quickly changed the conversation. Sue and I chatted well into the night after Sister Therese Marie had switched off our bedroom light. Sue had fallen asleep before me while I watched the statue of Our Lady of Lourdes illuminate the dressing table as it radiated a white and blue glow of light from the robes on the statue. I heard the chapel bells ringing out late into the night as my troubled mind eventually rested enough to sleep and I prayed to God that Sue would not wet her bed like she had done regularly at Miss Breen's.

Chapter IV

"Now girls time to get up," a brisk cold voice rudely interrupting my treasured sleep the morning after we had arrived at the Sacred Heart Convent. My thoughts quickly intensified sufficiently enough to discern that it was the nun's voice; she was now our newly assigned housemother. I slowly stirred in my bed, even though I was exhausted because of the turbulent sleep I had suffered. The constant changes of foster homes had taken their toll and now created even more internal demons for me as each new move seemed to be more unsettling than the last one.

"Now hurry up you two new girls and Mandy you are to help with the little ones," commanded Sister Therese Marie as she threw the bed sheets back which left me with a sense of shame and exposure as never before. I was however to become familiar with this routine from that day on.

"Now what's this?" she said to Sue as she threw back her bed sheets, "you have wet the bed haven't you. Miss Breen told me about this filthy nasty habit of yours; now it's got to stop, do you hear me as she tried in vain to push my sister's face into the wet patch. Every time you wet the bed, I am going to rub your face in it like this, do you understand."

"Yes," said Sue meekly bowing her head because she was clearly ashamed and upset about the bedwetting.

"Now you call me Sister Therese Marie at all times do your hear me, at all times you are to respect your housemother; and as I am your housemother make no mistake about it; you have obviously forgotten since yesterday, that you are to show me the utmost respect," she announced, with an air of utter arrogance and supremacy.

"Yes Sister Therese Marie," answered Sue in a dispirited unresisting voice.

"Next time you wet the bed, I will rub your nose in it," ranted Sister Therese Marie as she repeated herself.

"Come Sue, I'll help you to take the sheets down to the laundry room," I volunteered to her after the nun had left the room and we had recited our daily prayers and got dressed.

"But everyone will see me with these wet sheets," Sue protested as I saw the desperate tears swelling up in her eyes and begin their slow journey down her cheeks.

"Come on Sue, I'll be with you," I replied gently.

"I don't want the other children or the nuns to see me going down stairs with my wet sheets. They will know that it is me who has wet the bed and I already feel so ashamed," repudiated Sue.

"Look, I'm coming with you aren't I, so let's get it over with," I replied as I began to hurriedly gather up the sheets. Sue began to assist me and we started to descend the staircase together; going past the open door of the extensive kitchen, we then hurried across the landing, before descending the second flight of stairs.

"Where do you think you are going Mandy?" I heard Sister Therese Marie's voice bellow after me.

"I'm going to help my sister take her sheets down to the laundry room," I replied awkwardly.

"No you don't, she is perfectly capable of taking the sheets to the laundry room herself. After all she is the one who wet her bed, not you, you come back here and help wash the little ones, Caithleen and Bridget need an extra pair of hands," retorted Sister Therese Marie.

"It's OK Mandy, I'll manage on my own," announced Sue as she started to descend the second flight of stairs on her own with the bed sheets bundled up in both her arms.

"Now go and help Anne and Bernadette to wash themselves and make sure they are dressed properly afterwards and that their hair is brushed and combed, little Patrick and Daniel will be next in turn," riposted Sister Therese Marie.

I submissively did what I was told without question because instinct told me that I had no choice but to obey the rules and commands as dictated by Sister Therese Marie.

The next time I saw Sue was when we were at the dining table waiting for breakfast. Along with the rest of the children we resignedly stood behind our chairs and said our prayers before the meal with our heads hung over our praying hands.

"And I want you all to pray for Sue Mensan who is a bed wetter, we must pray that she will become a good girl in the eyes of God, so she will stop wetting the bed because we all know, don't we children, that only good girls and boys can enter the kingdom of Heaven," countered Sister Therese Marie, "now all say after me...please God make the new girl Sue Mensan a good and obedient child so that she will be answerable to you only; and not to the devil who with his evil ways makes her wet her bed…. Amen.

"Amen," chorused the children.

We sat down to the breakfast table where in the middle of the large table was long aluminium serving trays, which I had seen the evening before in the kitchen when requesting some milk from Sister Margarita for supper the previous night. The tray nearest to me contained what appeared to represent chipolata sausages however most of them were charcoal in colour due to their burnt and grossly overcooked condition. The second metallic tray contained very dried pieces of crispy bacon in it and the third tray had fried eggs in it. The majority of the eggs appeared overcooked and were swimming in lard, which looked like it had solidified around the pre heated eggs. The two remaining trays each contained black and brown pudding, which were cut in circular fashion.

"Now everyone pass the trays around to each other and make sure you eat up all your breakfast," demanded Sister Therese Marie.

I took an egg, some bacon, a sausages and one piece of black pudding. I was starving due to eating the bland and unappealing toad in the hole the previous evening but not taking a second portion despite still feeling hungry. I cut into the egg with my knife and proceeded to eat a piece of it. It tasted awful. The solidified lard sat in my mouth and refused to digest while the egg white was phlegmatic and unpleasant to the extent that I could not distinguish between the bits in my mouth that were the lumpy lard or the inedible egg white. I took one hard swallow but the piece of the egg I had put in my mouth obstinately lingered at the back of my throat. I knew instinctively that if I did not force it down I would vomit by virtue of having some alien substance in my mouth, for more that my taste buds could reasonably endure. I therefore forced myself to swallow with all my might however the eating of these fried eggs was to become my Achilles heel. I carried on eating the rest of the food on my plate as I looked out of the window as a means of distraction. I mercifully began to elicit fond memories of some of the meals Miss Breen had prepared. Those memories and the ensuing daydreams emanating a better existence that assisted in the distraction of that meal and many of the Convent meals until the poignancy of these memories became more and more evasive. Sister Marie

Therese frequently reproached me for staring out the window; I then ate what I could and left very little on my plate I was still hungry though because I only put on my plate the bear minimum of food so that I would not be told off. Afterwards I was instructed to help with the clearing up of the table followed by participating in the washing and drying up as part of the daily chores. I then assisted Bridget to throw the sops in the pigs' bins at the back of the institution if the other children had managed to escape such a task. Breakfast was the most ritualistic ordeal, which I was obliged to tolerate as a means of averting my hunger because all meals were compulsory. In time I discovered that stuffing myself with the tasteless white fluffy bread, which accompanied most meals helped to digest the fried eggs since the bread seemed to be the only food that agreed with my stomach. Even though the numerous times I tried to digest the egg while yearning for more substantial and nutritional food never wavered. Despite my efforts to pretend the horrid food was more desirable that it really was. I constantly retched and vomited the eggs up in the toilet after I hurriedly made my excuse to leave the breakfast table to carry out this laborious ordeal. Occasionally, I would try another burnt sausage but I had to eventually stop eating those because they were so hard that I could not even cut them in two with my knife, never mind desperately trying to chew them with my teeth. It was a defeatist task so I ultimately gave up despite my wishful desire to eat a tasty sausage, if only to fulfil my dream of eating a succulent sausage for once. The other children often broke the small chipolata sausages with their fingers that was a feat accomplished to the sounds of snapping around the table. In time, my appetite diminished and became less demanding of me because it seemed as if the sausages had won the day conclusively, due to their impenetrability and inedibility. Eventually they were abandoned on the breakfast plates. It was a struggle to eat anything remotely satisfying or pleasurable to my young palate at the breakfast table.

"Sue and Patrick why aren't you eating your breakfast," Sister Therese Marie remonstrated on many a morning.

"I don't eat meat," complained Sue before Patrick could formulate the words in his mind to respond to the sudden attack at the breakfast table.

"You eat what you are given, you don't eat meat, what kind of nonsense is that," scolded the nun.

"The egg is stone cold and all the fat is congealed," protested Sue.

"Children are dying in Africa every day and God only knows, they would be glad of good meal like this, now eat it up or you will go hungry, I don't know what the world is coming to," Sister Therese Marie castigated.

Oftentimes when we were so brow beaten by Sister Therese Marie's brand of parenting and her ninety nine percent of berating and belittlement, we made an huge effort to eat the breakfast with loads of bread, to disguise the taste of the congealed eggs; the burnt rock hard sausages; the black and brown burnt puddings, and the shrivelled up bacon. Sue never ate the sausages or for that matter any other meat, Kieran and Gordon always ate her portion when Sister Therese Marie was not paying attention; that was normally when her head was ensconced in her bible.

Surprisedly, we both settled into our enforced environment very quickly and ventured to follow the persecutory rules as best we could. Our ability to adapt to our immediate environment and our sense of survival ensured that this was the case.

"Now you must ask permission if you want to go upstairs and read in your bedroom Mandy," reproached Sister Therese Marie time and time again, "you just can't assume that you can do what you like you know, only lazy girls want to read, and besides you are only to read Catholic books apart from the bible and you also need to learn to pull your weight around here more like Caithleen does, in fact you are not to read at all in your bedroom apart from reading your bible."

"Permission, permission, permission, I am sick of Sister Therese Marie always telling us we've got to ask permission," bemoaned Sue for the umpteenth time, "even Miss Breen wasn't like that."

"And we never had to ask Miss Breen for permission for everything we did," I agreed with Sue, when Sister Therese Marie was no longer within earshot.

"It's a wonder that we don't have to ask for her permission to fart, since we even have to ask her permission to go to the toilet," responded Sue.

"Oh Sue that's funny," said Patrick who seemed to absolutely adore his new found friend.

"It seems as if we cannot have minds of our own anymore," I lamented in a frustrated voice.

"Well you haven't Mandy, even though you are becoming one of Sister Therese Marie's favourites because you never question what she tells you to do, in fact you are like her slave," declared Sue angrily.

"No I am not," I replied defensively," but I just can't stand the humiliation and the scolding we receive if we disobey her.

"Yes, but you are also afraid of her," replied Sue.

"No I am not," I answered unconvincingly, "and besides I don't want to go to hell when I die."

"She's always saying that if we are not good children we will go to hell," said Daniel who was listening to the two of us arguing.

"I don't know about hell, all I know it that to me Sister Therese Marie *is* hell itself," Sue contended.

"Oh Sue, don't blaspheme like that; you best tell the priest that you have sinned when you go to confession on Friday or else you will not be able to take Holy Communion next Sunday," I said genuinely feeling shocked at her response.

"Why should I go and confess my sins when Sister Therese Marie is always trying to brain wash us all anyway. I have really tried to be good this week because Sister Therese Marie said that mummy may come and see us on Sunday," said Sue who was now becoming visibly excited.

"Yes this will be the first time, we'd have seen her in a long while," I exclaimed sharing Sue's joy and excitement at the sheer possibility that our mother would be visiting us in our new foster home.

"Remember Miss Breen had said that one of the reasons we moved back to London was because our mother couldn't travel down to Kent to visit us, as it was too far, but instead she could come and see us here," Sue continued.

"It would be nice to see her before I start secondary school next Monday," I said in anticipation. All the children waited eagerly for Sundays. In fact we lived for Sundays in the hope that our families would visit us. Sue and I could not wait to see our mother after all these years. It seemed at last that our dream was about to come true.

"It looks like she is still coming Sue," I said on Saturday night with my hopes rising, "because Sister Therese Marie hasn't said yet that mummy's not coming tomorrow."

"I can't wait to see her and tell her how horrible this place is," answered Sue.

"I wonder if she has still got long hair that goes all the way down her back." I said remembering that was one of my last memories of my mother, "and I wonder if she still wears those fashionable suits that she used to wear."

"Don't be silly Mandy that was in the fifties, it's the sixties now and everyone is wearing more modern clothes, I expect that she is wearing similar clothes to what Estelle wore," claimed Sue.

"Like those full petticoats underneath those skirts", I said, as I fantasized my mother in the latest fashion.

"No, Estelle will be wearing mini skirts now but I don't think mummy will be wearing short skirts," reflected Sue.

"I don't like the clothes Caithleen wears or the other children," confessed Sue. "They are so old fashion, the sort of clothes my granny would wear if I had one."

"Oh stop it Sue," I responded with a smile.

"Well you better watch out Mandy being so tall, Sister Therese Marie might force you to wear similar clothes to Caithleen and if you do all the schoolchildren will start to snigger behind your back and laugh at you." warned David.

"I would hate that," I replied. The thought was not worth thinking about.

"Yes apparently a few renown retailers donate some of their clothes to the nuns for the children to wear and you know that room beside the chapel, all the children have to go there to try on the clothes and see which ones fit them the best, this usually happens on Monday evenings," continued David.

"How do you know that?" I asked.

"Because that's what all the children wear here," replied David matter of factly, "we all wear second hand clothes, which don't fit us very well."

"I hope we will not have to wear, second hand

clothes," I avowed miserably.

"Well they are clean," retorted David.

"Mrs. Gregory used to dress me in the best of clothes which were bought from shops off the peg and so did Miss Breen." I said.

"Yes and Miss Breen always bought us the latest fashionable shoes and plastic sandals for the beach," agreed Sue, again remembering the times Mrs. Breen had been kinder towards her.

"Well if they are nice clothes then I suppose it's OK," I found myself saying compromisingly.

"Oh Mandy you know they are not going to be nice clothes, girls of your age are wearing mini skirts out there, and I am not going to wear granny skirts which are down way past my knees," proclaimed Sue.

"What can I do?" I replied exasperatedly.

Sunday mornings brought its own routine and rituals, which as usual began with Sister Therese Marie marching briskly into our bedroom. With military precision she tore open the curtains at the same time as announcing that it was time to get up to undertake the inexorable chores assigned to me mainly. I could not help but notice on these mornings, the veil of Sister Therese Marie's habit flying around and about her as if it had taken on a life of its own.

"Come on you lazy girls, its time to get up and Mandy you are to help with the younger children, so get up and dress yourselves immediately."

The nun proceeded to throw back our bed linen as Sue and I slowly got up out of bed with last night's sleep still heavily weighing down on us. We took it in turns to go to the bathroom, which was conveniently beside our bedroom. The toilet though was at the opposite end of the corridor, which meant that as soon as we left our bedroom we had to turn immediately right and then carry on to the other end of the corridor.

"Now Mandy hurry up and get a strip wash first, then Sue can have hers' after you," ordered Sister Therese Marie as she marched out of the room and scurried down the corridor waking up all the other children along the way. We had baths on Saturday nights before we went to bed. While Sue had her strip wash I dressed myself before starting to lead the younger children to the bathroom for their washes. I then helped the younger children to dress themselves in their Sunday best ready to attend Mass. If it were a school day and we had to attend Mass I assisted the younger children to dress in their school uniform instead. Sister Therese Marie always escorted us to and from the Chapel before breakfast. Directly after Mass we promptly went to our bedrooms and changed out of our best clothes. Many a time we giggled together or joked as we raced up the flight of stairs. Certain distractions inevitable delayed us such as visits to the toilet, daring to lay on our beds for a while, or watching each other changing back into our everyday clothes.

"Now children hurry up, whatever is keeping you up there in your rooms, breakfast is ready, and Caithleen and Bridget have had to bring the dishes down from the kitchen themselves!" Sister Therese Marie shouted from the bottom of the two sets of stairs as we lost track of time because of our merriment. By the time we had sat down after reciting our prayers and Sister Therese Marie graced us with her presence as usual at the breakfast table, she persistently engrossed herself in her bible while we ate our meal in silence. However her oppressive presence did not always deter the children from sniggering at each other from across the breakfast table or for that matter, kicking or pitching each other under the table. As a rule though, we ate all meals in silence because we were acutely aware that Sister Therese Maria was watching our every move even when she read her bible. On the mornings when daily attendance at the chapel was compulsorily the overriding thoughts in my mind was the laborious and tedious Mass, which we were all, badgered to attend! Once we genuflected and found our seats along the benches, I usually followed the service intensively.

The evening meals were a remarkable improvement in comparison to breakfast in that the evening meals were not swimming in lard. Watery lumpy mashed potatoes were digestible while the fatty meat and vegetables the stomach could tolerate. At least the fat from the pork chops could be cut away from the rather dry but edible meat. Ultimately we concluded that the school meals were much more appetising. Sometimes however Sister Margarita, the cook sent down from the kitchen the remains of the food left from the nuns meals, especially when it was a special occasion such as a priest having dinner because it was a Saints day. The food was simply delicious. We ate asparagus, avocados, fresh fish, fruit flans, cream cakes and fresh strawberries and cream. There were other times when I sneaked into the communal kitchen after a special meal had finished and the nuns were all at chapel including Sister Margarita, this was usually when I made an excuse to go and fetch some more milk and when the domestic assistants had gone home for the evening. I saw this as my opportunity to look inside the two enormous fridges and help myself to the unfinished bowls of trifles, flans and fruit salads, in the hope that no one entered the kitchen and caught me helping myself to the glorious food. Even with the wrath of God hanging over my head, tasting the divine food, which undeniably was fit for gods; my poor mortal soul could not resist the temptation!

Holy week was in the month of November. The chapel bells rang every evening for six o'clock Mass and the ringing of the chapel bells was Sister Therese Marie's cue to usher us all from the dining table so that we were the first to arrive for evening Mass. The dark, often wet and cold nights exposed us to the fierce wintry elements as we were led through the Convent extension, then to the grounds outside, which was part of our walking route to the chapel. Occasionally we were allowed to enter the chapel through the main Convent but this practise was not often encouraged. Attendances at Mass during Lent were the occasions when we attended Mass early each morning for the six weeks prior to Easter Sunday. It was always refreshing to be greeted by the cool, crisp spring air afterwards particularly if the winter had been a harsh one. The chapel bells were always a reminder of Sister Therese Marie dedication to the chapel and the services she was obliged to attend. We observed her dashing off to join the other Sisters of the Sacred Heart at Mass or to attend the retreats that took place several times a year. The vow of silence during a retreat entailed that Sister Therese Marie had to withdraw into a world of silence and abstinence. Even so, this did not stop her from hissing at one of the children if she felt that the child needed to be pulled up for some shortcoming. We could not wait for these times anyhow when she withdrew from the world since this meant we were left more or less to our own devices. We were then reprieved from Sister Therese Marie's constant fault finding whether this was imaginary or not as children we could seemingly decipher the difference.

"Now listen children, as you know we will be going to Mass each evening for a week at the start of November, which begins in a fortnight's time. We, as usual will be praying for the Holy Souls in Purgatory;. They are the poor souls that are in a place of redemption but have not been good enough on earth to enter the kingdom of heaven because of this we must pray for them during Holy Souls week so that they can enter into that divine place of enlightenment. Now children I do not want any noise in chapel and none of you children are to act like heathens; that simply will not be tolerated. You all must behave like good Catholic children so that you can show an example to the outside world," Sister Therese Marie warned us as she rose from her chair.

"Yes Sister Therese Marie," we all responded meekly.

"Last Sunday I noticed Sister Agnes smirking to herself as she told Reverent Mother with great delight that Bernard and Gordon were talking to each other throughout the whole of Mass even when Father Murphy gave his sermon about obedience and good behaviour, and she told Reverent Mother that they even had the audacity to go up the aisle to receive Holy Communion," said an exasperated Sister Therese Marie. We were watched and observed by one or another of the nuns who attended Mass and we never knew which one of the nuns might report our antics to either Sister Therese Marie or the Reverent Mother. When the habitual attendance at Mass occurred, we always did our usual, which was to troop out of the communal sitting room in a mechanical fashion,and then out into the fresh air. We followed the footpath outside the main door opposite the adjacent primary school that stood as a constant reminder to us of the caged world of our existence, and the vast difference between the world we inhabited to the world other children from the outside world populated. The huge wire mesh fence reminded us that we were different from those children and that Convent life was a sheltered and desolate existence for vulnerable children. On our route to Mass we re-entered the building to past by Sister Veronica's care home in order to reach the steep staircase to the first floor landing. We then crossed over the landing to reach the fire door and out into the fresh air again, If the weather conditions were acutely severe alternatively we were given permission to walk through the arched entrance, passing directly on the right hand side Reverent Mother's office where we continued down the dimly lit passage way until we reached the reception hall again. We as usual proceeded across the hall, to the corridor on the opposite side where Sue and I passed the visitor's room, on the first day we arrived at the Convent when we sat with Miss Breen having refreshments. Any residual of sleep which still insisted on hanging over me despite my morning strip wash persistently lingered, especially if in summer the air was still warm enough not to disturb my clinging sleepy snugness. Although on wet frosty cold mornings, I was shocked from my sleepy hangover because stepping out into the air was like stepping into a cold icy shower.

"I hope we can play down the fields later?" Sue whispered to Patrick one morning when we took the outside route to chapel.

"Shush, stop that whispering," berated Sister Therese Marie as we walked past the French windows of the nuns' dining room. We often saw the silhouettes of the other nuns in their dining room which was only used on special occasions, for instance when nuns were visiting the Convent to spent time on retreat as part of their novice period. The permanent nuns taught at either the primary school or the secondary school which Sue and I attended. Sometimes we peeped through the French lace curtains, which hung majestically inside the windows to see the nuns sitting around the huge oval table. We knew the chair at the head of the table was the Reverent Mother's chair. The opposite chair at the other end of the table was where Father Murphy sat when he joined the nuns for lunch after Mass.

"Now come along Mandy stop peering into the windows, that's nothing to do with you. You should be setting an example to the younger children rather than being nosy and looking through windows. What would Reverent Mother say, I dread to think!"

"Yes Sister Therese Marie, sorry Sister Therese Marie," I replied in a customary embarrassed, apologist manner. Walking away from the French windows, we continued walking towards the chapel and on our left we passed the herbaceous borders and the vegetable gardens. The gardens were almost directly opposite the chapel. Rose hedges surrounded the small gardens and this area alluded to a place of privacy where, I noticed on a few occasions, one solitary nun sat on one of the benches by a rose brush reading her bible or just staring contemplatively ahead of her. The usual routine before we walked into the chapel after Sister Therese Marie was that she invariably stopped on the chapel steps to give us a final reprimand that bad behaviour in the chapel would not be tolerated.

"If you don't all behaviour yourselves you know what will happen to you don't you?" she said numerously.

"Yes Sister Therese Marie, each one of us will go to hell Sister Therese Marie," repeated the chorus of children.

"And what happens in hell," queried Sister Therese Marie.

"People get burnt forever and ever, Sister Therese Marie," reiterated the children.

Satisfied with our answer Sister Therese Marie led us through the chapel door and to the front row of the pews where we quickly knelt down to pray. We girls were told not to fidget and pull at our mantillas, while we were all told not to swing our rosary beads so that they could not knock against the wooden pews. As usual when attending the chapel, I prayed that my mother might come to visit us later that afternoon and promised God I would be the most obedient girl on earth if he would only let my mother visit Sue and me just this once. Father Murphy entered by the side door with the alter boys. We all stood up as the priest made his way towards the alter.

"Look at his shoes," stated Sue to me as she tried to muffle her giggles, "look they turn up at the toes towards heaven."

I looked down at the priest's shoes and sure enough his shoes curved at the tips as he rolled backwards and forward on them, before us while talking to the congregation. I looked around at the congregation in the chapel and saw opposite us Sister Vincent's group of children. I could not help but notice how much calmer and more relaxed they seemed compared to my group. Behind Sister Vincent's group of children knelt Sister Joan with her children. Sister Joan seemingly had a rather bemused look on her face. Not the strict look Sister Therese Marie always seemed to adopt. One time Sister Joan made eye contact with me; her bemusement so it seemed was directed at Sister Therese Marie who I immediately noticed was totally absorbed in her responses to the Priest's request from the congregation.

"Now say after me in *nomi padre spiritum sanctum, Amen.*"

Sister Therese Marie repeated the blessing in her normal pious voice, which was part of her overall demeanour. Sister Joan continued to look at me with knowing eyes, which I interpreted as her usual mocking manner towards Sister Therese Marie's sanctimonious attitude. Sister Joan's bemused look intrigued me for the length of time Sister Joan remained at the Convent. She was slender in physique with a marvellous sense of humour. Sister Joan made me feel somewhat visible because she seemed to acknowledge me; unlike the invisibility I felt the majority of the time in relation to my placement at the Convent.

"Now David and Gordon give me those comics you both have tucked under your blazers," demanded said Sister Therese Marie as soon as we had set foot outside of chapel to the two twelve year old boys.

"What comic Sister?" replied Gordon, shoving the comic further up his jumper and blushing as he did so. David reluctantly handed over his comic.

"Now don't get cocky with me Gordon, open up your blazer and give me that comic or I will ring and tell your father not to come to see you this afternoon," insisted Sister Therese Marie.

Similarly to David, Gordon opened his blazer and gave the nun his comic.

"Good morning Sister Therese Marie, I see we are in fine spirits today," Sister Joan teased.

"Oh Good morning Sister Joan," answered Sister Therese Marie looking both transgressed and startled.

"The sermon was very good this morning," continued Sister Joan.

"Oh Father Murphy delivered the sermon beautifully," replied Sister Therese Marie, with an ecstatic look in her eyes as she cast them up to the heavenly sky.

"Yes, the sermon was about forgiving the sins of those who do wrong to you," recalled Sister Joan, "and did you hear that bit Sister Therese Marie or at that point did we lose you as you took flight with the Angel Gabriel?"

"I certainly did not Sister Joan, whatever made you say such a thing, I was listening attentively as I usually do," replied Sister Therese Marie looking rather indignantly at the other nun.

"Well it certainly hasn't taken you five minutes to start tormenting your children has it?" said the amused Sister Joan.

"I am certainly not tormenting these children, I am merely correcting the boys which is something I don't see you doing much of with your children!" said Sister Therese Marie impertinently.

"Perhaps I allow them to be themselves, something that you seem incapable of achieving." responded Sister Joan quietly as she began to walk away.

"What like little devils with their unruly behaviour or, acting like heathens for that matter, children have to be disciplined and controlled or else they will be completely out of control," Sister Therese Marie retaliated by raising her voice slightly after Sister Joan.

"Perhaps if you spent less time in the chapel and more time getting to know the needs of the children they would not need to be controlled so much," remarked Sister Joan who had stopped to reply to Sister Therese Marie comment.

"Are you telling me how to look after my own children because God is the only person I am accountable to?" challenged Sister Therese Marie.

"Perhaps God is amongst us rather than up there," observed Sister Joan looking up to the sky.

"Really Sister Joan I do not think this conversation is suitable for children to hear such blasphemy, I don't want my children to hear such things!" said Sister Therese Marie haughtily.

"The sermon Father Murphy gave has really inspired you this morning."

"Father Murphy's sermons *always* inspires me

Sister Joan, now come along
children, I can't stop to chatter all day."

Sister Therese Marie march off towards the direction of our care home, with us children following close behind her in silence.

Roast Sunday lunch was a sober affair. The roast beef was dry and leathery as usual.

"Urg what's this?" proclaimed Sue" I'm not eating this it looks like a piece of leather from an old boot!"

"Now that's enough cheek from you Sod-dye," Sister Therese Marie snapped.

"My name is not Sod-dye," retorted Sue, "my name is Sue.

"You will go to bed if you continue to answer me back!"

"Don't mind her," whispered Bernard to Sue, "she's still angry from that conversation she had with Sister Joan."

"If I eat this I will be sick like the last time I was forced to eat meat," replied Sue.

"You eat that meat like everyone else and stop forcing yourself to be sick, you can stop wanting to vomit, if you try, sure you can."

"No I can't, so if I am sick I will tell my mother this afternoon when she comes to visit me."

"You eat that meat now and besides you mother telephoned this morning to say that she won't be coming because one of her other children is sick." said Sister Therese Marie triumphantly.

Sue and I were both devastated when we heard the news. Sue was sick and I helped her to clean up the mess. She kept pulling at her hair all afternoon until chunks of it came out. All the other children's parents arrived as usual. Sue and I were the only children whose mother did not turn up and this became the normal state of play. I consoled myself by undertaking the daily chores that had been assigned to me so that I could take my mind of the huge disappointment. Sue went down to the grounds to play with the other children from the other two care homes; a few of them were in the same predicament.

"I hate Sister Therese Marie," Sue later said, "and why didn't mummy come?"

"Well she has got other children now and she must look after them because they are younger than us," I stated in a matter of fact voice, "Look when I am thirteen I will be able to take on a Saturday job and then I can buy you some nice toys and sweets especially for Christmas and I can even buy you Easter eggs for Easter, just like the other mummy's do for their children who are living here."

My first day at Secondary school was strange, spending a whole day with children I had not been to school with previously, never mind not being remotely familiar with the local community.

"One of these days I am going to run away to mummy and tell her how unhappy I am here."

"The police will only bring you back again."

"Why can't we go and live with mummy?"

I could not answer her and I did not even try too. It would have been pointless to try and appease her with platitudes.

Before Secondary school started I spent the rest of the summer holiday doing household duties caring for the younger children and stitching the gold braiding on my dark brown blazer.

"Hasn't anyone taught you to sew Mandy?" Sister Therese Marie enquired one afternoon when I attempted to sew braiding on my new blazer for the first time.

"No Sister Therese Marie," I replied.

"Well let me show you because all girls must sew if

they want to be good Catholic housewives," said Sister Therese Marie elatedly.

So a few weeks before I started my new school and in between my morning and evening duties I sat in every afternoon and was taught to sew and darn the children socks by Sister Therese Marie.

I was inevitable confronted with a different world when I entered Secondary school with Sister Therese Marie walking in front of me on my first day to lead the way; I could not help but feel mortified.

"I've told Sister Mary Peter, the headmistress to keep a watchful eye on you so don't go disgracing yourself Mandy."

"No Sister Therese Marie."

"And you know Sister Cecilia by now since she plays the organ at Sunday Mass."

"Yes I do Sister Therese Marie."

Sister Therese Marie's comments reminded me of the time I heard Sister Therese Marie gossiping about Sister Celia to another nun. It was obvious to everyone that there was animosity between the two nuns but no one knew the exact history. I remember overhearing Sister Therese Marie say: "She pounds away at that poor organ like some demented creature."

I could hear Sister Therese Marie's sarcastic remarks in my head as she was forever joking about Sister Cecilia's attempts to play the organ. Sue on the other hand respected Sister Cecilia and had mentioned to me one day that Sister Cecilia had asked her to sing in the choir and that I could also join her, because she desperately needed more voices to lead the hymns and to make up the number of the dismal group of choristers'. While Sister Therese Marie was discussing her expectations of me, I began thinking about the conversation I had last week with Sue about joining the choir.

"Otherwise if you don't join Mandy, it will remain like a pathetic congregation of cats in heat howling on a hungry night."

"But I can't sing Sue."

"Yes, you can," encourage my little sister, "and besides Sister Cecilia will do anything to drown out Sister Therese Marie's screeching."

"Sister Therese Marie can always be heard above everyone else."

"She can't stand Sister Therese Marie's singing. She says she sounds like a banshee whose foot has got stuck in a mousetrap," continued Sue.

"Yes one of Sister Cecilia's missions in life is to ensure that the choir completely drowns Sister Therese Marie's screeching voice," interrupted Caithleen who had overheard the conversation.

"Sister Therese Marie is so unpopular with some of the other nuns," I acknowledged.

"Well I am not surprised are you?" Sue responded.

"No of course not, she is ever so critical and judgemental of everyone," I confirmed.

"She'd criticise her own mother if she had one and it's only because she thinks she is the right hand of God and in her view undertaking God's work means harassing everyone," attested Sue.

"Now Sue don't be nasty; you had better go to Confession this Friday after saying such a dreadful thing," reproached Caithleen and I nodded in agreement.

"Oh wake up Mandy, I expect that kind of blind worship from Caithleen because she does not know any better but you are my sister so I expect you to have more sense and not be so gormless. As you well know Sister Therese Marie often quotes from the bible herself and she is always quoting that *'none is as blind as the man who will not see'* and that includes you too, and yes I will go to Confession this Friday because it is expected of us; and anyway all Father Murphy does is waffle on and then dish out the same old prayers for my penance, such as half a dozen *Hail Mary's*; but half the time he is not listening anyway. I'm sure he nods off in the confessional box!" concluded Sue, "and I am sure I can smell alcohol on his breathe."

"You're making that up," I contested.

"You know what I mean, anyway I sing every Sunday with the choir and there are not many good singers apart from myself and Caithleen," said Sue, "so why don't you come along next Sunday?"

"Oh so I am not a gormless singer then or, for that matter sound like a cat in heat?" said Caithleen sarcastically.

"You know I can't sing to save my life," I replied amused at such an idea and trying to ignore Cathleen's comment.

"Well you can mime if you like or at least hum," said Sue " and you will get to see Sister Cecilia's veil flying around about her as she manically pounds, with gusto on her organ."

"Shouldn't she be playing drums then?"

"Oh yeah, since when have you ever seen a nun playing drums?"

At the time the three of us had fallen about laughing at such a prospect.

My days at secondary school were no different to my days at primary school in as much as I observed the other parents watching out for their children at the school gates and embracing them enthusiastically before going to school and when collecting them at the end of the day. At the end of my school day, I embarked on the solitary walk back to the Convent care home. After I had taken off my school uniform and changed into the second hand clothes given to me, I set about undertaking my chores as usual.

"How was your first day at secondary school?" Sue shouted to me as I ascended the stairs to fetch another two trays with shepherd's pie on them at the end of my first day.

"It's OK," I replied grateful that she had asked. No one else did.

The next Sunday I followed Sue up the stairwell to the balcony.

Joining the choir gave me the opportunity to remove myself from Sister Therese Marie's routinely watchful glaze. However I was to discover that I had not escaped entirely from her scolding because I had to listen to her afterwards briefing me about what a good young catholic soldier of the faith I needed to be now that I had joined the choir and particularly since I was at secondary school. Memories of my first day at school came flooding back again as I remembered Sister Therese Marie taking it upon herself to escort me to my classroom and handing me over to the teacher.

"What sort of things did you do on your first day at school"? Sue asked me, sometime later that evening.

"For one thing, I felt so embarrassed when I entered my class room the first morning because everyone knew I was from the Convent and I didn't want them to know my personal circumstances just yet," I had answered.

"It's bad enough the children in the primary school shouting *'here comes the Convent'* every time we walk past them," said Sue, "as if we are a building or something!"

"Anyway did you make some friends?" continued Sue.

"I think so and do you know that there is a black girl in my class called Laura and she seems to be good at everything because every time Miss Keogh asked a question or wanted something done, Laura answered the question correctly and also carried out to perfection what was asked of her," I replied. I did not want to admit to Sue that I felt far too timid to behave in such a brave manner as Laura. I also felt very much intimated by Laura but I was not willing to share that information with my sister either. After all, I was her older sister and I dare not expose my vulnerability to her to that extent because I was determined to remain a pillar of strength for her sake.

"What did the other children say when you told them you were from the Convent and did they realise that we live in the building at the back of their playground just beyond the tennis courts?"

"I think that they felt sorry for me and could not understand why I did not have parents to accompany me on my first day at school. They called me an orphan and did not believe that I had a mother." I replied.

"We are not orphans," protested Sue, "how dare they think that we are. I fed up with people assuming we are orphans!"

"But you don't remember much about mummy do you?" I asserted admitting to myself that I did not remember much more about our mother than Sue did.

"Even so she's still our mummy and I shall be going to live with her in two years time, I can't wait," declared an elated Sue.

Sue started the same secondary school as me a couple of years later.

"Hi Mandy," she greeted me whenever she passed me on the school stairs, on her first day, "that's my sister and she is a prefect."

I felt both a mixture of pride and trepidation when Sue started school because I had no illusions that Sue would make her mark at school. In fact I had given up trying to convince myself otherwise knowing that she would never conform in the way that I had.

I admired her determination and boldness when challenging the Convent's rules and practises, which to me seemed so absolute. Sue also had a knack at making herself very noticeable. She took risks, which I was far to frighten to take. I was as invisible as she was visible; as submissive as she was extrovert.

"Hi Sue," I said one day after she had sought me out at school during playtime.

"Here's a chocolate bar for you," said my sister putting the bar in my hand softly.

"Thanks Sue," I replied gratefully, not bothering to ask where she got her little extras anymore. Rather, I appreciated her little loving gifts she gave me.

Before Sue started secondary school I had to some extent established myself with my peers. Nina, Valentina and Bernice were the girls I mostly hung around with. Although I had mixed feelings about school it was a means of escape, a distraction from the institutionalised Convent's rules and rituals. I had assumed that school would be stricter in its codes than the Convent but it proved to be a refreshing contrast in general. So much so that there were times I felt that I could be myself once I was out of the watchful eyes of the teaching nuns. This was mainly because the majority of girls were day attendees so they went home to their families at the end of the school day. So although, I remained at the Convent just to be amongst normal schoolchildren had a tremendous affect on me. It was as if they were my mentors as I learnt codes of practise and behaviours, which were antithesis of those displayed at the Convent. Mixing with other children I could therefore allow myself to forget that I was 'the Convent' as the primary school children shouted out as soon as they saw me either playing in the Convent grounds or when we all went out for the day with our institutionalised stigmata imbued on us. During school periods I could lose my Convent identity and be just one of the many schoolgirls sitting at her desk learning literature or mathematic formulas. My school friends' discussions about their family lives outside school fascinated me even though I was reminded that I was the outsider, the disintegrated child. Their family lives proved alien to me and their family interactions perplexing as well. To have parents who loved them supposedly unconditionally was beyond my comprehension. Entry into their family world appeared to demand an entirely different way of being. A way of being that was not so rigid and to some extent offered peace of mind, subsequently I longed to have a family life like they did. Having parents, living in a house, parents buying Sue and I presents for our birthdays and Christmas, giving us pocket money and buying us bicycles, kissing us goodnight, hugging us when we were ill or when we cried instead of constantly being told by Sister Therese Marie that we did not deserve such things in this lifetime; but that we would be rewarded in the next life and that sacrifice and punishment was the order of the day.

"Making sacrifices in this life for Jesus Christ brings you children closer to him; that is what Jesus wants from you so that you can gain your reward in heaven when you meet him." Sister Therese Marie instilled in us.

"We've going out tomorrow to the science museum Mandy on a school excursion so ask Sister Therese Marie or whatever her name is to pack you some lunch," said Nina who was the school friend I have become particularly close with.

"I will ask her but I will also ask Sister Margarita the cook because I think she likes me, and she never tells me off when I ask permission to walk through her kitchen when I need to go to the chapel to get Sister Therese Marie, in emergencies," I replied.

"What's it like living in a Convent?" asked Bernice as the three of us sat on the grass near the netball court, "I can't imagine it myself."

"Horrible," I replied, "and you wouldn't last five minutes there with that hair style of yours and your skirt hitched right up over your knees, showing off your thighs like that."

"Yeah the school nuns are always telling me off about the length of my skirt, they are always saying," Bernice Hanrahan pull that skirt down, you heathen, *Jesus, Mary and Joseph,*" said Bernice laughing at her own mimicry, "and they even say what will your father say and you know what I feel like saying, that my father couldn't care less what they think because he can't stand nuns."

"Why is that?" asked Valentina who had come to join us.

"Because he was sent away to a boarding school run by nuns when my grandmother died in County Tipperary and he was beaten every day until he ran away to England." replied Bernice.

"Do they beat you there Mandy?" Nina enquired.

"No they don't beat me but Sister Therese Marie often hits the little ones with a hair brush. She makes them hold up their hands and hits them until they admit that they have done something wrong or naughty even if it's the wrong child," I replied.

"It's a pity you have to wear your school skirt so long even in summer," commented Valentina sympathetically.

"I can't help it, if I roll my skirts up as far as Bernice's I will be slaughtered by Sister Therese Marie because the other nuns at school will tell her and I will never hear the end of it, so I haven't got a choice but to be obedient and be submissive," I replied defensively.

"I wouldn't wear my skirt as short as Bernice's but you are the only one who wears them below the knee," pointed out Valentina.

"All my skirts and dresses are below the knee; Sister Therese Marie says any girl who wears them above the knee is following the devil's ways,"

I said flummoxed.

"But this is the 1960's not the 1880's, that nun is in a time warp, she sounds as old fashion as my maternal grandmother!" replied Bernice.

"Doesn't she know that our generation is breaking out of all those restrictive Victorian ways, can't she see what's going on all around her? Look men are growing their hair long, women are throwing their bra's away," stated Valentina.

"How can she know, she always has her head stuck in her bible," I affirmed.

"Well I like soul music particularly the *"Four Tops,"* declared Bernice, " in fact I love their music but it's a pity you couldn't be more white like your mummy or at least have straight hair."

"Are you girls going to chat all day or are we going to resume our game of netball," shouted Miss Wallis, the PE teacher.

"Coming Miss Wallis, and Mandy try and hitch your skirt up for the outing to the science museum tomorrow because you look like something out of one of Charles Dickens novels," shouted Bernice as she ran to catch the ball.

"Now children as you know Lent is upon us again so everyone as usual will be woken at six o'clock each morning so that we can all attend chapel for the seven o'clock Mass, and you will be attending chapel in the evening as well so that we can all follow the Stations of the Cross and say a pray at each one, and I do not expect any of you who have celebrated your first Holy Communion, to miss going to confession every week, do you hear my *every week,*" announced Sister Therese Marie one Saturday morning at breakfast.

"We will also have a discussion after tea about the number of Saints days there are in the remaining year. I want you to become familiar with each Saints good deed and how they became great martyrs. As you already know throughout their lives they sacrificed themselves converting heathens to Catholicism and you know that the Catholic religion is the most reverent of all, so you are extremely blessed and therefore very special in the eyes of God, and the more you suffer and make sacrifices the more you will be even more blessed, much more than any other person, in fact you will all be sitting at the right hand of God when your time for the next world comes," said Sister Therese Marie droning on and on in her euphoric, monotonous manner.

"Oh if I haven't heard this sermon once, I've heard it a thousand times." moaned Sue who was sitting beside me at the breakfast table.

"Shush Sue," I said as Sister Therese Marie's words of religious wisdom penetrated my psychic again and again subconsciously.

"And as you know children its simply so wonderful to be a saint and a indeed a martyr," continued Sister Therese Marie again adopting her familiar idolised ecstatic heavenly look as her eyes began to glaze over each time she glorified her favourite Saint as she persistently resurrected their lives; their sufferings and their martyrdom time and time again. "Of course I doubt if any of you will achieve such status, such reverence, perhaps you Mandy because you are so obedient and such a good girl so perhaps you will become a nun and leave this pagan world but as for you

Sod -dye, the day your mother had you, you were and are no doubt to remain a heathen, there is no salvation for you not with your devilish ways, the devil certainly lives within you doesn't he?"

"Yes Sister Therese Marie, he does," said Sue cutting her eyes at me as if to say what she is on today.

"There, I always know best and I am glad you have not chosen to question me on this rare occasion because, this time, no doubt you know I speak the absolute truth on this matter," proclaimed the nun.

"I'd rather be in hell dancing with the devil than in heaven with her," said Sue after we had all managed to regroup in the Convent grounds to play later on that evening.

"But you will burn in hell and who will protect me from the bigger children," said Patrick who was listening to the conversation.

"Don't worry Patrick, don't take any notice of Sister Therese Marie," Sue reassured the little boy.

"But she's our housemother and I love her," said Patrick.

"Oh you're just grateful that you have a substitute mother but how can she be your mother when she is always criticising us all, even you Mandy. If she is not criticising us she is telling us that we must always ask permission to do something, I am sick of it all, anyhow she is more like a grandmother, than a mother figure," replied Sue sounding exasperated.

"That's why I read most of the time," said Sheila who had looked up from her book as she lay outstretched on the grass underneath the huge oak tree. Sheila was another mixed race child who was younger than me. She had recently been placed at the Convent after Hillary had left and gone home to her parents. Sheila was an extremely bright and loved reading books. She could usually be found somewhere discreet;

totally oblivious to the outside world and she had passed her eleven plus to the surprise of the care home she had come from where she had initially be placed in a special needs classroom. Sheila had also told us that if it was not for the special needs teacher advocating on her behalf to place her in a higher class she would have remained in the 'backwards' classroom. Sheila was now going to the local Catholic grammar school.

"Well I can't read because Sister Therese Marie has given me too much work to do. I've got to wash all these white socks by hand and then go and bring down the tea on trays and afterwards wash and put the little ones to bed," I said resentfully getting up to make my way back to the laundry room.

"Well I have to do chores too but since I've been accepted into grammar school Sister Therese Marie has to let me have the time to read my books for school," responded Sheila.

"Anyway you just read to escape what is happening to you here and reading your books is a way of escaping from the way you are treated," said Sue.

"No I don't, "retorted Sheila sounding offended.

I hated getting up so early in March for chapel. It was cold and as I peered out the window, after Sister Therese Maria in her grand gesture, had majestically drawn the curtain as if she was expecting God to emerge from behind the curtains and bestow a knighthood on her. From the window I could see the cold blanket of frost covering the grounds. It did not help that the heating was often faulty which gave me no incentive whatsoever to get up any earlier than usual. These mornings only served to remind Sue and myself of the cold house we had left when we were separated from our parents and from each other. After we fought the panic attacks of these cold miserable mornings, we trooped down the stairs as normal and out into the cold morning air, bracing ourselves against the cold March winds which seemed to drive a piecing ice cold sword through each one of us, as we walked toward the chapel, the little children, still full of sleep. They appeared as if they were sleep walking, which was possibly the case at times since they either could not sleep the previous night because of talking to one another or because of their nightmares where they were left to fight their own inner demons alone, some of them frequently nodded off again to sleep in chapel, as Father Murphy's sermon was lost in words they did not comprehend.

"Now stop scratching your head Gordon," Sister Therese Marie could be heard hissing two or three rows behind the children.

"And Charlotte take that finger out of your mouth and stop fidgeting with your mantilla, "the nun continued as she picked on us all if we so much as moved a limb out of place; after we had entered the chapel and followed each other as we filed into the pews and sat down as motionless and as obediently as our despair and boredom would allow us to do throughout the Mass.

"Anne, your rosary beads are not to be used as your bracelet, take it off your wrist, whatever next child."

"That was torture," determined Sue once we had stepped outside into the open air again.

"I see you were in fine form this morning Sister Therese Marie, you never stopped hissing and whispering throughout the whole Mass," proclaimed Sister Joan as she walked briefly past Sister Therese Marie.

"Well children need to be constantly disciplined and learn to do what they are told in the eyes of the Lord," retorted Sister Therese Marie tossing her veil defiantly around and about her as if it was her mane of hair.

"You mean you want them to suffer like martyrs," replied Sister Joan.

"We all know that the Bible says suffer little children and come to me as you shall enjoy the fruits of heaven," countered Sister Therese Marie.

"Yes but that does not mean that you have to repetitively or endlessly henpeck the children who are placed in your care," said Sister Joan, "I note that you never give them praise or encouragement."

"Perhaps you should look after your children and I will look after mine, besides your Paul was out late last night and shouting in the grounds. I could hear him from the chapel," Sister Therese Marie accused.

"Paul is fifteen years old and is quite capable of going out on Saturday nights," Sister Joan answered.

"Fifteen or not, no child in my care is allowed out of the Convent and for that matter is given permission to make their way home by shouting raucously in the grounds at that time of night," Sister Therese Marie replied with an insinuating tone.

"Well you need to live in the real world or perhaps you should think of retiring from caring for children...?" said Sister Joan stopping herself short of saying anything else. She realised that perhaps she should not be having this conversation in front of the children and possible had over stepped the mark.

"What do you mean, what do you mean, you so called modern day nuns with your modern day ideas are misleading to the children and as for retirement, I will retire as and when the Reverent Mother says it is fit for me to do so!" replied Sister Therese Marie continuing in her recriminatory tone.

"Oh so we are a child psychiatrist now, are we?" Sister Joan responded moving closer to Sister Therese Marie so that her voice became instantly inaudible to most of the children standing around observing the altercation between the two nuns.

"I don't need any qualifications to look after children, it's natural to know what is best for a child," replied Sister Therese Marie airily glancing up at the sky.

"Even if you are a nun rather than a mother," stated Sister Joan inquisitively.

"Even more so. My absolute devotion to God ensures he guides me and shows me how to look after the children. It's a shame that you clearly are not as devoted as you think you are especially since it appears that you chose the life of celibacy rather than a married life and motherhood. Perhaps you should be the one to think about retirement," retorted Sister Therese Marie.

"Oh of course, you will be seated at the right hand of God the Father when your work is finished here on earth," said Sister Joan sarcastically ignoring the caustic remark about motherhood.

"Now don't be skittish but of course I shall get my dues in the next life since I have suffered so much in this one," Sister Therese Marie replied.

" Well I haven't got all day to listen to your self righteous platitudes but perhaps tomorrow I will be able to hear the Mass over your hissing," concluded Sister Joan as she walked briskly away. Turning around one last time she affirmed, "If everyone is seated at the right hand of God, won't it get just a little bit overcrowded?"

"I am sure you can always find a seat on the left hand side of God," Sister Therese Marie replied, raising her chest in the air with sheer delight that she had the last word, which no doubt she thought was in line with her quick, sharp tongue.

"Now children, I want you to be ready for six o clock Mass this evening so that we can all follow the Station of the Cross together. I want you to think of the pain Jesus suffered when he died for your sins," said Sister Therese Marie as she suddenly strode ahead of us, in an apparent huff.

We were back in the chapel every evening standing in front of the images of Jesus carrying his cross to his own crucifixion while he was being jostled and hounded by the soldiers.

"I wish I could be more like Jesus then perhaps Sister Therese Marie will love me enough to kiss and cuddle me, " Patrick said after leaving the chapel.

"Oh don't be silly Patrick she will *never ever love you,* and I'd never ever want her to kiss or cuddle me!" Sue acknowledged, "In fact I'd rather tango with the devil!"

"I just think it would be nice to be kissed and cuddled sometimes like other children are," attested Patrick wistfully.

"So do I," affirmed Gordon reticently.

"And me," I admitted.

"Me too," conceded Sue.

"But that's not going to happen," said Gordon regaining his valiant predilection.

"Why not?" inquired Patrick, "what have we done wrong?"

"Maybe we are just not good enough children," I said contemplatively.

"Well that's not fair," interposed David.

"Hey, who says anything has to be fair," replied Gordon sagaciously.

"Come on I'm hungry let's go and have breakfast," I said not wanting to dwell on the subject for one minute longer.

"You need breakfast Mandy became you are so skinny," noted Kieran who had not said anything until then.

"You know that's because I throw up each time I eat

one of those congealed fried eggs," I replied.

"Or when you are forced to eat the burnt sausages," added Sue.

"But I have to eat something although I normally constrain myself and wait until school dinners, and if I am lucky I can get second helpings. I then do not feel so hungry anymore but I sometimes get extremely hungry by teatime, then I feel I could eat a horse particularly by the time school dinners comes around the following day," I said touching my skinny arms as I began to walk towards the care home.

"You're legs are like matchsticks Mandy, you've got no calf muscles," continued Sue.

"Well I can't help it," I said apologetically.

We dwindled up to the side door of the Convent reluctantly and followed each other into our care home. We participated in the usual rituals at the tea table when we ate bubble and squeak in silence with Sister Therese Marie as usual peering at us intimidly over her treasured bible. Later on that evening we were greeted by a small group of children who were talking on the stairwell that led up to Sister Joan's care home. They wanted to know if we had been allowed out to play that evening. On this occasion I was able to join the group because Bridget O'Riley had agreed to wash the children's socks for me. That was because she was a live in domestic so she was able generally to undertake extra duties.

"Let's go down to the grounds to play now that tea is over and come on Mandy you've got no excuse not to come with us, we know how much you love playing with us even though at times you pretend playing is beneath you, or that you are far too grown up to play with us," said Sue.

"I love playing with you and climbing the trees especially the old ones.

"Well I can't see why you like old trees and besides all the trees are old," Sue observed.

"It's because the older trees have been on the planet so long that they seem wiser and so solid that I feel protected by them whenever I stand in their shade," I enthused.

"Anyway whatever, I just want to play conker games," said Sue as we all raced each other down to the Convent grounds.

"The last one to reach the oak tree is it," shouted Sue as we all raced each other running as fast as we could.

Chapter V

St Theresa's Secondary School was a relatively modern building with its spacious corridors and airy classrooms and, at the single sexed girls' school, Sister Mary John was the head mistress of the all female teaching staff. Despite my initial unsettling start at school I was relatively popular.

"Your sister is not like you is she?" alleged Bernice one day when we where sitting on the grass during the school dinner break.

"What do you mean?" I demanded.

"For one she wears her skirts far shorter than yours," confirmed Bernice.

"And she's always getting into trouble which you never do," Nina interjected.

"I like her because she's a rebel like me and she doesn't seem to care what people think of her," continued Bernice.

"She's blown away your good girl image as being inherited within your family," divulged Valentina who had been playing idly with the blades of grass by her ankles.

"I don't care," I stated not admitting that occasionally I felt annoyed at Sue's somewhat rebellious behaviour and her lack of discretion at times.

"Your sister is so unlike you," Sister Mary John remarked after cornering me outside the Art class one afternoon, following the discussion concerning the remarks my friends had also made about the difference in Sue's and my behaviour.

"Yes, Sister Mary John, I know she is unlike me, Sister Mary John," I admitted casting my eyes down to the ground in shame because I felt I had been put on the spot, as well as being held responsible for my younger sister's behaviour. I was becoming increasing frustration by the numerous remarks about Sue's attitude in general.

"She is very different from you and if she does not improve she will be expelled from the school," Sister Mary John warned.

"I will speak to her," I said feeling even guiltier about my sister's untoward behaviour.

"I have already raised the matter with the Reverent Mother."

I respected Sister Mary John because she was kind and gentle in her manner. She walked around the school gracefully and quietly. With her gently ways she had told me on another occasion how much she liked my artwork; observing how unusual she thought it was as her six foot frame stood over me smiling softly. I was thrilled because she was the only other person apart from the art teachers who had praised me for a piece of work I had done. Now that she had raised the matter of Sue's behaviour with me, I became confused. Part of me loved having Sue attend the same school as me but the other part of me begrudged it. I was proud that she took risks that I dare not take and that she blew her own good girl image to smithereens. In fact, she never invested in that sort of image anyway or tried to cultivate one in the first instance. It just was not a role she was prepared to favour or for that matter, consider internalising or needless to say, adapt to; never mind the idea of being conditioned by such learnt behaviour in the way I had been. I detested though, the perception that she appeared to tarnish my own submissive behaviour, which I assumed was the model of perfection compared to her rebellious one. My sister was everything I wished to be but I was too petrified to even consider. I felt I could not let down my guard, so I continued to suppress my feelings of anger at the treatment metered out to me and to my sister. By now I had convinced myself that at all costs, in order to protect my own self preservation I had to behave in an acceptable manner.

"You are like the Virgin Mary and you sister is like Mary Magdalene," continued Sister Mary John. "You set a very good example as a prefect but your sister will never be one."

Maybe the idea of being a prefect does not appeal to my sister I thought to myself as I turned to go into my classroom with my mixed and ambiguous feelings about Sue's behaviour and, the lack of duty of care afforded to both of us.

As the only other black girl in my class Laura had ebony smooth flawless skin and her athletic prowess was second to none.

"Now girls who can cut a straight line along this piece of fabric?" enquired Mrs. Fraser, the needlework teacher as she peered at the class through her spectacles one morning. None of the schoolgirls put their hands up because I suppose the task seemed too daunting. There was a long silence and then I heard a strong voice say.

"I can cut a straight line on that piece of cloth Mrs. Fraser," I knew instinctively that it was Laura's voice and we all somehow knew that she had never cut a straight line on a piece of fabric before. Similarly we knew that she was more courageous than any of us and her courage and determination to succeed surpassed us all. We watched with baited breath as Laura cut the cloth in a perfect straight line.

"That was excellent Laura," congratulated Mrs. Frazer when Laura had completed the unnerving task.

Although Laura was in the same class as me we hardly spoke to each other apart from the usual greetings. It was not that we did not like each other; I think it was simply that although there was a mutual respect for one another, she could not make me out and I had no understanding of her history or background.

"Where do you live?" she asked me suddenly, one day out of the blue as we queued up to go back into the school building, after our dinner break.

"Over there in the Convent," I replied feeling safe enough to reveal my personal circumstances to her although I was sure that she was already aware of where I lived.

"Where are you parents?"

"My father is dead and my mother lives the other side of London."

"Where were your parents from?"

"My father was from a country in Africa called Ghana," I said rather irritably, "and my mother is from Southern Ireland."

"Have you heard of St Kitts?"

"No, where is that?"

"It's an island in the West Indies, that's where my family are from and by the way I don't like Africans."

"I don't know anything about them myself only what I've been told and that is they live in mud huts."

"It's a pity you are not from the West Indies," Laura said as she stepped inside the school building.

"Why?"

"Because people like the way you look there."

"Why is that?"

"Because they like red skinned people with hazel brown eyes."

"I am not a red Indian.

"No, I know you are not silly, it just means someone who has a reddish brown complexion, who blushes like you do."

"Oh, "I said without fully understanding the significance of her comments.

"They treat people like you with privilege because

of your complexion."

By now we were in our history class and I walked over to find a desk at the back of the class while Laura sat near the front. The next lesson was PE and we gathered around Miss Davis our fourth year sports teacher waiting for her to announce the annual year's sports day events.

"Right girls the annual sports day is a few months away and you will need to compete against the different classes in your year as normal," informed Miss Davis. "Laura you will compete in all the sports events as usual and Mandy since you are the best runner in your year; you will also take part in the relay race."

"My parents will be coming to see me win," said Laura confidently to Miss Davis.

"Well every child's parent will be coming I expect," answered Miss Davis.

No they will not I could not help thinking to myself as year after year no one came to see me run or win or congratulate me, not even Sister Therese Marie, as I touched the finishing line with hope and expectation. In due course I learnt not to smile with satisfaction at my achievements. What was the point I told myself as I walked away from the finishing line after winning the race the previous year. I vividly remember sitting on the grass, watching the other parents kissing and hugging their children who had not done as well as me. I would have cut my right arm to be one of those children. At night I often dreamt that I was one of them. I fantasized night after night that Sue and I were at home with our own family and that we felt for the first time safe and secure with our peace of mind in tact.

"Mandy what happened to you this time, you normally always come first in the 200 metres race?" asked the astonished sport teacher in my penultimate year of school.

"I don't know Miss Davis," I replied as I walked away from the racetrack.

I was relieved that I no longer felt the pressure of putting myself in the position that whenever I won only my sports teacher and Sue congratulated me, apart from my school friends.

"What a disappointment to your class," Miss Davis exclaimed as I carried on walking away from her. "Oh by way Mandy, your sister Sue is a brilliant gymnast, she could go on and compete nationally".

Although Sue and I attended the same Secondary school we did not spend a lot of time together, however we often greeted each other when as a prefect, I stood standing on the landing by the staircase, making sure that all the girls walked in single file up the stairs and into their classrooms, without talking or pushing each other along the way. At times we would whisper something briefly to each other or chat in between our lessons or during the lunch breaks.

"There are three coloured girls in the year above me and they are always getting into trouble," claimed Sue one day.

"Yes I have seen them and they are always looking at me," I replied.

"The three of them always walk around together and I have discovered that they are a lot of fun, you know," informed Sue.

"They look a bit hostile and defiant to me."

"That's because the teachers are always picking on them so they have to be on their guard, that's why!"

"Why is that?"

"The teachers say that they don't speak the Queen's English very well, and the school girls keep saying that they smell!"

"Well do they?"

"No more than anyone else!"

"They don't look very happy."

"They are only happy when they are together but the teachers are always trying to split them up."

"They look strong together like nothing can touch them."

"They let me hang out with them sometimes."

"Why do you want to hang out with them?"

"Because they behave differently to the other girls and besides they make me laugh."

"I wish they wouldn't keep staring at me though whenever I walk past them because I feel intimidated by them."

"What do you think they will do to you, eat you?" said Sue laughing incredulously.

"No but I don't think they like me."

"Well they know you are my sister because I told them."

"They don't mix with the other girls do they?"

"No, they prefer to keep to themselves."

"I don't even know if they speak to Laura."

"I don't know either. Why don't you say hello to them when you pass them in the corridor next time?"

"I won't know what to say to them and if they ask me questions I won't know how to respond."

"Well they started to talk to me when I being reprimanded by Sister Cecilia because I did not do my homework for my music lesson last week, and she told me off in front of the other girls when I was on my way to the dining room."

"What did they say?"

"They wanted to know why I was always being picked on too."

"Well don't let them teach you bad ways."

"How can they teach me bad ways?"

"I don't know but everyone says they are badly

behaved and are a nuisance."

"Well everyone should leave them alone!"

"I'm glad they are at the school though," I found myself saying for no reason.

"They don't like rock music but they like soul and calypso music, and they also like the music from their own country."

"What music is that then?"

"Jamaican music!"

"I didn't know they had their own music."

"Well they do and it's called ska, bye Mandy, we better go to our class rooms as the bell has just gone."

We both hurriedly walked towards our respective classrooms.

"Mandy you will never guess what," said Valentina on the first day back from the summer holidays and which was the start of my fifth year at school.

"Well what's the excitement about?" I immediately wanted to know.

"It's our last year at school silly and I for one, am going to leave at the end of the next summer term now that I am fifteen. I can't wait to go to work so that I can buy the latest fashionable clothes; besides the school uniform sucks." she said repulsively looking down at her rather tatty short skirt.

"Is that it?" I replied trying to conceal my envy.

"Oh no, I nearly forgot we have also got a male teacher for English this year." Valentina continued.

"A male teacher we've never ever had a man teach us before," proclaimed Bernice, while we watched her mindlessly move her fingers towards the waist of her skirt and roll it up more than usual.

"You would, wouldn't you, hitch your skirt up even higher, you flirt," accused Nina turning to Bernice as we gathered in one of the alcoves in the school playground waiting for the bell to ring for our first lesson.

"Oh come on Nina we are not in Ireland now you know, so don't be so pious," responded Bernice.

"You are going to get yourself pregnant one of these days, sure you will, you Ejit!" retorted Nina.

"Your just jealous because I have a boyfriend and you haven't got one yet; and guess what Mike isn't a Catholic," said Bernice trying to shock us.

"What, not a Catholic," replied Nina in disbelief.

"And he wears his long hair in a ponytail, its lovely," continued Bernice.

"What have your parents got to say about that?" asked Nina.

"I haven't told them about Mike because when I go out with him, I tell them I am going to my cousin's house and she covers for me."

"I want a respectable Catholic boyfriend with short back and sides when I start dating," informed Nina, "and I am not jealous of you contrary to what you think!"

"Oh come on you two haven't you heard the bell go, let's go to our English class," declared Valentina growing tired of the conversation between Nina and Bernice and having been the only one to heed the school bell ringing. We started to make our way to our new classroom since we were particularly keen to meet our new English teacher.

Mr. Higgins was about forty-two. He was slim and tall and I knew most of us fancied him simply because he fulfilled our fantasy of an educated older man.

"Now girls your first assignment will be to write a poem so that I can determine your talent for literature. This will be your first homework for my class and it will need to be finished for the English lesson next week," announced Mr. Higgins.

"What shall the theme be?" asked Valentina putting

up her hand swiftly.

"It can be anything you chose," replied Mr. Higgins who was standing behind his desk.

The rest of the school day was pretty uneventful. The domestic science teacher showed us how to make a Victorian sandwich cake while the sewing teacher informed us that we would be making a dress this term, which we could wear for the school prom, so we had to buy a dress pattern and dress fabric.

"I have to write a poem for next week's English class," I mentioned to Sue while I collected the younger children for bed; who had been enjoying themselves on the swings playing, that evening.

"What are you going to write about?" asked my sister.

"I don't know I've never written a poem before," I told her.

"Oh well, don't worry about it, let's go on the swings before you have to put the little children to bed," suggested Sue climbing down from the branches of the huge old oak tree whose branches, along with the apple trees hung over the school fence and on to the tennis courts. We often climbed the oak tree to see how far we could get towards the top and then sit on the strongest branches and shout down at the children playing down below or look across at our school. Over the next few days, I was preoccupied with the poem I had been assigned to write and this had put me in a contemplative mood. I intuitively wanted to write something reasonably acceptable, but I was afraid I would fail and consequentially be humiliated in front to the class. Nevertheless the following evenings I sat down at the dining room table after tea time was over and before my evening duties, and tried in earnest to create meaningful words and verses in the hope that they would make sense as well as rhyme. I borrowed a dictionary from the Convent library and for the first time used it in order to find suitable words to convey the profundity of my feelings in poetic terms. I finally found the discipline to write a poem, which ended up quite lengthy and dense and despite my anxieties, afterwards I felt a sense of achievement. I put my work away and handed my poem in along with my classmates and thought nothing more of it.

"Now girls I have read all your poems which you handed in to me last week and the standard was rather average apart from two that were exceptional so I shall read them out to the class," disclosed Mr. Higgins the following week. I was partially listening to Mr. Higgins since I had been daydreaming whilst looking out of the window as was my usual stance. It was September and an Indian summer ensued; pleasantly hot which allowed me to indulge even further into my daydreaming world, which was my favourite past time since it allowed me to escape for a while from the affliction of my circumstances. So when Mr. Higgins commented on the two poems I assumed unreservedly that he was referring to the two cleverest girls in the classroom. They always radiated confidence and did consistently well at their lessons while I struggled at mine, so it did not surprise me that the first poem was by one of them.

"And now the second poem which in my view is by far the best, and is written by Mandy Mensan, it is called *"The lonely journey of the soul,"* decreed Mr. Higgins. I was immediately embarrassed when the English teacher read my poem. I felt exposed and shy and lowered my head to stare at my desk, in front of me. I was relieved when Mr. Higgins had finished and we could resume the rest of the lesson.

"Why were you surprised that your poem was one

of the best?" probed Sue later on that evening, "after all last year you won the first prize of that national chocolate company for your short story and you won it this year in March again."

"The only reason I decided to enter the competition was because the first prize were Easter eggs and that meant that I could give you an Easter egg just like other children's parents give to their children, at Easter each year," I replied.

"Admittedly I did look forward to getting one of those Easter eggs again this year because the one last year was bigger and of better quality than the Easter eggs we are given by the Convent, and this is the second year you have won first prize," remarked Sue.

"That's because the local shops donate those Easter eggs and I am not sure that they necessarily give the nuns their best ones," I replied.

Sue and I spent many nights talking to each other after Sister Therese Marie had turned our bedroom light off, which was after we had knelt down to say our prayers before getting into bed, following Sister Therese Marie had completed her rounds. We discovered in due course, Sister Therese Marie's own bedroom was on a lower mezzanine floor beneath our bedrooms. At different times, the children curiously tried to peep into our housemother's bedroom when we were either going up or down the staircase. We observed that her bedroom was sparse and unprepossessing, consisting of a single bed, which was in the centre of the room. Situated at the far end of the room was a small drab bedside table that was located near the window. The only other piece of furniture was a small wardrobe. The nun made her own bed every morning and Bridget O'Riley cleaned the room once a week. I assumed that this was the general practise for the other nuns as well. It was particularly on the nights when Sister Therese Marie could be heard retiring for the night that Sue and I had our long nightly reflections of our plight.

"Miss Davies says you're a good gymnast Sue."

"I love gymnastics it's so easy to do and Miss Davies always encourages me to try the more difficult somersaults," replied Sue sounding pleased with her efforts.

"Have you told Sister Therese Marie how well you are doing at sports?"

"Why would I want to tell her that Mandy, she's not interested in sports or in anything we do at school?" answered Sue laughing at the very idea of my suggestion.

"I suppose you are right."

"She doesn't seem bothered that you won the national writing competition this year and I bet that competition has never been won by many children in care, if any. All Sister Therese Marie says when giving you your prize is, 'here you are Mandy, here's the Easter Eggs you have won again."

"I cannot understand why I won those competitions though because there must be much better educated children out there who are far more able than I am."

"Why should they be better than you?"

"They no doubt are better at their school work than I am. I am not very good at any subjects at school and as a result only get average marks."

"How can you say that particularly when you wrote one of the best poems at school recently?"

"That doesn't count because I can hardly spell and besides, my pronunciation of certain words is extremely poor unlike some of my class mates who are much better performers at school than me."

"So what!"

"If I didn't have to wash the children's white socks

every night ready for school the next morning or have to wash all the collars and cuffs of their school shirts, perhaps I could read more often," I whispered to my sister since I was aware that we had better lower our voices a little bit just in case Sister Therese Marie might hear us.

"How many socks did you wash tonight?"

"About eight pairs as usual."

"Oh that is so boring having to wash all those socks every night. It not fair, especially since you are always expected to wash them by hand."

"There's no chance trying to get out of my chores, Sister Therese Marie stands her ground when she says at my age these are the chores girls should be doing."

"That cheap detergent is no good for you hands, look how dry and callous they are becoming?"

"It takes me sometimes over an hour to clean the dirt from the socks."

"Bridget O'Riley should be doing that job, not you!"

"I detest having to take on these tasks especially when you and the other children are out playing and are having so much more fun than me, but there is nothing I can do to change my workload."

"You do make a good job of them and besides I have to polish the stairs every Saturday morning along with the other children, so I do some chores although not as many as you do."

"I know you do Sue, anyway Sister Therese Marie is so fussy about the socks and she always inspects how well I have washed them afterwards, so I have no choice but to scrub them so hard with my hands so that they are as white and as clean as new."

"That harsh detergent and bleach the Convent buys is going to ruin your hands permanently Mandy, I bet it is the cheapest one in the shops."

"Probably."

"You never guess what Bridget was trying to do to Patrick's knees tonight when she was bathing him because he fell over in the mud."

"No, I can't guess so tell me."

"She was scrubbing his knees with vim because she thought his skin was dirty and he was screaming until I came into the bathroom and shouted at her several times to stop it before she'd take any notice of me; she had been trying to scrub his skin off even when the mud had already been washed off."

"What a terrible thing to do, doesn't she know that that is his natural skin colour."

"That woman is so ignorant, I could hear him screaming from the sitting room downstairs and Patrick never screams because he is ever so placid."

"We should report her to Sister Therese Marie in the morning."

"Come on Mandy what will she do, nothing as usual. She is just like Bridget they know nothing about children who are from African or the West Indies."

"We can't tell Patrick's parents because they seldom come to see him."

"They would not believe us anyway."

"Oh what's the point?"

"Bridget won't do that again in a hurry though because I told her that I won't help her ever again with completing her pools coupon."

"Sister Therese Marie wants us to be perfect all the time."

"That's because Sister Joan is always having a go at her about the fact that she doesn't know anything about bringing up children."

"She never stops telling us off. In her eyes we can never do anything right!"

"I know but we have got to keep trying to please her

otherwise she will fly off the handle and stamp her foot and when she does that she is so scary."

"I detest the way she always sneaks up on us by walking quietly into the sitting room in her little black lace up ankle boots, and any way why do we have to please her when she is so cruel to us?"

"I don't know why perhaps we will have a better life when we leave here."

"I want a better life now."

"Let's dream of a better life Sue, Good night and God Bless."

Good night Mandy and 'God Bless' you too."

As the fully-fledged in house sock washer I carried out these chores and the other ones assigned to me like the obedient servant that I had become. I washed the socks in the sink in the laundry room every night, in silence since there was no one else there to talk to. The chores were a penance for me that I accepted because I had no choice, and the art of negotiation was incomprehensible to me at the age of puberty. Each evening I dutifully gathered up the socks from the children's bedrooms once they had come back from school; after hanging up their school uniforms in their wardrobes and having changed into their casual clothes. Following the evening meal at five o'clock, I picked up the basket of socks and proceeded to walk passed Sister Therese Marie's office to the laundry room that was adjacent to her office. The task was not undertaken until I had assisted Bridget O'Riley and Caithleen O'Sullivan to clear and wash up after tea, which was the last meal before a light supper that was eaten at seven o'clock. The serving trays were taken back to the kitchen and the crockery and cutlery put in the cupboards and drawers in the dining room. If I had homework to do I generally washed the socks first and then did my homework before going out to the grounds to call the children in for supper and then put the younger ones to bed. After the Easter holidays we were decked out in our summer school uniform and changed from our long knee sock to ankle ones. By September we changed back into knee socks. To reach the laundry room from the dining room, I descended the three steps, which took me back into the sitting room where I turned right into the corridor passing the partitioning door. A further few metres took me further down the corridor past the doorway and staircase leading up to the kitchen and further up the staircase to the bedrooms. If I had turned immediately left rather than right after leaving the sitting room, the fire door opposite me would have led me outside of the care home; and another door would have led me back into the Convent, pass Sister Vincent's care home. This was the route Sue and I originally took when we first entered our new care home, which was the last time we ever saw Miss Breen, although she had sent us several postcards from her travels after the first year at the Convent we never heard from her again. Sometimes on my way to chapel, especially if I had to go and get Sister Therese Marie, if the Reverent Mother had come looking for her in the care home, I would go to the chapel through the dark dimly lit corridor that made visibility difficult. Often in the semi darkness I saw a shadowy figure walking towards me. I intuitively knew it was a nun who I did not recognise until they were practically face to face with me. Other times I did not recognise who the nun was even when she was within the closest proximity to me; the reason was because she would be a visiting nun. However, we were always expected to greet the nun coming towards us whoever she was.

"Good evening sister," I greeted each nun especially if I was not familiar with her name.

"Good evening child and God bless you," was the response.

Sometimes 'God Bless you,' would be replaced by: 'Peace be with you'.

I then crossed over to the reception hall and on to the chapel. The evenings when I stood at the large old sink in the laundry room, bent over, while washing the socks invariable fantasying about how I wished my life could have been different, was the means of getting through the excruciatingly boring and immutable task. When I had finished my duties, I put the socks and the school shirts with the blouses on the pipes in the boiler room, this being the last room along the corridor, to dry. Bridget O'Riley ironed the clothes in the morning ready for the children to wear the same day. My daydreaming and fantasies were always about living within a family setting, something I earnestly longed for; because I so desperately wanted to have the lifestyle my school friends had. Instead I felt alienated in the solitude of my evening chores.

The boiler room located at the dead end of the corridor was part of the building that was built during the Reformation period. If the children were not in the grounds playing, they could be found either in the sitting room or in the boiler room, where we normally retrieved the clean clothes that were put on the washing lines, or on the huge boilers pipes to dry. We congregated in the boiler room more so in winter because it was the warmest room in the building and was held in great intrigue by the children. We either sat on the enormous lower pips if they were not too hot or leant up against the walls while watching Bridget O'Riley or Caithleen Sullivan fold the clothes in the baskets; when we assisted them we chatted about all sorts of things before taking the very warm clothes back to the laundry room for ironing. On the right side of the boiler room away from the entrance were metal gates where we could see a lower room, which was locked and sealed off.

"The cellars are down there," Caithleen O'Sullivan notified us when Sue and I had initially arrived at the Convent.

"Does anyone ever go down there?" Sue had enquired.

"I don't think so, its' far too scary," Caithleen O'Sullivan replied.

"I'd love to go down there to explore the cellars," Sue had remarked.

"Sister Therese Marie says the devil lives down there," Caithleen O'Sullivan had warned us as if she almost believed what she was told to be true.

"Of course Sister Therese Marie would say that wouldn't she," Sue had replied.

On that particular evening before we could say anymore we heard Sister Therese Marie's foot steps beginning to descend the staircase close by. We then continued with our chores in silence.

"Have you children collected all the dry clothes ready for ironing," Sister Therese Marie had inquired as she entered the boiler room.

"Yes Sister Therese Marie," we responded.

"Now you children should be grateful that the Sacred Heart nuns took you in," Sister Therese Marie persistently stated, precisely when one of us tried to challenge a rule of hers, which perpetually were imposed upon us, "but I only want to wear some clothes that are a bit more modern," I protested to her one evening after I had accepted an invitation to one of my friend's house for tea after school. This was one of the rare occasions I had dared to challenge her after she had agreed that I could accept the invitation and naturally I wanted to look my best, but plucking up the courage to challenge her choice of clothes for me or indeed, to question my house mother's rules was clearly not admissible.

"This new generation is far too promiscuous: those girls wearing such short skirts are godless creatures," Sister Therese Marie inferred. "Now, Mandy a good obedient Catholic girl like you asking to wear such clothes surprises me. That sort of thing I would have expected from your sister since there is no hope for her."

I knew in my heart that it was useless to argue with Sister Therese Marie since she was adamant about her views on contemporary fashion, so I left her in her room under the stairs and went to sit down on the broken settee to join the other children while we waited for Sister Therese Marie to give us permission to switch on the television. My only consolation was that Nina was not into wearing mini skirts either, instead she wore her rather plain dresses just above her knees. But if I did not roll up my skirts they would always end up mid calf on me because some of the clothes Sister Therese Marie gave me to wear were for middle aged ladies; they were so old fashioned. If I had been invited to Valentina's house I would have cringed with embarrassment and probably have made some excuse not to go. However I was never invited so that was the least of my concerns.

Sister Therese Marie's office consisted of a desk directly opposite the door to the room and on the right wall, away from the door, there was a display of shelves with all sorts of boxes on them. Boxes of underwear, boxes of odd bits of clothing, boxes of cotton reels, packets of clips, bags of ribbons, buttons, note paper and other sewing paraphernalia. In fact Sister Therese Marie's office reminded me of a very untidy Victorian haberdashery shop. I never knew quite how Sister Therese Marie spent her time there but I knew she would be in her office for hours, which was her second best past time after her bouts in the chapel. Our housemother frequently summoned a child to her office and consequentially tugged this way and that way at their clothing, informing the child that they had not kept their clothes clean, or that there was a button hanging lose, or a tear in a boy's trousers which needed stitching. Sister Therese Marie spent hours in her office alone busying herself with her curiosities. At times when I was on my way to the laundry room, I dreaded having to walk past her office when she was there for fear of being summoned into her office to be scolded or picked on. Her office was permanently locked when she was not inside it.

"Yes, Sister Therese Marie, sorry Sister Therese Marie," I said, apologetically on far too frequent a basis whenever I was summoned to her office.

The sparse laundry room was in desperate need of repair and I often heard the scurrying of a mouse while I silently scrubbed the dirty cuffs and collars of the children's school shirts or blouses. At these times, I could hear the television in the sitting room as I impatiently scrubbed away so that the tasks were completed more quickly, in the hope that I would be given permission to go and join the other children, to watch a favourite children's programme. I never managed to finish the washing in time; this was always a great disappointment to me. A few of the other children were convinced that rather than mice living in the laundry room, there were instead rats that resided in the creaks of the floorboards.

My institutional conditioning as the submissive convent girl was all consuming, so much so that it was some time before it became evident that Sue was no longer conforming to the Convent principles of obedience, subservience and endurance.

"Sue you are not stealing again, are you?" I asked her many times during her final year at the Convent.

"Oh dam it," she'd replied, "I am sick of living this life of hell, it's so unreal. All my friends don't live like we have to; they don't have to always constantly ask permission to do this or to do that, so why should I?"

"But you only have a few more years left and then you can leave," I repeatedly told her.

"Yeah until I am fifteen, sorry Mandy I cannot wait that long. I'm just thirteen now and I want out of this prison once and for all. By the way, the Temptations have a new song out and it's great."

"How do you know that," I replied feeling slightly resentful of the fact that Sue always seemed to be ahead of me with the contemporary updates of which bands were in the charts and the latest sounds from the States.

"Because I sneaked out last night and spent most of the evening at Shirley's house. Her dad's into soul music and her mum works in a record shop.

'Here you are, here's the record you wanted," said Sue handing me the vinyl.

"You didn't steal that record from the record shop, did you?" I asked her.

"Oh yeah, as if I would steal from my mate's mother's record shop!" responded Sue with a look of disbelief. "Nah, I stole it from a departmental shop in the West end."

"What you have been up to the West End on your own?" I said trying not to sound envious.

"No, a gang of us went," Sue answered nonchalantly.

"Where are you going now?" I enquired trying to sound authoritative.

"I'm back out over to Shirley's so cover for me by

saying that I'm down playing in the Convent grounds."

"Oh Sue, I can't lie for you," I piously answered my younger sister.

"You should try it sometimes," she replied, giving me a cheeky grin as she ran off.

"I might get into trouble," I shouted after her as I played with the metal bar on the fire door while trying not to shout too loud in case one of the nuns heard me. I knew that Sue had not heard me since my voice was inaudible to her because of the speed she was running at and the distance she had already covered.

It was usually at Saturday's lunches that Sister Therese Marie announced when our social workers were due to visit us after school or during the school holidays. The announcement normally came the Saturday before they were due. Sue and I had spent our entire childhood being visited by social workers and they represented our link to the outside world. It was during my time at the Convent that I began to realise that they were people rather than just middle class ladies talking a language I did not comprehend. Before then I did not appreciate their role apart from the fact that I perceived them to be some sort of government figure. Undoubtedly they intimidated me; yet again I felt that I had to be on my best behaviour in order to impress them as somehow they had the key to the secular world as well as links to my mother. Similarly to the other children Sue and I were expected to dress in our Sunday best clothes whenever our social worker visited since a visit from a child's social worker or a parent was treated as a special occasion. As usual Sister Therese Marie used the means of controlling the children's behaviour by dissenting to emotional blackmail in order to insist on subordination from her charges. This tactic she applied to the children when their parents were due to visit. She alluded to her ability to persuade their parents not to visit their child. We had no reason to believe that this was not within her power to do so.

"How are things with you?" the social worker inevitably asked when visiting.

"Very well thank you, "I perpetually replied obediently. The social workers never asked if we were happy at the Convent. They just assumed that we were. Since they equated finding a placement for a child as the same as making a child happy.

"The two 'Mensan' sisters, you have a new social worker and she will be visiting you next Wednesday after school, so as usual you are to be on your best behaviour and you are to wear you Sunday clothes as usual," Sister Therese Marie announced one Saturday during lunch. It was hopeless to dream that our mother would come to visit us frequently throughout our childhood in care, and no matter how much I willed her to come by praying in chapel, and fervently promising God that I would try even harder to be an obedient girl; it was to no avail, she only ever came twice. At Miss Breen's home my mother could not travel so far because of the distance and the responsibilities to her other children, and with another baby, her situation was arduous enough, Miss Been had informed us. The retired teacher had also informed us that our mother had divorced our father and remarried once our father had returned to Ghana. With resignation Sue and I had little alternative but to wait patiently for the time when our mother would be in a position to visit us, and moving to London was considered to be that opportunity. Although we were nearer to her now that we were in London with five other children who were younger than us, we were told that it was not possible. Sister Therese Marie eventually stopped threatening that she would tell our mother not to visit us, as a stick

176

to emotionally beat us with when Sue or I were considered wilful, because of the realisation that our mother would not be visiting us anyway due to her other family commitments. With the other children whose parents and relatives came regularly Sister Therese Marie continued to threaten them; stating that she would contact their parents or their aunts or uncles if their bad behaviour did not stop. She harangued the children so that they felt that they did not deserve their parental visit. Sister Therese Marie never threatened to stop the children's social workers from visiting interesting enough. Instead she threatened the children that she would tell the social worker how badly behaved they had been. At times I assumed that a visit from my social worker confirmed my bad behaviour although I could not always determine what form or act my bad behaviour had become conspicuous. On one level, I had grown accustomed to thinking that my social workers represented smiling assassins or kindly prison officers who controlled my personal circumstance from a distance. Such was their roles completely perplexing to me as was it ambiguous.

"Go and tell Mandy and her sister that their new social worker is here," I heard Sister Therese Marie announce to another child as I was changing from my school uniform into my Sunday best clothes, after Sue and I had arrived back from school. I went down stairs to the sitting room slowly wondering what news the new social worker would have about my mother and my family generally. So despite my reservations with social workers, I always looked forward to their visits.

As I entered the room I saw a very slim, attractive Asian woman in a sari sitting gracefully in the armchair in the farthest corner away from the window, where the six foot wire mesh fence could be seen looming outside as I continued to enter the room. It was an unexpected surprise to me that the social worker was Asian since it had never occurred to me that I would have a social worker allocated to me who was not white. As I came and sat down near her on the settee I was completely struck by her elegance and unlike my previous social workers, she did not exude an air of authority but rather a pensive tenacity. I found myself initiating the usual greetings, which were a new gesture for me. As it was more common for me to wait dutifully for the social worker to introduce themselves first, and they always seemed to do this without hesitation. Her approach was so uniquely different to the expectations I was accustomed to that I was quite bewildered by her quiet manner. At that précised moment Sue came into the room and sat down beside me. Before I met Neeta Patel, I told my social workers that I was happy when I was acutely ambivalent about how I felt about my situation. I simply could not dare tell them about the things I was profoundly unhappy about because I firmly believed Sister Therese Marie would be alerted to our transgressions, and as a result we would be punished, even more severely, by God if not by her. However I immediately decided that I liked Neeta Patel; for one she told us her first name, which I did not recollect that any of my previous social workers had done. They were always a Mrs. So and So. We talked about our school reports and the progress we were making and Neeta seemed genuinely interested in our educational development. She listened intensely to us which, I appreciated and by the same token, I felt I could relax and feel comfortable in her company.

"Gymnastics and art are my favourite subjects," Sue replied when Neeta Patel had asked us both what subjects we liked best at school.

"You also like music particularly organ music and singing Sue," I interrupted remembering how Sue also loved singing and listening to music. She certainly had panache for church organ music.

"Shall I sing to you my favourite soul song?" Sue suddenly proffered.

"Yes please, that would be nice," replied Neeta Patel.

With that Sue started singing her favourite song. She stood up and sang the song in the middle of the room and since all the other children had been requested to leave us alone with our social worker, Sue sang confidently and unabashedly.

"You have a wonderful voice," acknowledged Neeta Patel when Sue had finished.

"I want to go into show business when I leave school and become a soul singer," said Sue enthusiastically.

"You are very talented and I am sure that you will do very well," replied Neeta Patel.

"Can you sing as well as your sister?" Neeta Patel enquired turning her attention towards me.

"No, I can't sing to save my life," I declared.

"Mandy can write though, she has won national writing competitions for the second year running and I bet she will win again next year," replied Sue proudly.

"Writing is a wonderful talent to have," affirmed Neeta Patel.

"Oh, I am not that good a writer because I cannot spell very well and my grammar isn't up to much," I said suddenly feeling acutely embarrassed.

"Oh come on Mandy, no one else won first prize and you don't get any help from the nuns," defended Sue.

"Don't you get any encouragement from your house nun?" asked Neeta Patel sounding surprised.

"Of course not," answered Sue, "Sister Therese Marie spends half of her time in the chapel especially when she cannot cope with the children screaming and shouting or when they fight with each other. She leaves Mandy and Caithleen to look after the children and to sort out their problems."

"I have joined Sue singing in the choir at Sunday Mass now," I said trying to change the subject.

"Yes, I love singing in the choir and the hymns I love the most are *Ave Maria* and *Lead Kindly Light amidst the encircling gloom,"* said Sue.

"She sings them both so well that the music teacher who plays the organ lets Sue sing some of the hymns solo especially those two hymns because she sings them so beautifully, so soulfully," I said in earnest. As we were talking I began to cast my mind back to the school choir and how I had sat in the school hall watching Sue's class singing the *Hallelujah chorus.* Once more I had felt enormously proud of her singing talents as she took the vocal lead. For all my disparaging concerns I had about her behaviour, at times she excelled herself when singing and playing the organ.

"I don't suppose you can come to Mass on Sunday to hear me sing," enquired Sue as an afterthought, "you'll be able to see Sister Cecelia who attacks the organ like a mad women while Sister Therese Marie screeches like a scalded cat when she joins in the singing."

"I am afraid not because I do no work on Sundays," replied Neeta Patel trying to suppress a smile.

You have a very Asian face," she suddenly remarked to me unexpectedly after Sue had excused herself from the sitting room to go to the toilet.

"Do you think so?" I replied utterly amazed at her remark.

"Yes if it wasn't for your afro hair you could be Asian," she continued.

At her last remark I hung my head crestfallenly because I felt that there was always something wrong with me and therefore never quite acceptable to people. When Neeta Patel got up to leave after saying her goodbyes and informing us that she would be visiting us every six weeks from then on, both Sue and I went to bed feeling remotely happy for the first time in many years. We both agreed how much we liked Neeta Patel and had high hopes that she was the person who would rescue us from our predicament. Consequently we could not wait to see her again. The second time she came to she told us that this was her last visit.

"I'm going back to India," she informed us towards the end of her visit.

"Why?" I asked resentfully as Sue sat beside me on the settee looking at her social worker in stunned silence.

"I want to go back and help my own people, many of them are poor and hungry," she answered quietly.

"Why do you want to do that, we need you?" I continued baffled that anyone should want to leave England. But I knew somehow that she had to go.

"We must have done something wrong to upset her," said Sue after Neeta Patel had left us.

"We just don't seem to do anything right do we?" I responded despondently.

"No we obviously cannot," Sue, replied disheartened. That night I could hear Sue crying herself to sleep. I did the same but I did not want my sister to hear me as I cried quietly into my pillow.

Thursday nights was Irish dancing nights. It was also fruit night that meant that Caithleen was responsible for bringing down the two trays of apples and oranges from the kitchen. We could either choose an apple or an orange but we could not have both because there was only enough for either one or the other. I always chose an apple because I debated to myself that an apple would fill me up more than an orange due to the orange consisting of more juice than an apple. Occasionally I would be tempted to take an orange from the tray because they looked so tantalisingly large and appealing. Although afterwards I instantly regretted choosing the orange because it never quite addressed my hunger in the way an apple did. We always ate the fruit after our Irish dancing session had finished. Every Thursday at about seven o clock when all the chores where done, we would assembly in the sitting room while Caithleen went to Sister Therese Marie's office to fetch the Irish dancing costumes, and to notify our house mother that we were ready for the entertainment of the evening. We dressed up in the green tartan kilts, white blouses and black pump shoes that needed to be laced up correctly before we danced. Once we were ready to begin the Irish jig . Each one of us was required to dance solo around each other, which meant that at times we would be dancing back to back to each other.

"Now kick your legs up higher Bernadette and you Caithleen, you both look like elephants instead of graceful and nimble dancers. Now show some finesse in your movement, *Jesus, Mary and Joseph!*" Sister Therese Marie scolded the girls as she peered from behind her spectacles after looking up from the chapter she was reading from her Bible in order to check our Irish dancing abilities.

"Now Kieran Heggarty, stop smirking, will you now."

"Why are we doing Irish dancing," I overheard Daniel whisper to Caithleen on one occasion.

"We've always done Irish dancing on a Thursday, it's traditional,"

Caithleen replied.

"That's madness," retorted Gordon who everyone knew scorned the weekly ordinance. Despite the general protestations, the dancing activities were fun. Due to the Irish dancing ritual Thursday night was recreational night and as a result we enjoyed ourselves immensely. As soon as Sister Therese Marie returned to her Bible, we would usurp the dance routine by linking our arms with our partners and spinning each other around much more rapidly than was required. We then dissenting into playing pranks with each other and making faces at Sister Therese Marie whenever she was so absorbed in her Bible that she had no idea what we were up to. Even I could allow myself to descend into silliness like the other children who saw a side of me that was only revealed on Thursday nights. We laughed and giggled gregariously; dancing faster and faster .Whenever the Reverent Mother or another nun summoned Sister Therese Marie away while we were practising our dance steps solemnly, we waited until she had disappeared from our care home and then we would shout, laugh, tease each other and jostled with each other as we progressively degenerated until our look out shouted out from the bottom of the stairs, near Sister Therese Marie's office that she could be heard beginning to descend the stairwell to return to take up her place in her appointed chair, where she positioned herself as our singular judge and spectator. There were times though on a Thursday night when even Sister Therese Marie allowed herself to relax. This was when Caithleen and Bridget sang some of the old Irish rebel songs after our Irish dancing session was over. They sang songs such as *Old Danny Boy, The Rose of Tralee* and *We are off to Dublin.* Sue was invited to sing along as well and Sister Therese Marie also joined in with the rest of us and oddly enough her singing voice was less raucous. It was on these nights that she read letters to us from her brother in the United States of America who was a priest. He knew all our names and asked how we were progressing. He often sent us sweets and always sent us a Christmas and Easter card each; Sister Therese Marie also shared with us a little bit about her family background. She told us that she was from the generation where it was traditional in Ireland for parents to choose one of their daughters and one of their sons to be a nun and a priest and in her family she had been chosen to be the nun and her brother a priest. Thursday recreational nights with the smell of fruit had a long-term affect on me.

I daydreamed continuously during the day whether it was at the Convent or during school time. Most of the times I was not consciously aware that I was daydreaming at all to the extent that I often looked at friends and acquaintances I knew, with unfamiliar eyes as I escaped into my world of daydreams.

"Mandy, come up here to the front of the class please," I thought I heard my geography teacher call me one day. She was looking at me as was the other woman who was standing beside her at the front of the classroom. I had been daydreaming as I looked out of the window watching the rain falling since I was bored with the lesson. I thought I had heard at one point though, something about a missionary in India as I observed myself getting up from the chair and shyly walk over to the front of the class in response to my name being called.

"You're nice and tall," observed the woman as she started to wrap the silk material around my thin waist. The sari was made of beautiful shades of reds and greys with silver threads running through it, although my shyness did not allow me to hold my head up and smile at the classroom of girls' faces. Instead I found myself smiling to myself as the woman continued to wrap the sari around my thin body, while talking to the girls about the secrets of how to wear a sari securely without the aid of pins. I went back to my chair afterwards feeling extremely pleased that I have been chosen to demonstrate how a sari should be worn. I was beaming with gratitude that someone had chosen me to wear the sari.

We were notified several months later after the departure of Neeta Patel, by Sister Therese Marie that social services had assigned a new social worker to us and she was coming to visit us after school that week. Sue and I had lost interest by now and could not really be bothered with any more social workers especially since Neeta Patel had been the only social worker that had formed any impression on us whatsoever. The afternoon of the visit we intentionally made ourselves unavailable by disappearing to the Convent grounds, where we sat on some branches of the oak tree until Caithleen had almost exhausted herself when shouting at us to climb down and come to meet our new social worker. The sullen walk back to our care home was both deliberate and debilitating: eventually we arrived at our care home to be greeted by Sister Therese Marie initially scowling at us for keeping our new social worker waiting. Albeit the scowl was immediately replaced by a mystified look on her face as she stood back to let us pass through the care home door. Our new social worker was nothing like I imagined her to be since I had assumed that after Neeta Patel we would be allocated another undistinguishable person. However we were both pleasantly amazed to see a young woman who wore her blond hair long and who although was rather on the plump side, was wearing a white mini shift dress. She appeared pretty settled in the armchair she sat in as she waited for Sue and I to sit down on the sofa near her.

"Hello girls, my name is Julie Morgan and I am sorry to drag you away from your play time to come and talk to boring old me. Now you must be Sue and you must be Mandy," Julie Morgan said guessing correctly.

"Yes, that's right," replied Sue as we both smiled at our new social worker.

"You have been here for quite sometime now; how is it for you both?"

"It's OK," I said not wanting to say too much although no one else was in the room.

"No, it isn't Mandy, I like your mini dress Miss Morgan," Sue informed Julie Morgan.

"Oh, call me Julie," insisted our new social worker.

"It's not that bad being here," I told Julie.

"It's horrible, when we can see mummy?" demanded Sue.

"Yes, I thought you girls would like to visit your mummy and your other brothers and sisters, so I am going to arrange for you to see your family as a matter of priority."

"We can't wait to see mummy and our brothers and sisters," stated Sue.

"Why is it horrible here?" Julie asked turning directly to Sue.

"The rules here are far too strict and besides I want to be with mummy," insisted Sue.

"Well I need to set up the visit first," Julie informed us.

"It's been a very long time since we have seen her and we have never seen our other brothers and sisters," I said.

"Yes, it has been a long time although she did come to visit us once while we have been here but I want to see her more now, even though Mandy has been like a little mother to me," said my sister.

"Yes, I expect she has and who has been a mother to you?" asked Julie this time directing her question to me.

"Mandy doesn't need a mother, she is very mature and independent you know," replied Sue incredulously.

"I think most children need a mother," Julie said looking at me while I looked at the floor. I did not know what else to do since I felt awkward. The idea of having a mother to care for me seemed now to have been a lost opportunity completely, and Sue was right I had been put in a situation where I had mothered her in the absence of our mother, although I knew that I could never replace our own mother and it was a role I did not want anyway, even though I had been indirectly assigned to such a position while in the care system. We chatted with Julie Morgan until Sister Therese Marie came sheepishly into the sitting room to remind us that it was teatime soon. The two of us were surprised how quickly the time had gone since we had been so relaxed with Julie Morgan. It was the very first time I had really seen my sister so animated with one of her social workers.

When Sue and I were in bed that night we talked at length about Julie Morgan's visit, to the extent that we dared to hope that she would keep her promise to arrange a visit to see our mother and that she would not let us down, as had been our familiar experiences of rejection, which was a practise we had endured throughout our childhoods. Needless to say, there were no tears for us that night.

Chapter VI

Julie Morgan drove us to the wimpy bar in Kilburn the second time she came to visit us. It was enormously exhilarating to be driven out of the Convent gates; down the hill past Chiesman's, the large departmental store that I had visited a few times on my own. The store was always noisily busy with families buying gifts as I stood watching the children out shopping with their parents. I could not afford to purchase any of the quality products in the shop, despite my earnings from my Saturday job. Nevertheless, I was content to spend the time people watching as family groups wondered around the store and through the swing doors. Once again, I could not help but acknowledge to myself my feelings of envy at the children who were out shopping with their parents. With the money I earned from my recently acquired Saturday job I was able to buy a few reasonably fashionable clothes for myself and sometimes for Sue as well from the less expensive shops.

On that particular day, I remembered it was a hot May afternoon and the sense of freedom and anticipation was unimaginably captivating, that had an immediate effect on me, as we drove away from the Convent gates.

"Will we see our mother today, Julie?" enquired Sue who was clearly elated about the prospect of seeing our mother. At the time, I was rather equivocal and slightly piqued about seeing her after such a long time, and although I tried to portray an air of diffidence at the likelihood of seeing my mother, deep down inside me, I was naturally curious and as excited about seeing her as my sister was. Especially, since our mother had recently visited us for a short time on a Sunday. If the truth be known we were both so overwhelmingly excited about the prospect of seeing our mother again that our long worn out patience seemed to have dissipated now into thin air.

"Your mother is looking forward to seeing you two girls again therefore, after we have eaten at the Wimpy cafe, the one that is nearest to your mother's home, we will visit her afterwards, although I am not sure where along the high street the Wimpy is located, so you two keep an eye out please?" Julie Morgan informed us from the driver's seat of her mini. Sitting in the back seat with the window rolled down and feeling the summer breeze on my face, I was even more delighted. The idea of someone asking me to join in the fun of looking for a place to eat out in town was beyond belief. Sue was more openly ecstatic in her excitement while I expressed mine more cautiously. We had no problem identifying the Wimpy café and quickly found ourselves a table by the window.

"Can we have one of those ice-creams after our hamburger? " Sue asked, chatting incessantly as she glanced at the separate ice cream menu.

"You mean one of those knickerbockers glories," replied Julie Morgan, "yes you can and in fact you can have anything you want."

"What, anything on this menu?" I stated sceptically.

"Yes anything," repeated Julie Morgan smiling.

My feelings were indescribable as I sat there mingling amongst the other diners, knowing that they had no knowledge or awareness of the Convent lives Sue and I shared. In fact, the general public had no idea of our personal circumstances, therefore were entirely indifference and non judgemental towards us. In this almost quasi sacrosanct environment I was able to concede that I did not have to put up with the children from the primary school taunting us with the words:

"Here comes the Convent, here comes the Convent," whenever our secondary school had a day off school and the primary school did not. There were times when all the Convent children embarked on either a one day excursion, or sometimes a short holiday, which invariably took us away from our group homes. On these occasions, Sister Therese Marie unfailingly took it upon herself to march off ahead of us whenever we went on these excursions. On this particular occasion, I recall that we were off on a weeks' holiday to stay at another Convent, which was located at Godmington, in Surrey.

"Now come along children, keep together in twos and hurry up," the nun shouted from the head of the line of children who were following her begrudgingly.

"That's right Mandy, take the hands of those two little ones?" she commanded.

"Now you Daniel keep in line or else you will get a clip around the ears, sure you will, if the devil doesn't get you first!" Sister Therese Marie was off with her usual platitudes of fear evoking scenarios that invariable made us scared and fearful. We perceived the nun to be omnipotent and that her platitudes were absolute. We believed she knew the whole truth and spoke nothing but the truth; after all Sister Therese Marie never ceased to remind us how, after her death; her place in heaven was designated beside God the father because of the many sacrifices she had endured while on earth. She ruled absolute power and authority over us.

"Jesus was the greatest martyr to have saved the world from all the evil doings of people," she pronounced, delivering her sermons, her truths, reproachfully to a wretched audience.

"And suffer little children to come unto me; they will be rewarded in the next life," she delivered her biblical quote, somewhat oblivious to her small gathering of children, who intermittedly turned their attention to the pending adventure which the trip alluded to.

"Oh, you're such a cracker," declared Sister Joan who with her group of children was making her own way along the gravelled driveway to the coach, which was parked further down towards the far end of the driveway. I remembered that occasion so vividly because it was the second summer Sue and I had spent at the Convent.

"I'm surprised Sister Vincent and her children are not already on the coach," announced Sister Therese Marie, who at that point was glancing ahead of her as she tried to peer into the back window of the coach; "and in the meantime we are minding our own business as usual, aren't we Sister Joan?" responded Sister Therese Marie sarcastically as she stuck her nose up in the air which was her usual style whenever she encountered Sister Joan; especially when trying to outwit her opponent who had almost caught up with her.

"I'm surprised that you managed to drag yourself away from the chapel in order to accompany your children on this holiday," continued Sister Joan in her usual mocking tone

"I don't live in the chapel?" proclaimed Sister Therese Marie now sounding quite acerbic.

"Maybe not, but you are always fleeing off to the chapel whenever the children need you," reminded Sister Joan.

"Well, Bridget, Caithleen and Mandy can look after the children while I am at chapel," retorted the nun.

"May I remind you, that Mandy is only a child herself and besides it's not her duty to care for the other children," answered Sister Joan glancing at me with a look of sadness in her eyes.

"She's thirteen now although she looks fifteen. She appears to have just shot up overnight!" exclaimed Sister Therese Marie defensively.

"Just because she is tall does not mean that she is not still a child," stated

Sister Joan who by now was sounding quite exasperated, "and as for Caithleen she can't tell a pig's ear from a donkey's tail!"

"Now, now Sister Joan, there is no need for rudeness, that is unchristenian of you," responded Sister Therese Marie chastising her adversary.

"There's no reasoning with a nun such as you", replied Sister Joan, shaking her head as she quickly walked towards the coach door, ascended the steps and disappeared inside.

We usually spent one week during the school summer holidays' at Our Lady of Lourdes Convent in Surrey. The children from the three group homes, accompanied by each nun, chatted together during the journey to the other Convent. Travelling to our destination was fun because apart from finding our own amusing activities we were also entertained by Sister Joan and Sister Therese Marie. Even though the three nuns conversed with each other Sister Joan and Sister Therese Marie as usual threw each other snide remarks across the coach and more often than not, whenever they passed one another in the grand corridors of Our Lady of Lourdes Convent; particularly since they could not necessarily avoid each other so easily whilst on holiday.

I noted that the only real difference in the regime of the two Convents was that Our Lady of Lourdes was set in the countryside. The location was lusciously green and peacefully quiet. It was where we children, spent the long summer days exploring the idyllic countryside surrounding the Convent. The nuns who resided at the Convent were extremely taciturn due to the fact that they had taken a vow of silence during their retreat; so they simply bowed their heads whenever they passed me along the labyrinth of corridors. Some smiled when they bowed their heads, while others did not.

Sitting in the Wimpy cafe with the sunshine shining brightly through the large windows made me feel abidingly optimistic, feelings of which I had not been able to express before then because they had been repressed for far too long, so much so that they were now predominately unfamiliar to me. The window we sat close to looked out on to the high street and I could not help but notice the shoppers were out in full force. It was strange watching so many people going about their business because it was such an extraordinarily unfamiliar sight to me. Merely, because my life at the time could be described as being socially excluded, hence it was not a sight that I was accustomed to. Rather, I felt as if I had been let out of an extremely enclosed environment and catapulted into a very unrestricted one which was perpetually spontaneous and free flowing where the social rules of engagement were to be learnt in earnest. Out of my enclosed world a mental door had opened for me, simply because my social worker had driven my sister and I out through the Convent gates and repositioned us, in the middle of a busy eating house; which was located in a bustling high street in central London. This new world was the antithesis of Convent life. Flower power was making itself visible ubiquitous on the streets with hippies mingling conspicuous with the rather less gregarious crowds. I knew that intuitively my unconstrained, radical freedom was time limited. I could therefore not fully relax despite Sue's continual prattle of excitement and optimism. I was intrigued and continued to observe the myriad of people on the streets, several of which were dressed in some of the most outrageous clothes I had ever seen. They did not seem to have a care in the world or if they did they had discarded their inhibitions for flamboyant clothes, public displays of affection and happy generous smiles.

The visit to our mother was pleasant although she made it clear that due to her impossible circumstances she could not offer us a permanent home. It was sufficient for me that we had at least visited our mother and her new family. Julie Morgan drove us back to the Convent and back to the routine life I had become inherently familiar with.

Bridget O'Riley took her role as the second in command very seriously whenever the situation warranted. The domestic spent a lot of time on her hands and knees scrubbing floors, dusting and polishing the banisters and scrubbing clean the baths and wash basins with scouring powder which made her hands even coarser than they needed to be. Bridget O'Riley always seemed to be preoccupied with cleaning up after the children since Sister Therese Marie did not tolerate any untidiness whatsoever. One Saturday morning Sue called me into the bathroom:

"Look Mandy look," directed Sue pointing at Bridget O'Riley's false teeth, which were in a glass of water. I recall the shudder I felt yet the fascination, the first time I saw the pink and white dentures laying at the bottom of the glass beaker with bits of food swimming around the water.

"They could almost be real!" I stated after closely examining the grisly sight.

"Don't be silly Mandy, how can they look like real ones, they are certainly false teeth, look at the pink gums!" Sue exclaimed.

"Well, I have never seen false teeth before," I retorted defensively.

"Look at the bits of food in the glass, floating around in the water, how disgusting," continued Sue.

"I better clean my teeth harder than ever from now on because I don't want to end up having to wear those scary things," I replied.

"Nor me neither," agreed Sue.

It was not unusual for the children to tease Bridget O'Riley because she was not very bright. We often used her poor educational background to blackmail her when trying to get her to protect us from Sister Therese Marie's abrasive condemnations.

"I grew up on a farm near Galway and my parents just let us run around, there was such freedom," she told us frequently.

"And did you go to school at all?" one of the children asked Bridget, knowing full well that Bridget had disclosed that she had been called a dunce at school and had to stand in the back of the class until the lesson was over, because she was told that she was too slow a learner at school.

"We didn't need to go to school that often because we educated ourselves

by looking after the animals on the farm," Bridget asserted.

"Is that why you can't read or write, very well?" Sue affirmed.

"Well it's not my fault."

"Oh never mind, but you must stop trying to cover up by telling me you have forgotten your glasses."

"Sue, don't start because you are the only one who does not make me feel so stupid!"

"And you are so unlike Sister Therese Marie in that you don't castigate me when I wet the bed!"

"You can't help wetting the bed, just look at the life you have had; taken away from your mother at such an early age, it's a sin, it really is," Bridget acknowledged.

"I detest Sister Therese Marie, I really do, she is always saying how evil everyone else is, but she is the evil one," Sue remonstrated, with a hurt look in her eyes, that made me double up in emotional pain.

"Now, now Sue, Sister Therese Marie cannot help it," Bridget instantly came to her employer's defence.

"Yes she can, she should never have been a nun because she doesn't know how to love anyone apart from God and how do we know God even accepts her love?"

"Sue, Sue, we can't question Sister Therese Marie's love for God, she is greater than us because she took the vows of absolute obedience to God when she became a nun, she is therefore nearer to God than any of us!" Bridget stated, as we observed her eyes clouding over with reverence and admiration.

"But she always crucifies us because we can never do anything right in her eyes, she expects us to be perfect just like the saints that she worships but we are only children."

"But she doesn't mean it Sue."

"You always stick up for her because you are so afraid of her; you are also afraid you will lose your job if you do not grovel to her."

"Sister Therese Marie is a living saint and I won't have anything bad said about her, do you hear?"

"Oh bollocks, you are as mad as she is!" responded Sue who ran off down to the grounds, to join the other children, knowing that her last comments, had fallen on deaf ears.

"I love Sue very much but sometimes I wish she was more like you Mandy."

"Maybe, I need to be more like her" I declared to

Bridget, becoming tired of people constantly comparing Sue's behaviour to mine. Yet, I told myself that it was wrong to think negatively of people even when it seemed obvious to me their assumptions were wrong. I had told myself more or less from the time I had moved to the Convent that it was wrong to think at all, so I repressed any opinions I had for fear that they would be denigrated by Sister Therese Marie, who was persistently critical of the children's behaviour, to the extent that none of us could really be ourselves, never mind being able to express any emotions of anger whenever she was around. Our emotional displays of any kind, were judged not acceptable, by the nun, instead we were expected to conduct ourselves at all times in a constraint and emotionally repressed manner.

"Now Mandy, I do not expect to hear that sort of thing from you, obedient girls such as you should never say things like that, whatever next, belittling the good food that you are given here."

"Sorry, Sister Therese Marie," I replied, her comments left me riddled with guilt.

"Now take yourself off to chapel, and pray to Jesus Christ to forgive you, I don't need to tell you that he died on the cross to save sinners such as you."

"Yes Sister Therese Marie," I said as I rose from my chair to go to chapel believing that this was the best way to address my disgruntlement; or at least exonerate my sinful behaviour.

Often, some of the nuns served at the alter with Sister Therese Marie being no exception. This happened when an alter boy failed to turn up for Sunday Mass. When observing Sister Therese Marie serving Father Murphy we sniggered amongst us from the moment she ascended the steps of the high alter because she appeared so transfixed. Her eyes glazed over as she prepared in her trance state the alter napkins and towels; to be used for the wine and hosts as part of the Holy Communion ritual. When Father Murphy began the rituals of the Mass, the nun, immediately turned the pages of the huge leather bound bible to enable Father Murphy to read the sermon for that particular Sunday, as she watched Father Murphy like a hawk, looking at him with pure adulation.

"Oh he is such a saint," she declared afterwards at breakfast and she remained on her ecstatic high for much of the day.

While Sister Therese Marie administered over the altar's tasks Sister Joan and Sister Veronica subsequently kept a keen eye on her children. For us, the pressures to behave were not so burdensome since the two nuns did not seem so perturbed when the younger children fidgeted, so we knew we could relax now that the atmosphere was less rigid. Secretly we envied the other children because their house nuns who cared for them were so much more congenial. These nuns engaged with their charges in a manner in which was inconceivable to Sister Therese Marie. At times I would lose tract of Father Murphy's sermon because my mind became completely distracted and I had to force myself to pay attention.

"I'm leaving the Convent," Sue told me a few months later.

"You're not?" I replied in disbelief.

"Yeah, the nuns are getting rid of me, they say that I am far too unruly and that they have had enough," said Sue nonchalantly.

"Where are you going to go?"

"Julie has found me a place at a reception centre which is near to where mummy lives."

"I hope you will be alright there."

"No matter where I go, anywhere has got to be

better than here!"

"I wouldn't know about that, when are you going?"

"A girl is leaving next Thursday so I will be taking up the vacancy, I will therefore be leaving here the same morning and I cannot wait. I've got to go now Mandy because I want to go and tell the other children who are out playing," she said as she walked towards the fire exit door and out into the grounds.

I walked back downstairs to Sister Therese Marie's group home with a mixture of emotions inside me. For one, I was glad that Sue was leaving because she had been so unhappy at the Convent and had never settled down. She had never really settled at Miss Breen's either so maybe she would settle down at the reception centre, I thought to myself. But I knew in my heart that was highly unlikely but at least she would be near our mother and that was want she wanted most. Thursday morning came in no time. I remember standing at the Convent front door, the door, in which Sue and I had entered five years previously, and that I had only ever been through again when the social workers came to visit Sue and me. Apart from these times the front entrance to the Convent was strictly prohibited. Children were not allowed to enter or leave from these doors. These main doors were the sole exclusive use of the nuns and of course, the domain of the local priest.

"Bye Mand, I'll ring you soon," my sister had said as she happily waved from Julie Morgan's car the following Thursday. I was happy for her to go and continued to wave to her as the car drove down the drive and finally around the corner. There was no doubt that Sue was embracing a new life ahead of me, so part of my excitement for her was tinged with resentment knowing that she was about to taste life outside of the Convent gates which I was not.

I walked back to my care home downcast and disillusioned and that night I lay awake looking at the empty bed beside me. Countless memories passed through my mind as the night slept on without me while I lay awake watching the luminous light glowing from the statue of Our Lady of Lourdes, which was perched on the chest of drawers by the side of the window. I thought of my first Saturday job at the age of thirteen when I had been employed as a breakfast cook in a working men's café. The position had been passed on to me by a girl at school who although she was in another class than I was, approached me one day out of the blue to ask me if I wanted her position became she was moving on to another job. Annette- Marie who was from Trinidad came across as clever, capable and self possessing. She carried her large matronly frame with formidable grace and when she approached me in order to establish as to whether I was interested, I instantaneously felt a panic attack coming on at the mere thought at such a proposition. Annette- Marie consequently spent hours re-assuring me and encouraging me that the job was simple and that I could easily manage the cookery tasks involved.

"The only thing you will have to worry about is making sure that the eggs you cook are exactly to the liking of the men who order them. They are very fussy about how their eggs are cooked," she assured me. Subsequently I worked at the café for almost two years. Whether I was obsessed with cooking the perfect egg for each customer who gave me their specifications, I am not quite sure however each customer complimented me on the fried eggs I produced. I had been working for almost two year at the café when one evening after work while walking back home to the Convent, I noticed a handwritten advert in an Italian restaurant that was seeking a Saturday waitress. It took me more than a week to muster up the courage to enter into the restaurant to enquire about the position. I was offered the job immediately so I gave in my notice to the café that very day. As it transpired I was extremely nervous as a waitress so much so that my hands visibly shook when I served the customers at their tables. I was simply unprepared for the ordeal of waiting at tables and no matter how much the manageress and her husband, the proprietor tried to encourage me to carry out the functions of a waitress, my nerves constantly failed me so that I visibly continued to shake and subsequently dropped the dinner plates. Consequently, I was more than relieved when the manageress reluctantly relegated me to a job in the kitchen peeling potatoes along with the West Indians and African men. The tasks were onerous but at least I no longer suffered from panic attacks.

"It's so easy daarling and you are such a nice girl, what are you so nervous about, you are such a pretty girl that you should be waiting on tables, so everyone can see you?" Carla, the manageress pleaded with me while her husband looked on sympathetically. It was to no avail; they simply could not understand what my trauma was about and I could not fight off my inner demons sufficiently enough to identify or even articulate my fears. No matter how the proprietors tried to encourage me to carry out the functions of a waitress, it was hopeless. All I could discern was that being placed in the spotlight meant that my inner demons went berserk. In time, I eventually deciphered that my inner battle was to do with an internal negative discourse, which repeatedly told me that I was no good, inadequate, undeserving and stupid. At the time I was not equipped with the coping tools required to control or at least, to some degree manage my inner demons. The only option for me finally was to work in an increasingly humid kitchen where I stood all day over a sink peeling potatoes. With the money I earned it allowed me to buy Sue and I birthday and Christmas presents that I could pretend were from our mother. Lying in the bed now, knowing that very soon another child would be sleeping in the bed beside me; in the very room that Sue and I had shared for the last four years made me think not only of the Saturday jobs but also of the annual summer holiday trips to Herne Bay. We arrived by coach at the seaside. Upon arrival we headed straight to the beach. Sister Therese Marie as usual positioned herself in a deck chair whilst instructing us to change into our bathing costumes for a swim in the sea. Never mind if the weather was more autumnal than the summer day we had been promised by her.

"Now every one of you is to get into the sea, this minute; a bit of mild weather won't hurt you," she commanded.

Sue of course was one of the first to take the plunge as the rest of us shivered on the beach.

"Come on Mandy, its not so cold once you are in the sea."

I was not convinced by her valiant gestures as I tried to find what little courage I had to follow my younger sister into the sea. In the end the constant exhortations by Sister Therese Marie gave me no option but to brave the cold seawater. It was nowhere near as warm as Sue had led me to believe. I was cold in the sea and even colder when I came out as I sat shivering even more violently as my teeth chattered uncontrollably for what seemed like hours, with a little inadequate bath towel wrapped around my shoulders.

There was no contention as to the fact that I missed my sister once she had left the Convent. I felt an intrinsic loneliness which none of my school friends could appease.

"Mandy, the Reverent Mother wants you to go to her office" insisted

Sister Therese Marie sometime afterwards when, I had arrived back from school. I hurriedly made my way to the Reverent Mother's office where I was handed the telephone.

"Your sister Sue is on the telephone and she wants to speak to you," said the Reverent Mother as she made her way around to the other side of her very large office desk.

"Hello Sue", I said, "how are you?"

"I'm OK and everything is fine," replied Sue sounding cheerful.

"What's the reception centre like?"

"There is more freedom here than at the Convent because there are not so many rules!"

"What do you do there?" I inquired wanting to hear more but conscious of Reverent Mother standing and watching me on the other side of her office.

"I go out a lot. I go to shabeens as well," she replied.

"What are shabeens?" I asked.

"They are clubs where ska is played, they are a bit like a house party and the only difference is that people pay a small entry fee as well as paying for their drinks.

"Most of the soul music I hear is the tunes that are played on the pirate radio stations."

"Gosh, Mandy coped up in the Convent means that you don't know what music people are listening to, in the shabeens."

"I can't help it."

"I know it's a shame because there are also some fantastic sounds coming from Jamaica such as studio one music."

"Now Mandy, you will need to hurry up and finish your conversation because I am expecting a telephone call shortly," interrupted Reverent Mother.

"Yes Reverent Mother, sorry Reverent Mother, I won't be much longer."

"Is that Reverent Mother having a go at you?" asked Sue, who no doubt had heard Reverent Mother's voice.

"I got stabbed in the finger the other day," continued Sue, deciding to ignore the Reverent Mother's request.

"What happened?"

"Some Jamaica girls thought I had stolen their money."

"Well did you?"

"No and besides everyone steals here, I've had a few of my records stolen."

"Are you at school?"

"Yes I go to a local school in Harlesden, but I don't go every day."

"Why?" I asked not wanting the Reverent Mother to hear that Sue was not attending school on a daily basis.

"I don't like it because it is far too rough and the teachers are hopeless, so I am going to drop out at the end of this term."

"But you are only fourteen."

"So what, none of the other girls at the reception centre go to school, some of them work in the local factory and some just steal from local shops."

"Mandy, that's enough now, say goodbye to Sue," interjected the Reverent Mother.

"Sue, I've got to go now."

"Yeah, I heard."

"Bye Sue."

"Bye Mand."

A few days after Sue telephoned Julie Morgan came to visit me.

"Sue seems OK," I told her.

"Yes she seems to have settled down as much as she ever can," replied Julie Morgan, nonplussed.

"She doesn't seem to be going to school much though," I said not feeling very happy about Sue's lack of schooling.

"Well the staff at the reception centre are doing their utmost best," answered Julie Morgan rather despairingly.

"But why are they not doing anything about her lack of attendance at school?" I declared, annoyed at what appeared to be their lack of concern about my sister's educational welfare.

"Sue seems to have got in with a bad crowd of girls," continued Julie Morgan.

"She said one girl stabbed her finger," I decided to mentioned to my social worker.

"Yes a couple of girls accused Sue of stealing something of theirs," replied Julie Morgan.

"Well I hope she will be alright," I replied unconvinced.

"She is certainly becoming streetwise since she left the Convent," responded Julie Morgan.

"But that cannot be a good thing."

"No, it's not, but Sue does not seem to want to listen to anyone in authority especially since she has left the convent."

"It seems that she has gone to the opposite extreme, being coped up in here and now doing the complete opposite out there."

I cannot quite remember the exact details as to when I succumbed to my emotional outburst. I suppose in hindsight the turning point had to be when Sue left the Convent. What I do know though is that it coincided with Sister Joan leaving the Convent a few months after Sue left. She was replaced, by a rather portly nun called

Sister Pauline, who oozed motherly affection what with her sunny disposition. Sometimes, when I passed the landing to go to chapel or to collect the younger children for bed I saw Sister Pauline carrying the most delicious food up to her charges. No doubt these were the left over food from the nuns' meals and not the meals the children ate that were cooked by the kitchen assistants because Sister Margarita was too preoccupied with the nuns' meals. I knew instinctively, that whatever Sister Pauline was giving to her children albeit a type of mother's love or some appetising food. I was hungry for some of it as well. The delicious food reminded me of the time when I had sneaked down to the kitchen one night after everyone was in bed because it was a very humid night and I have wanted some iced water. In the fridge were fresh cream gateaux, smoked salmon sandwiches, trifles and fresh fruit salad. As I was helping myself to some ice cubes I felt someone enter the kitchen. I turned around and was startled to see one of the nuns standing by the door in her dressing gown. After a while I recognised Sister Mary Peter who was standing watching me; her blond grey hair hung down the side of her shoulders and stopped just past her hips.

"Child, you should not be in the kitchen at this time of night," the headmistress informed me.

"I am sorry Sister Mary Peter but I wanted some iced water because I was feeling so hot and thirsty," I had replied at the time.

"Well hurry up and get the water and then go to back to bed."

"Yes, Sister Mary Peter."

The headmistress watched me as I put the ice in the beaker which I filled with water.

"Goodnight Sister Mary Peter."

"Goodnight child and God bless you."

Sister Therese Marie had started to correct me about something I had done. The rights or wrongs of the deed were irrelevant only that it was the catalyst I had been waiting for. I suddenly started shouting at her; telling her that I was sick of her picking on me. In the back of my mind I had plotted the scene in my head sometime ago because I was determined to change my care home in order to go and live upstairs with Sister Pauline and her children. It was a day when I knew the Reverent Mother was alone in her office since I had already checked previously that afternoon. After the outburst, I subsequently marched upstairs to her office with Sister Therese Marie running after me. I knocked on the Reverent Mother's door and, without waiting for a reply I entered. I warned both nuns that if I was not moved to Sister Pauline's care home I would commit suicide such was my clinical depression. My tears of anguish expressed my sheer determination to get my demands realised. In fact I was surprised by the wrath of my own anger as both nuns stood staring at me baffled, while I ranted and raved on about how unhappy I was and that I was always being picked on. When I had nearly exhausted myself, I looked across at Sister Therese Marie and I was quite taken aback by the hurt look I saw in her eyes; but for the first time in my life, I was determined, to get my needs met.

The change of care home was swift. I was given permission to move to Sister Pauline's care home that evening. The times afterwards that I saw Sister Therese Marie we were both clearly embarrassed. She never seemed so confident anymore. I sensed that despite my embittered relationship with her there was without any reservation, the fact that she had held me in high esteem. I assume to some extent that I was considered an achievement to her.

There was little doubt the liberation I felt once I had been transferred upstairs what with the physical layout of living in an upstairs flat that was psychologically empowering for me. It was my sixteenth birthday a week after my move to Sister Pauline's care home and normally the children's' birthday passed uneventfully; there was never a fuss made either on mine or Sue's birthdays. Usually, my birthday would be celebrated with a few sandwiches and a small impersonal sponge cake that seemed to belong more to the group than to me. Imagine my profound surprise when Sister Pauline came into the living room with the most beautiful birthday cake I had ever seen. It was covered in white icing with pink icing etched around the sides together with pink rosettes on either side of the inscription which read; *Happy 16th Birthday Mandy.* I was so moved by the gesture that I was lost for words, yet alone able to smile at my good fortune. To my mind it was the first birthday cake I had ever had because it had been made especially for me nevertheless the gesture overwhelmed me hugely.

"Now Mandy you need to think about what you want to do when you leave school in July," exclaimed Sister Pauline as we walked back to the group home from chapel one Sunday morning.

"I am meeting the school's career advisor next Monday so perhaps she will help me decide what I can do." I replied.

The following Monday saw me sitting outside the career's advisor's office with my classmates.

"What do you want to do Jane?" I asked the girl sitting opposite me. Jane was someone I had always admired in class. She was petite with straight dark brown hair, which she wore in a page boy hair style. Jane was always smartly dressed and had the knack of adapting her school skirt and blouse to the latest fashion so that her skirts were at mini skirt length and her blouses were not the traditional school ones, but lovely fashionable white tailored shirts. She had a panache for black silk stockings and smart shoes with just an acceptable high heel. Jane always seemed to stay within the confines of the school uniform yet was able to put a more fashionable spin on her clothes. The school girl never broke the rules and was extremely bright as well as displaying the required respect towards the school rules. It was not unheard of for Jane to get top marks for her school work which clearly met the teachers' expectations of her. She was the school's model pupil and enjoyed the status of the head prefect. The admiration for her was extended to all the teachers including the teaching nuns. Their star pupil was selective in terms of who she hung around with, which was only with two other girls of a similar calibre. Although she was always polite to me she merely gave me a cursory acknowledgement.

"I don't really need to see the career's advisor, "Jane proffered,

"My mother has already helped me apply for a position as a salesgirl's girl with one of the most famous chain stores in the country. I was interviewed last Thursday after school and was accepted straight away. I will undertake their management training programme as soon as I finish school."

"That's nice," I found myself saying, surprised that her future was already secure and mapped out in contrast to my career prospects, which seemed to hang at a balance with countless directions and possibilities but with no clear pathway or purpose.

"I' also hope to work for a chain store in the photographic department because I want to train as a photographer. The Company can also offer me apprenticeship training." said Noreen who was one of Jane's selected friends, "mother helped me complete the application form yesterday."

Again, I was surprised at the headway they had both made.

"You are next Mandy," instructed Valentina as she came out of the career office.

I got up and walked towards the door. I placed my hand on the doorknob to open the door and went inside. "That's it come in, sit down, and make yourself comfortable," beckoned, a rather large lady with black hair that looked too dull to be natural, "you must be Mandy?" she said as she glanced down at a list of names in front of her rather ample bosom. There was no question that I was nervous as I entered the room and sat down on the chair opposite the career's advisor.

"I'm Mrs. James, now have you got any ideas what you would like to do when you leave school this summer Mandy?" she asked. "What sort of things are you good at, at school?"

"I am not really very good at anything," I answered knowing that I did not have a clue what I wanted to do.

"You must be good at some things because your school report shows that you are expected to gain a few CSE's to the standard of O levels."

"I thought I might join the Navy," I said since the idea suddenly seemed to pop into my head.

"Hmm, the Navy isn't a bad career but you may need to consider another job before signing up or at least just to give yourself an opportunity to try something else before you finally make up your mind," said Mrs. James.

"Oh, the navy seems fine to me," I insisted suddenly wanting to get this meeting over and done with as well as my career choices because suddenly it all seemed rather scary.

"Why the navy?" asked Mrs. James who did not seem to want to get me off the hook so lightly.

"Well I can travel which is something I have always wanted to do."

"It also offers you a room over your head and food."

"It will save me trying to find somewhere to live then," I said satisfied that I had made the right decision.

"Yes but you will need to sign up for at least two years if not five years," said Mrs. James hesitantly," and if it is five years that is a very long time to make such a commitment."

"At least I can travel," I said not so sure now that joining the Navy would be such a good idea.

"You will also be trained in military tasks."

I was lost for words now because I didn't know what to say or what I wanted to do.

"I think it is the right career for me," I eventually said feeling rather intimidated by Mrs. James. After a long pause, Mrs. James said kindly, "Perhaps you need a bit more time to think about other career choices; after all you don't want to swap one institution for another one, do you?"

"What do you mean?" I asked the career's advisor, now sounding a little defensive.

"I understand that you are one of the Convent girls," she continued gently.

I resented everyone knowing that I was a Convent girl. I felt exposed by the lack of privacy afforded to my personal circumstances.

"Yes, I live at the Convent," I said conceding to my circumstances.

"You may like to experience the world a little bit, by choosing another career before you finally make up your mind about joining the Navy."

"What exactly can I do otherwise?" I asked now getting a little bit impatient that my ideas about joining the Navy weren't considered to be such a good idea by the career's advisor or by myself after all.

"You could be trained to make wigs."

"Make wigs," I said not knowing whether to be insulted.

"There is lots of money in making wigs."

"No, I do not want to make wigs," I replied adamantly.

"I will make enquiries then for you about joining the Navy," said Mrs. James as she looked at her watch, "can you please ask, Mary Heaney to come in next?" she requested indicating that my time was up.

I walked out of Mrs. James' office feeling more confused about my career and my future prospects than when I first entered her office.

"How did you get on?" asked Noreen as we sat on a bench in the playground sunshine.

"I didn't," I replied.

"Well I am definitely going to join the Company I told you about earlier and my mum has bought me a new outfit to wear for my interview."

We got up from the bench to queue up to go back to class. Jane came up behind us to join the queue with her friends.

"By the way Mandy, you know it's my sixteenth birthday in two weeks' time and I am inviting you to my birthday party," Nina informed me several weeks after my meeting with the career's advisor.

"I will ask Sister Therese Marie if I can come and what would you like as a present?" I enquired feeling much more confidant now that I was working in the Italian restaurant.

"Oh, buy me the latest record by the Temptations," Nina answered, "and I'll get my mother to telephone Sister Therese Marie, to ask her permission so that you can formerly come to my birthday party. My dad with take you home afterwards."

"If your mother's telephone Sister Therese Marie on my behalf, she is more likely to let me come to your party," I replied.

"That's not a problem anyway, you know my mother is from Limerick which is the same County as Sister Therese Marie's originates from and she knows most of Sister Therese Marie's family over there," replied Nina. " By the way have you decided what you want to do Mandy regarding your career prospects?"

"I want to join the Navy but the career's advisor was trying to put me off."

"Don't let her if that's what you really want to do," interrupted Jane. "I definitely know what I want to do and once I start working in my new job I can save up and get married and then have children."

"With Richard," said Nina.

"Of course, we have been dating for over a year now and as soon as we marry I will give up my job to have children," continued Jane.

"Will Richard be able to support you?" I inquired.

"He had better since he works in the local bank anyway if he doesn't then his parents can help out because they own their own house and I can't possibly work and bring up children and, run the home all at the same time," Jane declared categorically.

"Are any of you girls thinking of staying on for the sixth form?" queried Sister Lucy our class teacher as we sat down for our next lesson.

"No Sister Lucy," we responded, "we want to go out to work instead."

"Well as long as you get good CSE grades, then that's all that can be expected of you," Sister Lucy asserted, sounding very pleased with our response. Deep down inside me, I had contemplated staying on at the sixth form because I was torn between furthering my education and leaving the Convent. In the end I decided that I could not bear staying on at the Convent for anymore time than was necessary despite moving to Sister Pauline's care home. The lure of another life, another existence: to follow in Sue's footsteps, who was living a life with fewer restrictions was far too beguiling to resist.

I arrived at Nina's birthday party with my present in my hand which had been wrapped up expertly by Sister Pauline. Nina's house was approximately a twenty minute walk down the bottom of the hill and so it was always much more motivational walking away from the Convent, than walking up the hill towards it again. On this occasion, my self esteem was pretty high because I was able to wear some new clothes which I had bought with my hard earned Saturday wages. One thing I was extremely grateful for was that I could spend my Saturday earnings more or less how I pleased. Being given permission to keep my pocket money was the incentive I needed particularly because the money gave me a degree of choice in terms of what clothes I wore when school was finished.

"Hello Mandy," greeted Nina as soon as she opened her front door to me. I could not help but notice her surprise when she observed how fashionably dressed I was. I followed Nina into the sitting room and immediately felt self conscious about my clothes because all the other girls from school were wearing far shorter mini skirts. Even though Nina's dress was not as finer a quality as mine, it was certainly shorter. My dress had not quite made the grand entry I had hoped for especially since I was not allowed to wear anything shorter than an inch above my knees. At one point during the party Nina cornered me into her bedroom to show me all the clothes her mother had bought her for work. Although I did not particularly care for the styles of the dresses laid out before me on her bed, I was envious of the number of dresses she had to wear.

Afterwards, I returned to the living room and sat on a chair beside the settee and watched Nina's extended family talk and share jokes with her and her other friends.

"I am Nina's aunt," a middle aged women of Asian appearance suddenly said to me. She had been sitting next to me at the end of the settee nearest to me for sometime but I had not paid her any attention until then.

"Oh, "I replied not really knowing what else to say to her.

"I know you are surprised that I am Nina's aunt, aren't you?" she commented and before I could answer her, she went on to say, "and over there are my two daughters; they can pass as white, don't you think? That's because their father is Irish. I am married to Nina's mother's brother, the one over there and both my girls have blue eyes. She pointed to a blond man talking to Nina's father over by the sideboard, which was covered with party treats. Both men had a whisky glass in their hands while another man who I assumed was another uncle of Nina's went around with a bottle topping up the men's glasses.

"All my brothers and sisters have married white people as well so there is hardly a trace of Asian blood in my family now," the Asian lady remarked sounding pleased at this achievement.

"I see," I replied trying to fathom out why she had decided to talk to me.

"You can do the same too," she continued.

"Thank you," I replied as I reached for my glass of home made lemonade.

I continued to sit and make my observations. Every so often I was offered food and more lemonade as various members of Noreen's family came around with plates of sandwiches, birthday cake and biscuits. Everybody was friendly and when it was time to go home Noreen's father drove a few of her friends' home including me.

Shortly after the party Julie Morgan came to visit me.

"I am here to discuss with you where you will live once you leave school in July and since it is May we do not have much time. I have also invited Sue around to my flat next Sunday so you might like to come along as well," Julie Morgan said as we sat on the settee together one afternoon after school.

"Since there are still issues with Sue, I will be discussing her behaviour with her."

"Sister Therese Marie always accused Sue of being unruly but she seems to have lost control completely now that she has left the Convent," I proclaimed trying not to sound somehow as if I had gained the moral high ground.

"Now your housing options when you leave here is that I can probably find you a hostel near Sue which will also be near your mother," Julie Morgan informed me.

"I don't want to live in a hostel or a reception centre," I remarked not wanting to admit to Julie Morgan that I felt safer where I was than in an environment that seemed far too unfamiliar and unsafe, particularly as I was not sure that I had the coping skills to survive such a placement.

"You do not have any other options," declared Julie Morgan.

"Hum."

"Where do you want to go Mandy?" Julie Morgan persisted after a long silence between us.

"Where do I want to go, you know I'd really love to

live in a house with a family because that is something that has been denied to me," I answered trying my hardest to swallow the lump in my throat and the tears from swelling up in my eyes. I was taken aback at the unexpected emotional pain I felt, which seemed to paralyse me, to the extent that all I could do was to look down at the floor in shame at the sudden and unexpected display of deep feeling within me. Up until that point I assumed that I had been utterly immune to feeling hurt about my predicament anymore, particularly since I thought I had been so thoroughly conditioned to repress the emotional turmoil of being separated from my parents. It had been drummed into me repeatedly that I must act like the grateful girl I was supposed to be and any feelings of negativity towards those who had provided food and shelter was deemed the ultimate betrayal and a cardinal sin. I thought I had learnt to repress my emotional pain well. It appeared that I had not.

"You're a bit old to be fostered now Mandy," replied Julie Morgan compassionately.

"Oh well it was just a thought and it was silly of me to even consider it," I commented quickly trying to cover up my disappointment.

"Look, I cannot promise anything but I'll put something in the fostering circular and let's see what happens," replied Julie Morgan.

I looked up at her because I was amazed at her last reply. I could not help but notice that she was wiping something from her eyes.

"What's the matter with your eyes?" I asked in astonishment when I saw the tears in them.

"I think I am getting a bit of a cold," she answered rather briskly.

I was perturbed because I could not for the life of me begin to think why she should have tears in her eyes.

"I hope I have not upset you by being too demanding," I said now feeling guilty about the possibility of upsetting her.

"You can never be too demanding Mandy, never," she replied getting up to leave.

It seemed to me remotely doubtful that I could be fostered now that I was about to leave school that year, after all it was late June and it was to be the final term of my last year at school and the end of my fifth year. There were times after the meeting with my social worker that I reprimanded myself for even thinking of such a possibility as being fostered at nearly sixteen years old. Sister Therese Marie had always accused me of daydreaming and after waving Julie Morgan goodbye from the Convent's front door I started to make my way to the chapel to say a prayer for Sue. For a good many years afterwards, I could hear Sister Therese Marie's voice in my head scolding me as she did on numerous occasions about daydreaming and walking to the chapel was no exception.

"Now Mandy, stop that vacant glassy look in your eyes; it's as if you were yearning for salvation. Day dreaming won't get you anywhere so go and wash the socks for school tomorrow that will stop you day dreaming and longing for something which is far beyond your reach.

"Yes, Sister Therese Marie," I agreed, straightening myself up as I went about gathering up the socks from the bedrooms. I immediately snapped out of my daydreaming state for a while to resort back to the obediently submissive girl which Sister Therese Marie had groomed me to be.

"Set the example Mandy," she continued," so that the other children can look up to you!"

It was funny I thought to myself as I opened the

chapel door and entered inside although I had been resettled upstairs in Sister Pauline's group home, Sister Therese Marie's scolding narrative remained in my mind. There were so many times that I found myself turning around just to make sure that she was not behind me because she was renowned for creeping into her group home when we could not hear her, and then telling us off for being lazy or noisy. Despite the liberation that leaving Sister Therese Marie's care home brought me I was so enormously haunted by her chidings; her berating was a permanent fixture in my mind since her voice was my predominate internal demon. I knelt down on the pew and prayed that Sue would be all right. I also prayed that if my behaviour was acceptable to God, then I would be rewarded by a foster home placement.

"Mandy," Sister Pauline called me as I was finishing off my homework in preparation for my forthcoming CSE exam the following week.

"Julie Morgan is coming to see you again. She is coming on Friday," informed Sister Pauline.

"Thank you Sister Pauline," I answered thinking that as it was Tuesday I had another three days before I saw Julie Morgan.

"Do you want some help with your homework?" Sister Pauline enquired.

"No thank you Sister Pauline, besides, I am used to doing my homework on my own since Sister Therese Marie never dreamed of offering to help me, or the other children," I replied, somewhat bewildered that anyone should offer to help me with my homework.

"I am not, Sister Therese Marie," remarked Sister Pauline, "and I like to help all my children with their homework."

"Thank you," I replied again not quite knowing where to begin to ask Sister Pauline for assistance with my homework so I did not bother.

A few days later the Reverent Mother came up to my new group home to inform me that Julie Morgan would be coming back to visit me the following week instead of Friday. I did not think anything of it apart from the fact that in the not too distant future I was due to leave both the Convent and my secondary school. I could not imagine what lay beyond the Convent gates on a long term basis. Sue had not telephoned again since her last conversation so I assumed that she was getting on with her new life.

The following week I arrived home from school on the Wednesday and changed out of my school uniform. Afterwards, I went and sat on the comfortable sofa in the front room to wait for Julie Morgan. While I waited I looked at the electric fire that had been placed in the fireplace. The room was sparsely furnished as had Sister Therese Marie's group home been. The only difference was the furniture was not so threadbare which made the room more homely. There were also pictures of some of the children placed on the mantelpiece. One particular photograph must have been taken at Herne bay the previous summer. The children were all cuddling Sister Pauline who was trying to embrace all of them at once. As I sat there I felt a deep sense of sadness. I felt sad that neither Sue or I had benefited from this relaxed and caring environment because Sue had left the Convent before ever moving from Sister Therese Marie's group home, and the nine months' that I lived in the new group home before leaving seemed far to short a time for me to readjust to a completely new regime, which to all intents and purposes was a loving one.

"Hello Mandy," greeted Julie Morgan as she entered the room and interrupted my thoughts.

"I will leave you two to talk while I make you both

a cup of tea," insisted Sister Pauline as she hurried out of the sitting room.

Apart from thinking to myself how completely different Sister Pauline's attitude was compared to Sister Therese Marie's, their physical make up was completely opposite as well. While Sister Therese Marie was thin, bony and had become rather wrinkly, Sister Pauline was pump with a youthful gait about her with rosy cheeks. She was jolly with an infectious smile and I hardly ever saw her angry either. In comparison Sister Therese Marie's immutable anger emanated a phobic dread of her that was exacerbated by her somewhat temperamental nature. As a child growing up I found it perplexing when deciphering that adults did not hold the absolute universal knowledge or truth about the world around them, even when it was evident to me that to contemplate questioning or even challenge Sister Therese Marie was deemed sacrilegious. When living in Sister Therese Marie's group home it was not unusual for Sister Therese Marie to eavesdrop on the conversations the children had with their social workers. She sometimes found ways of interrupting our meetings so that she could remind us of how she had undertaken a little task for our benefit, as she gave us the cue to offer praise and appreciation for such a task. The social worker appeared oblivious of the interactions between us. No doubt seduced by the nun and the environment in which they were in. In these instances, I sat quietly like a statue with my hands folded in my lap and my back straight waiting to answer any questions asked of me. Sue did likewise albeit in her own fashion but after a while she became bored and would cross her legs and complain about some of the house rules. In response Sister Therese Marie answered any questions or queries piously and manipulatively as the situation allowed. Sometimes she would mockingly reproach Sue if she did not rise to the bait. Afterwards, she gave Sue hell for the negative comments Sue had made in front of the social worker, to the extent that Sue would be beaten into submission by the emotional denigration imposed on her by Sister Therese Marie.

"Sue, you filthy disgusting girl, you wet the bed yesterday and all last week," she often reprimanded Sue at the dining table.

"Oh shut up Sister Therese Marie," Sue retorted to conceal her embarrassment.

"Don't you tell me to shut up; I've a good mind to rub you face in the bed sheets, a big girl like you, all of thirteen and wetting your bed every night.

What kind of man would want you as a wife; no descent man only the dregs of society; I am sure," Sister Therese Marie endlessly goaded Sue before and after the mealtime prayers while the rest of us ate our meal in silence. I was distraught over my younger sister's humiliation and affliction.

"What makes you think I want to get married anyway?" Sue retaliated.

"It's just as well because no Catholic man would want you only some heathen," Sister Therese Marie remonstrated.

The altercations continued until finally Sue ran out of the dining room.

"You are very thin Mandy," some of the social workers commented.

"Mandy has never been a big eater since she came to us," Sister Therese Marie announced, smiling her gleeful empty smiles as she perched herself on the arm of the broken down sofa, have you Mandy"?

"No, Sister Therese Marie," I replied meekly in the belief that Sister Therese Marie had my best interests at heart. Anyway I knew my place and if I did not agree with the nun, the veiled threat that I was lucky to have been taken in by the nuns was endorsed ruthlessly as soon as my assigned social worker had left.

"But she is, very thin Sister Therese Marie," said one of the social worker's emphasized on one such visit.

"Oh, but you are rather a fussy eater, aren't you Mandy and I do have to coax you to eat, don't I?" continued Sister Therese Marie sanctimoniously.

"Yes Sister Therese Marie," I replied obediently. Later that evening, Sister Therese Marie recanted her pious pseudo caring attitude until reverting back to her normal behaviour by instilling in us her usual diatribe.

"If it wasn't for the goodness of nuns like me, you and your sister Sue in fact all these children would be out on the streets, or in some godless, forsaken home," Sister Therese Marie ceaselessly reminded me of the perils of the outside world and the alternative to the Convent, which seemed to me to be far too horrible to envisage.

"Your mother couldn't keep you because she has far too many of your other brothers and sisters to look after. It was because of the goodness of my heart that I took you and your sister into my care home and what thanks do I get from your sister, you need to compensate for her wilful behaviour because if it wasn't for you, I would have got rid of her a long time ago." The nun ranted.

"Yes, Sister Therese Marie, thank you, Sister Therese Marie," I repeatedly stated from the time I arrived at almost eleven years old to the time I threw a tantrum at fifteen years old and managed to get a transfer to Sister Pauline's home out of sheer desperation.

"Your sister is a nasty piece of work," Sister Therese Marie consistently told me.

"Yes, Sister Therese Marie," I whispered in a guilty voice because of the betrayal towards Sue.

"You're the nasty piece of work," Sue answered back defending herself.

"Now you will never go to heaven but to hell for answering me back," Sister Therese Marie barked back at Sue in a rage, never ceasing to sound incredulous that Sue had dared to answer her back.

"Who wants to go to heaven with you there, I'd rather go to hell" Sue retorted clearly becoming even more agitated.

"And burn there undoubtedly," Sister Therese Marie taunted.

Sister Pauline put the two china cups of tea on the small coffee table and then went off to chat to the other children.

"How are you Mandy?" Julie Morgan asked as she sat opposite me in one of the armchairs.

"I am fine."

"Your CSE's are coming up soon aren't they?"

"Yes that's right."

"What subjects do you think you will do well in?"

"I think I might do well in English literature, Art and English language."

"Well good luck and apart from wishing you well for you're forthcoming CSE exams, I've come to give you some good news."

"What's that, has Sue decided to go back to school?"

"No I am afraid not but I think I have found you a foster placement."

"Are you sure?"

"I am sure; it's a placement with a Mr. and Mrs. Lewis who have responded to the advert in the local paper written by Social Services. They say that they can offer a room to you within a family environment."

I suddenly felt panicky because I was not sure if I could integrate into a family environment anymore given my institutional background. I became acutely aware that I was not equipped and had little understanding of what social skills I needed to be socially included into a nuclear family setting.

"What if I don't fit in?"

"Well let's arrange to visit the Lewis's after your exams first. I can arrange for you to visit the family for tea immediately after your last exam and then we can see how you get on."

"What are they like?"

"I am afraid I do not know much about them at the moment."

"I hope they like me."

"I've got to go now and visit some other children so I will come and collect you in the next few weeks."

Julie Morgan rose up from the armchair.

"I will see you to the front door."

"Thank you Mandy."

I recall that it was another reasonably hot day when Julie Morgan drove me to Middlesex. The day had started out as one of those very English summer days when the defining white clouds drifting lazily across the topaz blue sky. The whole world seemed to glisten and sparkle: it was as if the sun was sprinkling the tiniest of diamonds everywhere which then laid randomly over trees, across roads, on top of cars and buses, as they gleamed rhythmically in the hot responsive sun shine. We continued to drive towards a number of semi-detached houses that were situated on either side of the road.

"This is the house," said Julie Morgan pulling up to one of the houses on the left.

I got out of the car slowly and looked around at the

row of houses until my eyes settled on the one Julie Morgan had pointed out. I liked the house immediately because of its continental appearance: it was painted in a pretty pale green with a terracotta door and window frames. We walked up to the porch and Julie Morgan looked around to find the doorbell that she proceeded to ring. Shortly afterwards the front door opened but the seconds before the door opened, in my mind I had run away and hidden around the nearest corner a thousand times because I was so nervous. The door open wide enough to reveal a woman who had light olive skin and dark brown wavy short hair.

"Hello, I'm Lydia Lewis," she said with a smile as she walked into the porch to open the second door.

I looked into her warm brown eyes and felt uncannily as if I had known her previously; from another time and another place; from somewhere that I could not fathom out. Needless to say I was not the least bit phased by this revelation as it did not seem to matter anyway as I entered beyond the porch and into the hall.

"You go straight through into the breakfast room while I'll go straight through into the kitchen to make a nice pot of tea," Lydia Lewis informed us as we followed her from the hall and through into the breakfast room.

The hall was light and sunny as we walked through it and there were a number of pictures displayed on the walls. Some were prints whereas others were posters from the 1930's cinema era. Suddenly from nowhere a rather large white French poodle playfully bounced up to greet me almost knocking me over.

"Oh don't be afraid of Jason, he won't hurt you, down Jason down, there's a good dog, he is absolutely hopeless as a guard dog, do you like dogs? Mrs. Lewis enquired as she led Jason away by his collar.

While tea was being made, Julie Morgan and I sat down around the circular wooden table.

"Now Mandy, do you take sugar?" Mrs. Lewis asked.

"No, thank you Mrs. Lewis, I gave sugar up for Lent last year and have never taken it since," I said directing my reply to the table.

"That was very determined of you," commented Mrs. Lewis as she lit a cigarette.

There was a momentary silence as we watched Mrs. Lewis pour the tea.

I did not know what to say although I was conscious that Mrs. Lewis was observing me while pouring the tea into the three teacups. Undoubtedly I felt intimidated so I found solace stroking Jason; afraid that I might do or say something wrong.

"I like your dress Mandy," remarked Mrs. Lewis after a while.

"I made it at school," I replied shyly.

"You are very talented to make a dress like that," she declared.

"Is your husband here?" I asked trying to think of something useful to say.

"Jim is at work," answered Mrs. Lewis ,"and he won't be home until 7pm."

"You have some nice pictures on your walls in the hall." I commented trying to make a conversational effort.

"Did you notice the one of Jim, a student friend drew it, Jim is wearing a farmer's hat that is far too big for him," said Mrs. Lewis shrugging her shoulders and laughing, "now Jason stop licking Mandy's feet."

I smiled because the picture of Jim was extremely amusing, what with his large green eyes looking forlorn underneath a rather over sized farmer's hat and Jason obsessively licking my feet.

"We better go now Mrs. Lewis, I will be in touch next week," stated Julie Morgan sometime after we had finished our tea and biscuits.

"It's been very nice to meet you Mandy and I do hope that you will come and stay with us for a while," said Mrs. Lewis as she waved us goodbye and then closed her porch door behind us.

"She seemed very nice doesn't she?" suggested Julie Morgan.

"Yes I liked her," I replied although I did not disclose that I felt hugely intimidated by Mrs. Lewis because she seemed so knowledgeable and so sophisticated. It seemed like a dream come true the possibility of living in a proper family house.

"I like your artwork; it has always remained of excellent quality." Sister Mary Peter noted when she walked around the fifth year classroom, commenting on the schoolgirl's artwork and now here she was standing very tall beside me, admiring my artwork as she towered over me.

"Thank you Sister Mary Peter," I replied.

"You should think of going to Art College because I can see you are very talented," she observed.

"Thank you," I said again to her. Any ideas I might have had of staying on at school or going to college seemed far too remote to me especially since I assumed I would have to stay on at the Convent, and I knew I could not do that. My visit to Mrs. Lewis had given me a glimpse of other possibilities and an alternative lifestyle that, I sensed that I was more than ready to leave the Convent and discover a life outside its walls. It looked like the beginning of a very hot summer and I wanted to put the Convent behind me forever.

I was not surprised that the day I left the Convent the weather was somewhat hazy. I vividly recollect Sister Pauline helping to pack a small suitcase for me. I included the pale lemon dress Mrs. Lewis had commented on so favourably amongst the few clothes I had to my name. I was very proud I had made the dress at needlework class, it had helped that Sister Therese Marie had transferred the sewing duties to me because of her frustrations with Bridget O'Riley. The needlework teacher had also praised my needlework skills telling me that I was doing very well in class. I wore the dress to the school prom where the local Catholic boys' school were invited to attend. Many years later I realised that the dress was awful and that Mrs. Lewis had merely been polite in commenting on it.

My reflections on my Convent life as I walked across the marble floor were exonerating. I was no longer a child who had been placed in the care of nuns I thought to myself as I walked across the foyer hall for the very last time, out into the hazy summer's day. All in all my childhood years of institutional care together with several foster home placements, up until the time I walked out of the Convent with my social worker had been from 1957 until 1967. It was the first week of August and Sister Pauline walked behind me, carrying in her hand a small gift box that was the piece of cake she had persuaded Sister Margarita to make for me the previous night as part of my farewell meal. Again, I had been taken by surprised by Sister Pauline's goodwill gesture. The culinary baking skills of Sister Margarita were consummated with her ability to produce the finest of meals for the nuns. Adversely, the meals produced by her staff for the children clearly indicated that they could not cook. The sun began to shine down from the generous blanket of blue sky as the freedom I felt was reminiscent of the time I had spent with the Gregory family and to some extent at Miss Breen's foster home. It was a freedom that I had forgotten existed and that I had assumed remained enduringly elusive.

"We must go and buy you some clothes Mandy," Mrs. Lewis declared at the beginning of the second week I arrived at 17 Chase Park.

"Yes Mrs. Lewis."

"I have asked Julie Morgan to ask the social services financial department to give you a clothing allowance because the clothes you came with from the Convent are not entirely suitable and you cannot keep wearing the dress you made from school can you?"

"No Mrs. Lewis."

"And you can call me Lydia dear if you like because it doesn't sound so formal."

"Are you sure you don't mind?"

"I wouldn't have said so, silly if I hadn't minded, would I?"

"But I don't want to be disrespectful towards you."

"And calling me Lydia is disrespectful, is it?"

"I don't know?"

"That's settled then, it's Lydia and Jim from now on," she said as she put the book she was reading on the window sill in the breakfast room.

"Shall I help you with the tea?"

"Yes you can help me set the table, so you will need to get the crockery from the kitchen dresser."

"I like these plates," I commented as I carefully handle the expensive looking plates because I was so afraid I might break them.

"I am glad you like them, I bought them in that famous shop in Oxford Street, you know the one I mean; they are china and I bought them in the second's department, or was it in the sales," Lydia pondered to herself as she took the casserole out of the oven. The grant I was given from Social Services bought me a few clothes I took back to Chase Park to show Lydia

Lewis.

"Do you like what you bought Mandy?" she asked me at the dinner table that evening.

"I don't know," I replied in an ambivalent tone.

"The shop assistant didn't force you to buy that dress did she, dear?" insisted Lydia Lewis when I showed her the dress I had purchased. I had no idea when I would wear the dress but it seemed a good idea to buy it just in case the occasion presented itself.

"What happened after you tried the dress on?" persisted Lydia.

"Well, the shop assistant kept saying that I should buy the dress because it suited me," I replied.

"That's it, I am not having you bullied into buying that dress, we are going to go back to the shop together to change the dress so you can buy one you really like," proclaimed Lydia Lewis.

We went back to the shop the following day and spent time trying on other dresses.

"Oh that's looks nice on you dear," maintained Lydia as I came out of the changing room and showed her the purple dress I was wearing.

I liked it too and it was the best dress in the shop so I bought it with my grant money.

"We need to help you find a job now that you have left school, any ideas Jim?" inquired Lydia looking across the lunch table at her husband who was reading the newspaper.

"What dear?" answered Jim as he peered over his reading glasses at his wife.

"Mandy needs to get a job, any ideas?" she repeated.

"Well, what does she want to do?" he asked looking at me then returning to his newspaper.

I found myself smiling at Jim because whatever Lydia said or did her husband seemed happy to go along with. They adored each other. When Lydia suffered from migraines these generally took up to three days to run their course he attended to her every need. I had worked out from the early days when living with the Lewis family that Lydia was the extroverted one while Jim remained reticent. He loved nothing better than reading whilst smoking his roll ups. Lydia was sorely missed when she suffered from migraines and a sense of normality only really resumed when she recovered, and was back on her feet again. I could not help but feel empathy towards her when she suffered from migraine attacks. Thankfully my own migraines had stopped once I reached puberty.

"If you observe me while I am cooking, you will learn a few recipes," Lydia assured me at the dinner table after I had complimented her on the meal she had prepared. We had eaten smoked salmon accompanied with Spanish olives and mixed salad.

"I love the food preparations, you do," I told her frequently. Lydia's food presentations were a work of art: each time I sat down for a meal I felt as if I was eating in an exclusive restaurant. Her meals were a far cry from the numerous metal trays of burnt sausages and congealed eggs that had been my daily diet at the Convent.

"Mandy do you want a fried egg for breakfast for a change?" Lydia asked me one Saturday morning.

"No thank you."

"Wouldn't you rather a fried egg instead of a scrambled egg just for a change?"

"I don't like them."

"If you don't like fried eggs what about a boil egg instead?"

"I am fine with scrambled eggs thank you, besides there is cereal, toast and marmalade on the table," I replied, astounded that she should worry about giving me anything else.

"Well at least you are having a proper breakfast especially now that you are working at the Tin Box Company in Baker Street."

I had started at the Tin Box Company about a fortnight earlier after both Julie Wigan and Lydia Lewis had assisted me to complete the application form. The first day I felt extremely anxious as I tried earnestly to follow every instruction I was given as if my life depended on it. One of my tasks was to collect the mail from each department and take it back to the typing pool. Lydia Lewis had also managed to arrange a day release course for me. Consequently, I attended day college, to gain an O level in English and Stage One typing. Attendance at college every Tuesday while working the rest of the week was a new experience for me. When I returned to my office job each Wednesday the girls in the typing pool welcomed me back wholeheartedly since every Tuesday they were left to carry out their own mail and filing duties. They had accepted me from the day I commenced my junior clerk position. I was the only black girl in the office and at lunch time we sat in the canteen chatting about the office politics.

"I thought you were Spanish when I first met you," I informed Lydia Lewis one night when we had caught each other sneaking down the stairs for a midnight feast of her homemade rice pudding. Neither one of us had planned to meet up with each other during the night but I had woken up feeling peckish. I had remembered the delicious rice pudding she had made which we had eaten at the evening meal. The slight aroma of cinnamon and nutmeg had captivated me completely. The rice pudding was delicious and had left me craving for more during the night.

"What are you doing down here?" asked an alarmed Lydia as soon as I opened the door to the breakfast room.

"Oh, I didn't think anyone was here and that the light had been left on by mistake," I replied feeling just as startled.

"I couldn't sleep and felt a bit peckish so I thought I would come down and have some rice pudding," Lydia Lewis continued laughing, "do you want some?"

"Yes please," I answered without hesitation.

We both sat and finished off the rest of the rice pudding while we chatted about Lydia's job as a personal secretary to a director of an American cosmetic company.

"I've got some free samples of expensive foundation cream which I will give you tomorrow."

"OK, but I don't think I need foundation cream."

"I might as well give them to you, the colour will suit your complexion and I have so much of it you might as well use it up. It would be a pity to waste the samples especially since the product is very expensive and of high quality," Lydia asserted, "I use it but this particular one is a bit dark for my complexion but it will suit yours."

"Thank you."

"Let's turn the lights off and go to bed now."

"Good night."

Good night dear."

The Lewis family afforded me a tremendous amount of trust which meant that I could go out with friends to parties at weekends as long as I informed them where I was staying. In hindsight, I was living in supported lodgings, rather than within a foster home environment since at seventeen I realised that I did not need a foster family but rather a family who offered me positive mentoring and coaching. Most weekends after finishing my Saturday job in Oxford Street, a group of us met at our regular pub in Swiss Cottage. By the time the pub closed, we had a number of party invitations to chose from. It was on one of these weekends that I met a boy at a friend's party who invited me to hitch hike with him to the Isle of Wright festival over the August bank holiday.

"Please come with me, you know the Who and Jimi Hendrix are going to be playing there, it will be like the British version of Woodstock."

"I don't know I have never hitched hiked before," I replied hesitantly.

"Come on, don't be scared, if we travel together we will be alright and the concert is a must because there are so many artists performing at the festival."

"OK." I said knowing that wild horses would not stop me from going to see Jimi Hendrix perform.

We were on the road early that morning and hitched several lifts until we arrived at the Isle of Wright. Gerard set up his tent at a suitable spot before we mingled with the crowds. The festival was electrifying and Jimi

Hendrix's performance was spellbinding. On Bank holiday Monday I said goodbye to Gerard in the evening and decided to hitch hike back to London because I had to be at work the following day. The money I had with me was spent pretty quickly so I was unable to eat anything that day. Luckily I was picked up by two guys in a Mercedes on their way home from the festival. I sat in the back of the car and was given cheese and chocolates to eat after I told the guys that I had not eaten all day. They dropped me off at the Lewis's house just after midnight.

"Mandy, did you enjoy yourself at the Isle of Wright festival," Lydia Lewis enquired at breakfast the following morning.

"How did you know I went to the festival," I replied astonished that Lydia Lewis knew where I had spent the weekend.

"That's because I saw you on television yesterday at the festival,"

Lydia replied.

"I didn't know the festival was televised,"

"It wasn't silly but you left a sugar bowl with the Isle of Wright written on it as a gift for me this morning," Lydia Lewis laughed as she told me.

The following weekend I visited Sue at the reception centre to tell her where I was living and about my new job.

"Mandy, why are you wearing that foundation, it is far too dark for you," observed Sue the instance she set eyes on me.

"Lydia Lewis gave it to me as a gift," I replied.

"Take it off; it is far too dark for you,"

"No, I cannot do that Lydia Lewis will be very offended if I don't wear it."

"I'm so happy that you have found a foster family but it doesn't mean that you have to wear a foundation cream which is far darker than your own skin tone."

"The Lewis's are so nice and their home is beautiful, it is full of antique furniture and Jim Lewis is so funny he has such a dry sense of humour." I responded determined to change the subject.

"I'm fed up living here. Julie Morgan has found me a placement at a Convent in Southampton."

" You are leaving London?"

"Yeah, I will be going to Southampton by the end of the month."

"I thought you have had enough of Convents' by now."

"Oh, but this one is so different, you must come and visit Mandy because you wont believe how different it is."

"Why, have you seen it already?"

"Yes, Julie drove me down to Southampton last Tuesday."

I travelled by coach down to Southampton to visit Sue the following month. I eventually arrived at the Convent where Sue greeted me at the door.

"Come and meet Sister Charlotte, she's in the kitchen washing up." proposed Sue as I followed her through a complex of contemporary buildings.

"Sister Charlie, this is my sister Mandy, you know who I have been telling you about," said Sue proudly as she led me into the kitchen.

"Hello Mandy, pleased to meet you at last, Sue never stops talking about you," enthused the nun who looked no more than in her mid twenties. She was drying some plates with a tea towel. Sue was right the Convent was the antithesis of the Sacred Heart Convent.

"Hello," I said exchanging greeting whilst feeling completely relaxed, "you don't look like a nun since you are not wearing a habit."

"No, my Order does not require us to wear a habit so we wear just a pleated skirt and a blouse, we also only partially cover our hair," Sister Charlotte replied, "how was your journey from London and I expect you are hungry?"

"The journey was fine, the coach was a bit slow due to the traffic around Victoria and yes I am hungry."

"Sue, go and show Mandy the fridge so she can choose what she wants to eat."

"What, you get to choose your own food," I said to Sue astounded after thanking Sister Charlotte.

"And we get to eat when we want."

"What between meals."

"Yes if we are hungry and we can agree our own meal times so if I go out at night Sister Charlotte leaves me something to eat."

"Supper was also left for us in the Convent in London," I reminded my sister.

"Yes, but only if we came back before eight o'clock if we had attended a after school event" replied Sue, "here we can stay out until eleven and Sister Charlotte still leaves us food, sometimes we girls have a midnight feast when we come home."

"Where do you go at night?" I said my curiosity getting the better of me.

"We go to the Shambeens, parties and to the cinema," Sue replied.

"Sister Charlotte allows you go to parties," I responded.

"Of course and sometimes I stay out all night."

I could not believe the freedom and fun Sue was having. The house was so completely without rules.

"It's so peaceful here," I remarked to Sue as a group of us set off down to the local pub.

"I know, I love it down here and Sister Charlotte is my best friend," remarked Sue happily.

"I never thought I'd hear you say that Sue, a nun as your best friend," I observed amazed by her comment.

"Sister Charlie is not like a nun she's more like a big sister, a bit like you and guess what she is teaching me to play the guitar and she is arranging to pay for singing lessons for me because you know that I have always dreamed of becoming a singer."

"Oh, you lucky thing."

"Sister Charlie said she'd do her best to promote me as a singer and you know that Aretha Franklin is my favourite singer now."

"You have so many talents, you are athletic, you can draw brilliantly and you can sing just as well as any of the soul singers. I wish I had talents like you."

"But Mandy, you are an excellent runner and you

are good at helping people, besides what about those Easter eggs you won from those writing competitions."

"Yes but I gave up running when no one came to see me to cheer me on and as for writing well I only entered the competitions so that you and I could be given Easter eggs if I won. As for Christmas presents you know I bought those with my wages from my Saturday jobs. Anyhow I can't write that well and as for caring for people well I don't have a choice. At least if you are a singer or an artist people can see your talents straight away!" I replied not convinced that any of my talents were of any worth.

The pub was crowded when we entered however we managed to find a table in the corner near the jukebox. Marianne one of Sue's newly acquired friends walked over to the jukebox to play some records.

"Hey Sue, what sounds do you want to hear?" Marianne shouted at Sue.

"Play the latest ones, not the old tunes." Sue shouted back.

"What do you all want to drink," I offered gallantly.

"Oh I'll have a treble gin and tonic," replied Sue immediately.

"A treble gin and tonic?" I said in shock.

"Well a double then," responded Sue resentfully.

"I'll have a lager," said Deana who was very thin with red hair and freckles.

"I'll have a lager too," said Marianne coming back to join the group at the table.

I ordered the drinks and bought some crisps.

"Oh get some packet of nuts too Mandy," requested Sue as I made my way back to the bar to collect the rest of the drinks. In no time at all the local guys were chatting us up. We were invited to a party later on that night and arrived back at the Convent well after midnight. Sue was merrily drunk and had been the life and soul of the party. I watched her during the evening being chatted up by the guys but she made no commitment to any one of them as my sister downed her drinks rapidly. By the time the four of us went to bed it was well past two o'clock. The next night we got ready to go to a Shambeen.

"What's a shambeen like?" I asked.

"They are similar to a house party but people pay a small entrance fee to get in and they pay for their drinks, the disc jockey specialises exclusively in ska and studio one music, remember Mandy, I told you this on the telephone when I phoned you at the Convent."

We arrived at the shambeen about ten and entered inside. It was dark and once my eyes had adjusted to the dimly lit room, I noticed that there were small groups of people in various parts of the room. The majority of them seemed to be prompt up against the walls while swaying rhythmically to the music. After the pubs closed the shambeen became suddenly packed with all sorts of people.

"That's the local street women with their pimps over there," pointed Sue discreetly to some white and black women in the far corner who were laughing and joking together as they danced to the music. There were students, US sailors, couples and single people mingling collectively. The deejay played the sound system loud enough for the drum and bass to vibrate across the room. I observed the West Indians dancing with keen interest since the steps and rhythms they were dancing were excitingly new to me. One of the men, who were dressed in an Italian designer suit, pulled me towards him to dance. I did not have a clue how to follow his rhythm, his body movements seemed so refine and deft yet complicated because of his rhythmic manoeuvres which derived from his hip movements. I knew instinctively that I had to master the hip movements in order to gain any credibility from the other dancers who I perceived were watching me as I self consciously battled to follow my mentor's dance style. I convinced myself that if I was to stand up and be counted I had to be adept at the particular dance style; besides I had been put on the spot as I told myself that I had to survive this ordeal with dignity. My dance partner not only wore a suit, he wore a hat in fact looking around the dance floor, I observed that most of the Caribbean men were dressed in suits unlike the white men who mainly wore jeans apart from those who were in uniform. My initiation of the rites of passage into the reggae dance style was not any easy one. My dance partner moved one way while I moved the other.

"Where you from, you're not from Jamaican then?" he said looking rather puzzled at me.

"No, my mother is Irish and my father was from Ghana," I replied nervously, pre-empting the fact that he was probably going to ask me where my parents were from.

"You're a half caste, then?"

"I am not half of a caste," I replied indignantly, "but I am half of a race, in fact half of two races!"

"Just follow my rhythm," he whispered clearly ignoring my last remark.

"I can't."

"That's because you are not relaxed, you are too wooden."

"I can't seem to follow your rhythm."

After a couple of dances he left me to go and dance with other women. I could not help but notice that some of the white women were able to follow his rhythm without consternation so I felt slightly put out by my revelations.

He came back from time to time to dance with me.

Each time he went away a white guy would ask me to dance. His rhythms were easier to follow and I often took the lead because some of his movements were not as tight as the Jamaican's. Whenever the Jamaican man came back to me I was determined to improve my dance style. He assisted me in this dance inauguration since he always took the lead and guided my hips in harmony with his. He added stomach dance movements to his repertoire and finally with his persistent lead I was able to follow his style confidently by the end of the night. I was drawn to his sophisticated movements because he hardly moved his feet only to take short elegant steps.

"You dance differently whenever you dance with him," declared the white guy who had been dancing with me intermittently.

"Do I? "I replied not knowing what else to say. What I did know was that a few white guys were dancing similarly to the Caribbean men while several others were dancing all over the place. Their uncontrolled movements appeared out of time with the incessant pulsating staccato beat of the music. Nevertheless, the reggae sounds were so enticing that whatever movements, were made by the dancers, enjoyment was clearly illustrated on their faces. Those who were not dancing just stood at the bar in their mellow stance while the singers sung songs of love and of the racial, social and economic discriminations in their bitter sweet harmonies. Circumspectly, it seemed to me that at some point the drum and bass was instrumental in transcending our individual movements so that everyone's manoeuvres on the dance floor sublimely crescendoed into one universal rhythm. When I left the shambeen that night, I looked out at the world through different eyes. Not only had I been inducted into a completely new dance form, I had also been initiated into a sub culture which I had not known existed before then.

I travelled back to London the following day and back to work on the Tuesday morning. While at the Tin Box Company I became friendly with one of the typist's from the typing pool and along with her sister I went partying with Deborah and Jean at weekends. Deborah and Jean rented a flat in trendy Earl's Court and where originally from County Durham. By now I was relatively independent since I was earning a wage while social services paid my weekly rent to Lydia and Jim Lewis. I hardly saw Julie Morgan although Sue saw her regularly.

"You know Jim's parents were from Russia and my parents were from Poland originally," Lydia Lewis revealed to me one day when we were eating lunch.

"When did your parents come over to England?" I asked.

"Both sets of parents came during the Second World War because they had to escape from Nazi Germany," she added.

"My parents' were emigrates as well," I replied.

"Yes dear they were. Jim has a sister in Israel," continued Lydia.

"He must miss her when did he last see her?"

"Jin does miss his sister and only see her when she travels to England but her health hasn't been all that good lately."

"Why doesn't Jim travel to Israel to see her?"

"He won't go to Israel, he won't travel there."

"Why not?"

"He just won't go. You know Jim used to be actor and he used to act at the Unity theatre."

"Was he a very good actor?"

"He certainly was and he was very funny as well but he wasn't able to bring up a family on the wages he earned as an actor due to work not being regular enough."

"What sorts of plays were shown at the Unity theatre?"

"The Unity was a socialist theatre so the plays were about social and political issues, many of the productions spoke out against fascism in Europe."

"I went for an interview today at a restaurant and was offered a job as a waitress. My mother told me when I went to visit her recently that she had once been a waitress when she first arrived here from Ireland. She worked at a Lyons tea house," I said wanting to emulate my mother in someway.

"With due respect to your mother becoming a waitress, waitressing does not seem much of a career Mandy!"

"Well, it pays more money than what I'm earning now and I do need to buy some descent clothes because I am fed up with not being able to buy similar clothes to my friends especially since they all earn far more money than me" I replied defensively.

"Yes I know dear, but they are three or four years older than you and they are secretaries," replied Lydia sounding a bit disappointed.

"It's called the Boulevard and Mr. Benjamin the proprietor seems very nice. He offered me the post immediately so I will be starting in just over a fortnight's time."

"How did you find out about this job," asked Lydia inquisitively.

"One of my friends' has a friend who is Australian and she told me about the vacancy, apparently a lot of Australians and Polish girls work there," I exclaimed not quite understanding why Lydia wasn't as enthused as I was.

"I suppose you have already given in your notice at

the Tin Box Company."

"Yes I have and I leave in two weeks time."

"I hope you will invite Jim and me to lunch at the Boulevard one day?"

"Of course I will!"

The boulevard was located in one of the side streets, which ran adjacent to Oxford Street. The main entrance to the restaurant was through two glass sliding doors that in summer allowed the sun to shine through so the front tables on either side of the sliding doors were very popular with the customers particularly since a few tables were placed on the veranda, outside the sliding doors, usually from May until late September weather permitted. There were four waitresses on duty at any one time. I worked from nine to five alternative weeks and from three to ten every other week. The shifts pattern included working weekends however I felt that it was worth it because although the wages were lousy, the tips were good.

I purchased the required black skirt, white blouse and white apron that made up the uniform. On my feet I wore black comfortable shoes since it was not long before I discovered that my feet ached from standing all day.

The early shifts were busy from 10 am onwards. French coffee and croissants were served until 12pm then the lunchtime menu was on offer.

"Chicken Kiev and veal dishes are very popular here," I stated to Judith one morning. She was one of the cashiers at the restaurant who was on duty that particular lunch time.

"Yes they are very popular with our customers although some people complain that we have veal on the menu because they do not agree with eating calf's meat. "

"Why is veal so popular? "

"Because the meat is sweet and tender."

"I don't like it because it's prepared in breadcrumbs and besides I don't really care for meat that much anymore."

"You mean to say that you don't like fillet steak because I've got one right here under my cash till."

"I was wondering what you were eating, what will happen if Mr. Benjamin finds out?"

"Oh, he won't find out, Ali the chef always makes sure I get a steak to eat when Mr. Benjamin is not about."

"I don't like Ali, he is always swearing and his long hair is really unkempt," I pointed out while wiping the glass cover which had the remaining fresh cream cakes underneath.

"Ali's always arguing with Mr. Benjamin because he refuses to tie his hair back and wear his chef's hat."

"Yes, I can hear them when I have to go downstairs to check my orders."

"But the main thing that get's Mr. Benjamin is the joints Ali smokes while he's on duty."

"Yes, I don't know how he gets away with it."

"He is an excellent chef though," replied Judith helping herself to another piece of fillet steak.

"Pia the Italian waitress is his girlfriend isn't she but I cannot understand why she is so moody, she hardly speaks to anyone."

"That's because he knocks her about and cheats on her by having relationships with other women."

"Why does she put up with it?"

"I don't know," replied Judith shaking her head.

"She never looks happy."

"Well he takes all the money she earns as well and her family are very wealthy in Italy. Her mother has come over from Italy and has been in the restaurant pleading with Pia to go back to Italy with her but she won't. She just keeps giving her money to Ali, and she had told me that he sometimes sends her out on the streets, if she has no more money left."

"Is that why she never seems to buy any clothes so always wears her waitress uniform instead of changing into something else after her shift?"

"I suppose so anyway my old man knocks me around sometimes, a lot of Jamaican men are like that you know."

"No, I didn't know that, why do you put up with it?" I asked as I saw some customers coming through the glass doors. I started to walk over to them to greet them and to take them to the vacant tables.

"What else can I do?"

"Leave him," I said moving towards the customers so that I could show them to my tables.

"He'll only find me. You look like you are from the Caribbean," said Judith changing the subject.

"So I have been told, but I am not," I managed to say before I greeted my customers.

Whenever I worked the day shifts I served meals to tourists as they made up the bulk of customers who ate at lunch times before going to a matinee show. Lunch times were always maniac as we waitresses raced around trying to serve each table almost simultaneously. At around 3pm most of the lunch time customers had left to be replaced by the older ladies who lived in Golders Green. The majority of them were sixty and over and they were the business in so far as they were exquisitely dressed with fully applied make up, painted nails and a large number of them wore some of the most expensive jewellery I had ever seen. The waitresses quickly cleared the tables in preparation for the afternoon pots of boiling tea along with serving new fresh cream cakes from the cake trolley. The ladies adored their tea and cakes and sat until five o'clock chatting to their friends and families who often joined them.

"I'll have that last miel foil, you know dear, the one with the pink icing on top and the layers of fresh cream in between the shoe pastry." Declared one of my regulars as she pointed over to show me the cake she wanted with her perfectly pink painted finger nail. I could not help but notice, the faint display of numbers on one of her arms as she pointed to the cake. She noticed me looking at her arm on that occasion so she discreetly pulled her blouse sleeve further down towards her wrist as she withdrew her hand.

"These women are very well dressed," acknowledged Leanne, a newly acquired friend of mine. Leanne was Australian and she had just popped in one day for coffee before she went off to work in one of the local pubs' around the corner from Baker Street.

"Yes, they are," I replied not taking much notice of Leanne's remark since I was preoccupied with clearing away the remaining crockery from one of my tables. The table was parallel to the one Leanne was sitting at so we could have a muted conversation that was not heard by anyone else. While she was drinking her coffee I was mentally counting the tip that had been left me. I was not disappointed.

"I hope I look like that when I am a pensioner?" observed Leanne.

"You need to cut down on your drinking then!" I mentioned teasingly.

"I couldn't help but notice that the lady you have just finished serving tea to a while ago, you know the one with the tinted hair, well when she introduced her son to another of the ladies on the next table, I was flabbergasted because she looked the same age as her son!"

"He's probably got a high flying, yet stressful job."

I declared again not paying much attention because I needed to get my tables ready for the evening crowd who would want dinner before they went off to the theatre.

"I heard him say that he owned a string of shops near Finchley Road."

"Really, I must say I didn't really notice him but that's because I cannot sit around like you being a lady of leisure," I joked.

"What cake can I have today?" Leanne asked changing the subject.

"Whatever you want and as usual I'll charge you just for a cup of coffee."

"Can I have a steak then like the last time?"

"If you like, but you will get me sacked one of these days."

"Oh come on all the waitresses do the same, don't they?"

"You know they do," I replied as I went to order her steak.

Timothy and Kevin the two deputy Managers and they were completely opposite to one another. In fact they were poles apart. Kevin lived with his wife in affluent Henley on Thames while Ian lived in a salubrious flat in Islington.

"Working class made good," said Jane the daytime cashier who detested Kevin.

"Why don't you like him?" I asked her one day as she was grooming her shoulder length blond hair with her jade comb while observing herself in her hand mirror.

"I can always tell those sort, the neavou riche, lots of money, no taste and have never heard of Elizabeth Browning or Shelley, in fact the only reading he does is to read the daily newspapers so that he can peer at the scantily dressed women and find out the football results."

"I was surprised to know that he was married since he's always chasing the new waitresses especially the Polish ones."

"Yes, he likes them blond and foreign, he thinks he's a proper Don Juan with his slick black hair, and you know he dyes it too." Jane exclaimed.

"He doesn't?" I said wondering to myself why I hadn't noticed it before.

"Yes, he's forty two you know and his girlfriends are all half his age."

"Doesn't his wife mind?"

"He told me that they only live in the same house because neither one wants to move out because the house is so beautiful although they live separate lives. They also have a son who lives with them."

"What about you, are you married? " I said noticing the ring on Jane's third finger of her left hand.

"What me, no, I prefer women I'm a lesbian; one of my ex girlfriends is now famous but I can't tell you who she is, I really miss her though but anyhow my new girlfriend is a doctor and we have only just met recently so its early days yet."

"You don't look like a lesbian," I said shocked by Jane's outspokenness.

"And what are lesbians supposed to look like?" she replied looking at me rather sympathetically.

"Rather aggressive with short hair," I said stammering over my words.

"Oh typical male press, you really need to learn to question what you read or who you mix with, you need to get your facts right before you form an opinion or judgment," said Jane now manicuring her unpainted finger nails after putting her mirror and comb away in her rather posh handbag.

Timothy was also gay, in fact he was outrageously camp and the older ladies simply idolized him as he fussed and flirted with them whenever he was on the afternoon shift.

"Timothy's coming to tea at my house next Sunday," one of my regular ladies informed me one afternoon as I was fetching her some more hot water to top up her teapot.

"He's very popular," I admitted, "since he is always being invited to tea by a customer."

"He is so attentive and kind; and is a delightful gossip: he knows a lot about the lives of the film stars who were famous when I was young and he has marvellous ideas about interior design and other bits and pieces; he is ever so entertaining. His knowledge of excellent food is superb and he has such good taste and impeccable manners. You know, the last time he came around for afternoon tea he even bought some of my mother's favourite perfume for her because it was her eighty seventh birthday. She was so thrilled that he bothered to think of her especially with her being so ill now, Is he, you know, a homosexual dear?"

"I think so."

"Such a nice young man, he'd have made a wonderful son in law, never mind, I've managed to book him for afternoon tea, this Sunday before Mrs. Jacob did."

Friday nights were when Timothy's crowd came to eat at the restaurant. After the theatre crowd had finished their meals and set off to see their favourite shows, his friends arrived. I found their theatrical ways amusing as they made their grand entrances into the restaurant and then finding their favourite seats, they sat down and proceeded to gossip about the latest fashion or who will be at the next party they were attending, or about the altercation they had with their latest boyfriend. Some arrived with their Pekinese dogs whose silk ribbons flapped against their ears. While others wore their lacquered hair in such a manner as to conceal their bald patches; a few had applied make up discreetly to their eyes while others were as delicate and discreet as they could be. It was the only time the radio was played when Timothy turned it on and we all listened to Billie Holiday and other jazz musicians of that era playing softly in the background. Undoubtedly when Timothy was on duty the atmosphere at the Boulevard was extremely relaxed since there was no need to be on our guard. Friday nights was the one night in the week that we waitresses were virtually ignored by our customers, so we sat down at the tables at the back of the restaurant chatting to each other while some waitresses smoked their cigarettes and helped themselves to a glass of wine knowing that Timothy was preoccupied with his cliental. We knew full well that he turned a blind eye to our capers. Besides, Judith was on the till every Friday night so whatever we wanted to eat, we sneaked downstairs to get it sometimes having the meal sent up by the dummy waiter where another waitress took the plate of food around to the back of the restaurant for us all to pick at. In the meantime Timothy either sat and talked with his friends or ran around after them. Ali was content to cook whatever was asked of him all we had to do was be prepared to walk past the blaze of heavy smoke of hashish when we needed to go downstairs to the kitchen.

"Mandy, your table three needs serving," Timothy proclaimed coming over to me one evening, "what's that smell; it must be coming from the kitchen!"

"No idea," I said as I got up to serve the two men at my table.

"Oh, it's Ali again with his joints I should have

known, I must go and tell him to stop smoking otherwise our customers will think that we are in a Turkish Kasbah rather than in a restaurant in London!" remarked Timothy as he walked hurriedly towards the steps which led down to the kitchen.

"Ali, Ali, I need to speak to you, or where has he gone?"

I heard Timothy calling after Ali as he daintily descended the stairs. We all knew that Ali would not take any notice of Timothy.

"Yes, what would you like to eat sir?" I asked one of the two gentlemen seated at my table.

"I think I might just have a cake," said the man who had a heavy French accent. "What do you think I should have Jeremy?" he asked, turning at his friend.

"Have whatever you want," replied the other man looking proudly and lovingly at his partner.

"I think I will be daring and have a cake from the trolley over there," he replied.

I wheeled the cake trolley over so that the two men could have a closer look.

"I think I will have that strawberry tart with the fresh cream," he requested, pointing a long elegant finger towards the trolley, is it fresh today?"

"Yes of course, the cakes are always fresh every day," I assured him.

"I must watch my figure though because I want to keep it slim like yours," he said.

The three of us laughed knowing that he had a fabulous figure and had every intention of keeping it trim.

One Friday night on my way home from a day shift at the Boulevard I was looking through the evening paper while trying to get a seat on the underground train when I noticed the advert. It seemed to leap out at me. It read 'English girls wanted to work in bars in

Spain and Italy.'

I was intrigued because at nineteen years old and three years away from leaving the Convent, I wanted to take up as many opportunities that life could offer me. I was hungry for freedom and adventure and the idea of working abroad appealed to me. I had by now moved away from Lydia Lewis's home and set up home in a bed sitter in Belsize Square with my first boyfriend. However, Ossie, was pressurising me to get married and settle down with him but the idea of commitment was furthest from my mind. The problem was though that if I left him, I would be homeless. The opportunity to work in abroad offered accommodation as well. I suppose, I was also heavily influenced by the girls at the Boulevard who were always travelling and taking up work as secretaries, waitresses and doing bar work in between their travelling epochs. Before I realised what I was doing I was on the aeroplane heading towards Southern Spain. The only other time I had travelled abroad was to Holland when I was sixteen with Sue. Julie Morgan had arranged for Social Services to pay for the holiday and we travelled by coach to Holland to spend a week on a barge. Sue and I had pestered Julie Morgan so much so beforehand because we had desperately wanted to travel abroad. The first night of our holiday we had lost our barge because we could not remember the name of it. A group of Dutch teenagers spent most of the night helping us to locate it, which we did in the early hours of the following morning.

Chapter VII

I sat on my seat in the aeroplane feeling a sense of achievement because I had enough money in my savings account to pay for the airfare to Spain as well as having a sufficient amount for holiday money. Arriving in Malaga I had no idea what to expect insofar as to assume that Spain was not unlike Holland. It was therefore a tremendous shock to me when I discovered how overwhelmingly hot Southern Spain was. The dry heat hit me full force as soon as I disembarked from the aeroplane. To be greeted by numerous Palm trees when I stepped out of the airport terminal was another huge surprise.

"I must be in Africa," I thought to myself as I panicked in confusion, "or the West Indies, there must be some mistake, Spain cannot be this hot and with so many Palm trees, this can't be right!" I felt that I had walked straight into an over large and over heated glass oven. I looked around for my contact but could not see Pedro anywhere amongst the mass of unfamiliar faces. The lady who had organised the trip had stated quite clearly on the telephone that Pedro Rodriguez would meet me. As the Proprietor's assistant, he had been instructed to meet me when I arrived at Malaga airport. For my part, I had agreed to wear my red jacket so that he could recognise me although I quickly realised what a mistake that had been wearing such a heavy jacket in the blistering hot weather. However I had little idea that the weather in late September in Malaga was just as hot as the height of the summer weather in England, if not hotter. For instance the week I had left for Spain it had been decidedly cooler in England to the extent that the September evenings were markedly colder for that time of year but here in Malaga, I anticipated the weather to be approximately thirty eight celsius. Yet despite the soaring heat there was no way I was going to take off my jacket.

I had boarded the plane at 9 o'clock that morning and had arrived a few hours later. I waited until about 8 o clock that evening before I decided Pedro was definitely not coming to collect me. I had been standing around conspicuously for over seven hours. Common sense told me to take one of the many taxis that stood stationary outside the airport terminal. I walked over to the taxi driver whose cab was first in the taxi line and showed him the address of my destination. He in return peered at the scribbled handwriting and subsequently shook his head and said something incomprehensible to me. I spoke no Spanish whatsoever and he spoke a few words of English.

"No, No, Grenada, no," he said sounding exasperated.

"But why not, I've got money," I replied showing him my money.

"No, no," he answered as he opened the taxi door and I climbed in.

I felt disconcerted and disorientated but nevertheless, I was on my way to Granada, wherever that was. I noticed that it was quickly becoming dark as we journeyed towards the town. Suddenly the taxi stopped abruptly.

"Come, come, senorita," the taxi driver beckoned.

"Is this Granada?" I asked even more confused and not wanting to get out of the taxi until I was sure where I was.

"No, you here, tonight, tomorrow Grenada," he replied taking my suitcase from the boot of the taxi and beckoning me to come with him. "Come, senorita, come."

I followed him as he led me towards a very old

building with laced wrought iron gates. We entered a courtyard and walked through to the reception area. He spoke to the proprietor for what seemed like ages, who in turn looked me up and down while nodding sympathetically.

"Passport, signorita por favour," the taxi drive gesticulated.

"I want it back though," I stated not sure whether I should hand over my passport.

"Si, si, manana, manana, tomorrow," he replied resolutely.

"How much for the taxi ride?" I said holding out a bundle of Spanish money while we stood at the reception. I later realised I was in a bed and breakfast hotel. The taxi driver took what he wanted and waved me goodnight.

"Buenos notches senorita, esta manana."

"Goodbye, I mean, adios."

I was escorted to my room by the proprietor in silence. The room was of moderate size and somewhat basic. The building may well have been an eighteenth century building but was now rather dilapidated. The French windows opened out onto a balcony, I noticed had window shutters that were semi shut but I could still observe the people below through them, as they walked around enjoying their late evening stroll. The noisy plaza was filled with families who were implacably dressed some of who were eating at nearby cafes and bars. Although I was exhausted I was far too excited to sleep even though the semi closed shutters blocked out some of the noise. It seemed strange to me that people with children were out at that time of night especially knowing that if I were in London the streets would be empty of children who might well be asleep or at least indoors for the night. I felt as if I was on another planet never mind in another country. The room was extremely humid since there was no air conditioning available apart from a little fan that swirled the hot air around the room. Hunger pains unexpectedly kicked in as I instantly remembered that I had not eaten since the meal on the aeroplane and by now I was starving. Luckily, I was reminded of the packet of crisps in my handbag I had bought at the airport in London, hungrily I ate those after showering off the long sultry day. The antiquated room charmed me as tiredness began to engulf me and I finally succumbed to sleep with anticipation and apprehension of my new life.

"Signorita, signorita."

"Yes," I said as I heard the proprietor knocking on my door. His frantic knocks on the door woke me up from a profound sleep. I immediately jumped out of bed, showered and dressed in no time at all despite my disorientation. The urgency in his voice told me that I needed to be responsive and quick thinking. At reception I was promptly shown my bill and paid him diligently. To my utter amazement the same taxi driver who had driven me to the pension the previous evening walked into the reception area as I was handed back my passport. He greeted me as he picked up my suitcase and escorted me out through the courtyard then ushered me into his cab. I am now on way to Granada I assumed. Instead however we arrived at a coach station where the taxi driver gestured to me to pay for a ticket that he supervised. I gave him a wad of Spanish notes again he took what was required, paid for my ticket and then walked over to the coach driver to have a brief discussion with him while I followed in keen pursuit. Next he took my suitcase and gave it to the coach driver who put it in the back of the coach in the luggage department.

"Adios signorita, goodbye," he said smiling a

fatherly smile at me.

Goodbye," I replied as I waved and smiled back at him. No doubt I was just as confused as I was the day before but despite my confusion, I proceeded to climb the steps and find a seat on the coach amongst the loud Spanish chattering. I sat beside a large lady who was preoccupied with her thoughts so did not take any notice of me. The coach stood in its own motionless perpetuity while utterly fascinated I observed the social activities around me. Families boarded with what appeared to be their entire utensils and food provisions stuffed into large bulging bags. Unexpectedly amongst all the bustling, a man climbed on to the coach and started singing in a lamenters tone, raw and emotional. He then manoeuvred his guitar from his back to his front and subsequently started strumming it as he serenaded us. Following him another man climbed up the steep coach steps; he carried a basket with a very clean starched tablecloth covering the contents. I was amongst the people watching him as he meticulously unfolded the cloth to reveal bread rolls. Hunger saw me buy two cheese rolls. The cheese was hot and sweaty but I was not perturbed my hunger was as such. I bit into the bread and nearly broke my front teeth because the bread was so hard to the degree that I was convinced it was stale but after looking around and observing that everyone else was eating it; I assumed that this was the order of the day. As much as I tried I could not eat the hard rolls, this left me only the cheese to eat. I soon wished I was bought some more rolls so that I could eat more of the cheese because I was still hungry but I was satisfied enough to enjoy the scenery which was beginning to unfold spectacularly around me, as the coach finally pulled out of the coach station. I had the good sense to have purchased a bottled of mineral water as well and thankfully that was nice and cold. I promptly sat back to enjoy the most beautiful scenery I had every seen. Luscious green hills and valleys with numerous olive, orange and lemons trees together with jasmine brushes which threw up their fragrances to me almost simultaneously; by virtue of the open window and mercifully I was without hesitation seduced. I feasted my eyes on the rolling hills, the rich blue hot sky with its burning sun. Never had I been so convinced that I was in heaven. The euphoric view was staring out in front of me and all the people around me could do; were to laugh and chatter in their indifference. We passed fields and fields of sunflowers and the azure sea sparkled teasingly below us as we climbed higher and higher away from its cool refreshing breeze. Many times I found myself closing my eyes in order to capture the scenery; to store in my mind forever; as picturesque scenes constantly unfolded before me. Each time I opened my eyes, I took in more and more of the intoxicating beauty of it all. The journey was long and winding and seemed never ending; needless to say I did not want it to, hence my new life's adventure was so far removed from the life that I had known. This encounter was something completely new and magical and as much as I wanted to sleep and let the sunshine down on my sleeping face, I dare not accede for fear that this dreamlike realm would end brusquely. I was awake in a dream and felt for the first time a happiness that I had never ever known in my whole life.

The coach hummed its way along the mountainous roads that dipped down initially along the coastal roads. The trip took about six hours and it was only when I looked at my watch that I fully comprehended what the taxi driver had meant. There was no way he would have driven six hours to Granada and then back again especially after seeing the money I had shown him. I disembarked with the other passengers when the coach finally stopped at a plaza. The Moorish and old European architecture eminently embraced me with their magnificent and foreboding delicate details against the Sierra Nevada mountains in the background. Looking around and about me I desperately hoped that someone might emerge from the local population to greet me. Instead, I was informally and indirectly introduced unwittingly to people of whom a vast number of them were severely disabled and disturbingly disfigured. Admittedly not everyone bore such scars but those who did stood out. I quickly realised that in England perhaps I either had not noticed people with similar physical ailments or that they were treated for their conditions much more adequately by the National Health Service.

I waited for a while and then decided to get another taxi to the Bar Whiskeria, which was where I was supposedly to take up employment. Within five minutes I arrived outside a small indistinguishable building. There were no chairs or tables outside only a brown door. I paid the taxi driver and then opened the door and went inside. I was immediately affected by the darkness of the narrow room I had entered. My eyes took some considerable time to readjust from the burning bright sun outside to the almost midnight darkness, I now found myself in. Curiosity led me to walk further into the room.

"Who are you?" I heard a voice say as I turned around to see where it came from. The voice had come from a woman whose large thick wavy red hair framed a small oval shaped face.

"I'm Mandy," I replied introducing myself despite feeling hugely intimidated.

"Have you come to work here?" she enquired.

"Yes, I think so, although someone was supposed to

meet me at the airport but they didn't turn up," I answered now seriously wondering as to whether I had made the right decision to come to Spain.

"Pedro, Pedro," shouted the woman, "you were supposed to collect this girl from the airport, you silly man, by the way my name is Jan, and this is Kay and beside her is Mary."

"Hello, pleased to meet you," said Mary immediately" have you travelled all the way from Malaga on your own?"

"Yes," I replied.

"Pedro, Pedro, come here right this minute," demanded Jan.

I noticed that Kay just looked at me and then looked away. I thought that I had done something wrong so over the next few days I tried to make conversation with Kay but she ignored me. Eventually I gave up trying.

A thin wiry man emerged from the darkness and came towards me. I was struck, by his blond hair and green eyes because up until then all the other Spaniards I had encountered were dark in complexion without exception. After putting out his cigarette he smiled at me, shook my hand and then ushered me out into daylight again.

"Pedro, you forgot to collect her from the airport, didn't you, go on, admit it," I heard Jan shout, before Pedro closed the door behind him.

"You come with me."

Pedro gestured to me to follow him along the pavement as he picked up my suitcase. He wore a green thick cotton jacket which seemed out of place in the baking sun but that did not seem to bother him.

"You from London?" he asked in broken English.

"Yes I am."

"But where your parents from?"

"My mother is from Southern Ireland."
"Oh Erlandesa."
"And my father was from Ghana."
"Where?"
"From Africa."
"Then you are a mulatta."
"Am I."
"Theese way, pleese."
"What, that way?"
"No, no, theese way!"
"Oh you mean, we need to go up these steps?"
"Si, Si."

We climbed the many steps until we reached a door. It was open and we walked inside and up to the reception.

"Ola Paco," greeted the concierge.
"Hello Miguel."

Both men then entered into a long conversation in Spanish which left me feeling bored. Finally Pedro was handed a key and I followed him to a room at the end of the landing.

"You stay here and rest for a while."
"But I am hungry and when do I start work?
"Tomorrow."
"And food."
"I will go and get you some after I have returned to the bar. You know those foreign girls are too bad."
"Are they, what have they done?"
"They go out with married men and they flirt too much, and they are too cheeky, not like Spanish girls, but you, you are different, you are a good girl."
"Well I don't go out with married men, besides I grew up in a Convent."
"Hmm, some Convent girls are bad too, but not you, I can see that," with that assertion Pedro left. I settled down and fell asleep exhausted. The culmination of the

hot sun and the last twenty four hours events had finally worn me out.

The following day I woke up early, remembering where I was I opened the wooden shutters and looked out past the wire mesh to the streets below. I felt pleased with myself that I had made it to Granada on my own and now I was more curious than ever to meet the other young women who worked in the bar. I had an en suite shower and toilet so I showered and then decided since Pedro had not returned last night with food to go and buy some. I turned the handle of the door only to find that it was locked. I was locked in. I thought I had heard the key in the door turn last night but I had instantly dismissed it because I had no reason to think that Pedro would lock me in my room. I was wrong. He had.

I stayed in my room all day. Thank goodness I had a couple of magazines with me. The hunger pains came and went and the bread I had from the coach I proceeded to eat. The next day I spent on my own again. By now I was getting anxious and worried. I spent the time observing the people in the streets below. The little old ladies in their black garments fondling their rosary beads as their mantillas covered their hair and the few older men, also dressed in black sat with their wives on benches underneath trees, shading themselves from the sun. Similarly to my observations in Malaga, families strolled out in the evening after the sun had gone down in order to get some respite as the evenings turned into night became comfortably cooler. I observed the young girls being chaperoned by their brothers as groups of young men walked admiringly past them. I lay on my bed at night listening to the sounds and the whirring of the ceiling fan, swishing the air around the room. At least the walls were made of stone I thought feeling relieved that I was not outside during the day and under the mercy of the hot sun. However I wanted desperately to go walkabouts in the evenings like everyone else. There were times that I knocked on the door shouting for Pedro or for anyone to let me out. I discovered that in the daytime this was a waste of effort because it seemed so quiet. Everyone must be out and about I thought. At night I knocked a few times but no one took any notice.

At last when I was almost at my wits end and after I had just finished showering before getting dressed, I heard a knock on the door and then the key turn. At last Pedro had come back. The door opened and sure enough Pedro entered the room. Behind him was another man.

"This is Alexis, the owner of the bar."

"Hello," said Alexis.

"Hello."

"I have bought you some food," said Pedro as he began to lay out some enamel dishes which contained meat and lentil stew inside.

"I have been here for three days without food and locked up in this room, why?"

"I am sorry that you have been in this room for so long." answered Alexis.

His English was almost fluent although his voice was slightly inaudible but I did not care because I was fascinated by his appearance. He looked like Che Guevara. It was as if Che Guevara had stepped out from one of the posters that I had seen in Carnaby Street.

"That's OK," I found myself saying, knowing that it was not but I was lost for words.

"We have all your papers and passport approved so you can start work tonight." informed Alexis as he sat in front of me wearing a beige designer suit, with his flowing hair. I noticed that his dark brown melancholic eyes held secrets he kept to himself. Alexis left shortly afterwards while Pedro stayed and hovered around me.

"You my girlfriend, do you know that?"

"Am I?"

"Yes, I am very fussy and I only go out with good girls."

After finishing my meal, I followed Pedro to the Bar Whiskeria. It was a short enough walk from the Pension.

"Well, well, you have finally let her out of the pension," declared Jan as I came in to the bar to work that evening.

"Oh don't mind her, she talks too much."

"Talks too much, do I, if it wasn't for me you would still have that girl locked up in that room, hungry and alone because stupid Pedro had forgotten all about you," Jan proclaimed turning to me, as she tossed her thick mane of red hair and smiled at me with her emerald green eyes.

Pedro sulkily went to sit at the end of the bar presumably to keep an eye on us. I went over to chat to Jan and the other bar assistants including a young woman who name was Patricia in order to find out what I needed to know about the new job. Mary and Patricia were Irish and Kay and Jan were Australian. While Mary had mousy brown short hair, Kay's hair was ravishing black, and her eyes were a striking blue. In fact both Jan and Kay had a film star appearance about them. Patricia was blond and blue eyed. At six o clock, the bar opened and by nine, it was full with mostly businessmen. Both Mary and Jan seemed to have enough command of the language to have a descent conversation with some of the customers. I did not know where to begin.

"Don't worry," encouraged Mary "you'll soon pick

up enough Spanish to get your message across. So with a mixture of two Spanish words spoken by me; together with broken English spoken by the customers, my job as a bar maid commenced.

"What eeze your name?" enquired a rather short squat man with olive skin, straight black hair and equally black eyes.

"Mandy."

"Monday," Oh in Spanish, that is Lunes," he said sounding rather pleased with himself.

"No not Monday, Mandy," I declared, exasperated because this was not the first time I had difficulty explaining my name that evening.

"Mondy."

"Yes, that is a nick name, it is short for Amanda."

"A man da that is a South American name, why you don't call yourself by your proper name, Mondy, what kind of name is that anyways?"

"Just call me Amanda then!"

I soon settled in my job and often after work I went out either dancing or, at other times, a group of us went up to Sacramento where we found a local bar and watched the gypsies dancing. The audience clapped a staccato clap to the music and stamping of the dancer's feet. If I felt confident enough, I joined in. The fiery arm movements and technical steps, of the dancers; in conjunction with their rhythmic hip movements emanated an ambience of fiery passion as the mesmerising unbroken voices of the pubescent gypsy boys; singing lamentable songs that transcended high above us, way over beyond the mountains, to far off places; inevitably distilling within me a hauntingly shared memory of emotional lost love. The spell of bewitched enchantment cast numerous haunted memories over those who were there on those captivating nights. We were insatiably for all those beguiling nights could offer us; more sangria, more music, more dancing and even more mournful love songs.

One night after work, I found myself in such a bar with Jan and her boyfriend Jose: Mary and her friend Patricia had joined us later on with a couple of customers from the bar. Anna with her Lebanese boyfriend had also turned up an hour or so afterwards.

"Let's go on to the Feria after we have finished our drinks," suggested Patricia, "especially since I have to go to the airport tomorrow with you Pedro, to collect Kathleen who will be arriving in from Dublin so if we go now, I will not have to worry so much about getting up in time."

"Yes, you better go with him or else Kathleen will have to make her own way to Granada just like Amanda had to," replied Jan who had her arms wrapped around Jose.

"Don't drink too much wine tonight Jan," warned Jose.

"Well as long as you don't," retorted Jan.

"Don't answer me back," shouted Jose raising his arm to Jan.

"Amigos," interrupted Pedro "what's the matter? There is no problem, is there?"

"No, there is no problem," replied Jose looked aggrieved and somewhat embarrassed.

"Are you and Mary from Dublin?" I asked directing my question at Patricia.

"No, I am from County Cork, and Mary is from Wexford."

"How long have you been here?"

"Six months but we are heading for Rota soon."

"Rota."

"Yes Rota is further south, past Cadiz, near Cordoba."

"Why Rota?"

"Because an American base is there and we want to get to the States, we need a green card to work over there."

"Why do you want to go to the States?" interrupted Jan "who wants to be with those stupid GI's; they just get drunk all the time and go and fight in Vietnam and kill innocent people."

"Not all GI s are drunkens, not all of them volunteer to join the military neither some have been recently conscripted to fight in Vietnam," declared Mary.

"Yeah, but that's only because there are no more blacks to call up because the government is losing the war and so many US military are already getting killed in Vietnam," continued Jan, "and if the war stops it will be because too many middle class WASPS have been killed."

"Politics, politics you are always talking about this thing called feminism, the black civil rights movement and Vietnam, why?" protested Jose looking and sounding bored and bewildered.

"Because, don't you know, there is a revolution going on in the States but Spain seems far removed from it," replied Jan ordering another round of drinks as she lit another cigarette.

"Not you and politics again," proclaimed Kay, coming up to our table as the man she was with looked around for some chairs.

"Jan, this is Chris, he's from New Zealand and he is hitch hiking over to Morocco in a few days," said Kay, not bothering to introduce Chris to Pedro or Jose, or me.

"Hi," greeted Chris, to everyone.

"I'm thinking of going with him. I'm bored with working my way around Europe having to do bar work. Daddy said he'd send me some more cash and then I think I will head off to northern Europe, Chris says he will come with me, won't you Chris?"

"Yeah, why not, after we've been to Morocco though, then after northern Europe, I'll be heading for India."

"And I'll be heading for home, dear Australia, how I miss you!"

"I don't know why you bothered to come to Spain in the first place," questioned Jan.

"Well, all young Aussies want to travel around the world at least once, you know that Jan and if it wasn't for me who else would you have travelled with?"

"That may be the case but you haven't stopped moaning since you left Australian, I guess you are just too pampered."

"Well I can't help it, if Australia happens to be more civilised than Southern Europe."

"Civilised, my foot," responded Jan," how come the Aboriginals are treated so badly and you know that when my Aboriginal friend Martha and I were in a bar in Queensland one time, we were called the N word and told to get out. The men thought that I was part Aboriginal due to my frizzy wavy red hair."

"If you had straightened your hair like I told you to so then it wouldn't have frizzed, the men in the bar would have thought you were one of them, an Australian."

"My hair is naturally frizzy and I like it that way, and one of them, one of what, oh when are you going to join the human race," retorted Jan downing her fourth glass of wine.

"Let's go, you are getting drunk," intercepted Jose angrily.

"Whenever I challenge people you think I am drunk!"

"Well you are and in my country women don't get

drunk and, they don't answer their men back, you are asking for a slap."

"Jose please, por favour, hombre," interceded Pedro.

"Oh stop it Pedro, if you were more of a man instead of a wimp, you would be able to control these women instead of letting them speak to you the way they do," retorted Jose who was getting more and more agitated with Jan.

"Sure, Spanish women don't get drunk or answer their men back, and they are all virgins before they get married too, aren't they, then why is it that so many Spanish men prefer foreign women: is it because they think they can have their way with them?" continued Jan.

"This country is so backwards because of Franco, he is such a dictator!"said Kay suddenly deciding to pick up the mantle.

"Shush," whispered Pedro and Jose both at the same time as they looked around them.

"You don't know who is spying on behalf of the Civil Guard," murmured Pedro. "And if they hear us being derogatory we could be thrown in prison, and the bar will close because Alexis will have his licence taken away."

"It's that bad then?" queried Chris.

"Oh yes, you cannot trust anyone, not even your own brother," replied Pedro.

"Are you coming to the Feria or not," said Jose to Jan, "because I am leaving now and if you do not come with me our relationship is over!"

"Oh, again," giggled Jan.

Jose got up and threw back his chair and walked off. Jan got up, finished her drink and ran after him.

"I wouldn't want to fight with him, have you seen the muscles in his arms, Jan says he's a drummer in a band," said Mary.

"She always picks the rough types," said Kay nonchalantly.

"Let's go to the Feria!"

We finished our drinks and went to the Feria where we stayed all night.

I stayed in Granada for about three months and had become Pedro's unofficially girlfriend. This made it impossible for me to meet anyone else.

"You'll never meet anyone with Pedro around. I bet he is telling everyone in Spanish that you are engaged to him," Mary said to me one day as she was washing the glasses in the sink which was located just below the counter, and towards the till.

"I like Pedro and I don't want to hurt his feelings but he is not my type,"

I replied

"We can see that!" exclaimed Mary.

"We are off to Rota next week, why don't you come with us," invited Kathleen who was stacking the glasses on the shelves above the bottles of liqueurs.

"How are you getting there?" I replied interested at the prospect of seeing more of Spain.

"Hitch hiking love, we always do," answered Patricia.

"Don't the men try it on when you are travelling in their cars?" I asked.

"Of course they do and if we fancy them, well why not!" responded Mary.

"And if we don't, we just shout Franco," laughed Patricia.

"OK, I'll come but I don't want to be involved in one night stands."

"Oh you are such a Catholic, anyway hand in your notice tonight if you are coming with us," said Kathleen "I have already given in my notice even though I have only been here a short while."

"You're not going to Rota are you?" Jan asked me, when she discovered that I had given in my notice to the displeasure of Pedro.

"Yes, I want to see more of Spain."

"You won't see much of Spain in Rota, just a bunch of drunken and sexually frustrated GI's," reported Jan.

"I want to get away from Pedro."

"Just tell him to get away."

"I can't."

"You know you could stay here, learn Spanish properly and then travel to Madrid and perhaps work there for a while, and then travel to other Southern towns," persisted Jan.

"Not with Pedro, I can't."

The following week we were on the road. Mary and I set off as a twosome and Kathleen and Patricia climbed into the car behind us. We stayed in Pensions at night and hitched throughout the day. The journey along the coast took us about three days. This was mainly because we took our time, sightseeing whenever possible. We even stopped on beaches near Cadiz for swims in the sea. Before we arrived in Rota, Mary and I had been picked up by an English guy. When he dropped us off along a coastal road, we proceeded to collect our belongings from the boot of his car but Mary could not find her address book after the contents of her bag had sprawled out everywhere. She was clearly becoming frustrated as she searched amongst the items in the boot in order to find her address book. I had noticed it at first glance but assumed she had as well however after several more minutes I reached for it and gave it to her.

"You are very modest, aren't you?" observed Charles as I gave Mary her address book.

"I don't think so," I replied.

"Yes you are, why are you so modest?" probed

Charles.

"I have no idea."

"Do your family mind you travelling around Spain?"

"I grew up in care."

"You grew up in care, what age was you made a ward of Court?"

"At five years old."

"You know something, if you imagine that you are competing in a race and at the moment you are last in the race, but one day you will win the race because once you have worked out the system, you will overtake your counterparts.

"Is this it, is this Rota," I said incredulously when we arrived and I got out of the car.

"Yes, isn't it great," replied Mary.

"I don't know if you could describe the place as great. I can't believe it, it looks like something out of a film set, Hollywood perhaps, the bar doors look like salon doors from a cowboy film. They look just like stage props. Look at the bars; they look like saloons with those swing doors. I can just imagine a cowboy coming out of those saloon doors slinging a gun in each hand, aiming to shoot us without even asking us to put our hands up."

"It's fine," Kathleen replied clearly not sharing my disbelief and disappointment never mind failing to pick up on the stark artificialness of the place. I thought the whole set up was ludicrous if not hilarious. The idea of a western film set superimposed on a pretty small Spanish fishing village, seemed incredibly bizarre to me. I simply could not believe what was in front of my eyes, rows upon rows of bars which were all garishly painted: some had steps leading up to them while the majority of them had salon swing doors. They looked somewhat grotesque and completely out of character.

Their vulgar appearance, I considered tasteless. It was three o' clock in the afternoon and there was an eerie quietness to the village as we stood outside the first bar in the hot baking sun.

"We better decide which one of us wants to go into the nearest bar and ask if they need bar staff," Mary decided sensibly.

"The Pasapoga, here on the right, is the first bar, so I'm going to ask in there," responded Patricia.

I followed her into the bar reluctantly since I began to regret leaving the sophisticated and cultural city of Granada with its Moorish history and the Alhambra as its opulent centrepiece. Again I found myself having to acclimatize my eyes in order to view the bar I had just walked into because I was initially purged into total darkness. Once my eye sight had adjusted sufficiently enough I found myself in a relatively large dimly lit room. There was no natural light apart from the light emanating from the electric light bulbs hanging over the two pool tables which were situated in the middle of the room, apart from the electric light radiating from the lamps on the walls.

"Hi girls," said a voice that I could not immediately locate.

"Hello, we are looking for work," stated Patricia responding to the voice.

"OK, how many of you are looking for work exactly?"

"Four."

"I can take two only and maybe two more later."

"OK, Amanda, you and I can work here if you want."

"OK."

"You start tonight, OK."

"OK, how much will we be paid?"

We agreed with Patricia that the wages were pretty

reasonable and better than our wages were in Granada when we came out again into the hot sun. The four of us continued to walk down the street until Kathleen and Mary had decided which bar they wanted to approach. As we carried on walking down the road a group of three black guys walked towards us. They had their shirts knotted around their chests exposing their taunt midriffs. I noticed that their ebony skins gleamed in the sun like silk. Behind them walked two white men whose pale skins had not yet caught the sun so their complexions showed a mixture of raw red and chalk white areas.

"The black ones look sexier than the one whites," declared Kathleen.

"Yes they do," we all laughed in agreement.

The black men looked at me intensely as they walked by.

"Ola, signorita," they greeted.

"Ola," I replied.

"She isn't Spanish you know," said Kathleen.

"Where are you from then?" they asked sounding surprised and stopping suddenly in their tracks.

"From England," I replied.

"I didn't know that there were any blacks in England," said one of them.

"Well there are," I said not understanding my defensiveness.

"Gee, that's awesome."

I never knew Fernandez my boss very well but well enough to know that he was gay and moderately discreet about it. He was generally a very private man although very easy going and cheerful. I never saw him lose his temper even when the GIs' became uncontrollably drunk, Fernandez simply tried to placate them until the Shore Patrol came and took them back to base. Sometimes in a bored moment when either I was on an afternoon shift and no one had yet come from the beach to have an early afternoon quiet drink, or when the few customers I had already served, just sat in the bar staring at their drinks, no doubt preoccupied with their own private thoughts; I observed Fernandez in these sullen moments sitting in front of the cash till. Even when the hustle and bustle of last night's activities was long over and I was able to reflect on the scenarios of the previous night, I noted that Fernandez hated the arguments Miguel his boyfriend had with him. I gathered that the fights were to do with Miguel's frustrations with life. His uncontrollable mood swings often whirled themselves into a tantrum of a magnificent kind within the public arena of the bar. At these times Fernandez allowed Miguel's tantrums to exhaust him so that eventually Miguel became tired. Of course Fernandez knew what these turns and spins of his tantrum wheel were about. He knew that Miguel's inner battles would come to the surface from time to time. He understood his lover's struggles better than Miguel did simply because Miguel could not master his own demons. Fernandez read his eyes, knowing that they revealed all Miguel's confusions and frustrations within a world which Miguel felt was hostile and full of barriers. The pressures to conform as a child to something he was not had left their ineffaceable mark on him. His inability to engage in traditional or convention employment to make a living was part of his frustration. He also felt frustrated because he knew Fernandez kept him intact by providing him with both material and emotional support. He knew he could not pay his way because he could not conform to the conventional models that society had assigned him.

Fernandez knew all this. He also knew that in some other time, perhaps in some other life, Miguel had been a musician at a grand court. Playing his lute and reading poetry to the medieval spectators. It was because of this inner knowledge that allowed Fernandez not to worry too much when Miguel went off on his wonderings. Fernandez knew that Miguel would be with others and not with him. He had seen the scenario unfold many times before. Another person would entice Miguel and he would succumb to the other's charms. Fernandez knew Miguel's behaviour comprehensively to the extent that he could almost anticipate them. The mood swings, the tantrums, he watched Miguel struggle with his own beauty as Miguel tried forever to see it mirrored in the faces of others. Fernandez knew that Miguel could only ever find an illusion of his own beauty in the other because Miguel's charismatic beauty had been etched so artistically onto his own face making his beauty unique. Fernandez knew this in his heart for he was further down life's road than Miguel. For, had he not been just as exquisite an individual in his own time. He had been modelled just like a china doll with his long sweeping black eye lashes which only allowed so much of his eyes to be seen as they gracefully swept down to protect his pale chestnut brown eyes, that discreetly glimpsed green whenever they thought no one noticed. After fifty seven years Fernandez's looks had been lost in experience and self preservation. He always waited patiently until Miguel lost interest in his new love and came back to Fernandez. Fernandez then grounded Miguel's illusions and disappointments in sustaining love and appreciation. Fernandez had invested so much of his emotions into his love for Miguel that Miguel always found his way back into his embraces because ultimately he found solace in the unconditional paternalistic love Fernandez showered on him.

"What do I care," Fernandez said to himself every

once in a while. He knew all too well what the alternative offered. That would mean a life mapped out with a long lonely search to find another such delightful love that he knew he would never find if he lost Miguel. Not in this lifetime for sure he thought to himself as he got up from the cashier's chair to wipe the speck of dust from one of the wine glasses.

Jan was right Rota was occupied by the US Navy. The Enterprise, an aircraft carrier had docked there as part of its military operations in the Mediterranean and the marines, and other US military personnel were stationed there until they were either shipped back to the United States after returning from Vietnam, or were sent to fight in Vietnam. Some, had bought or rented apartments in Rota while others who wanted to get away from their fellow countrymen rented or purchased villas in Chipiona, the next village while others however lived on the base.

The first few nights were strange in comparison to working in the bar in Granada. In contrast guys were mainly rowdy and extroverted compared to the judicious Granadians. The young guys just wanted to party while the older guys were happy to have a drink and to chat.

"Hi, your new here aren't you?" asked a middle aged marine.

"Yes, I am," I replied

"Get me another beer please."

"An American beer, right."

"Yeah that's right, I don't care much for the Spanish beer," he said unapologically.

"How long have you been over here?"

"Too long."

"I guess you have been fighting in Vietnam."

"Yeah, I've been to Nam, who hasn't around here."

"You don't look very happy."

"You wouldn't be either if you had just seen a young guy cut in two by the aircraft cable which snapped when trying to bring it to a standstill after landing this morning. Shit man, what a waste of a young life and all he wanted to do was to go to college when he got back to the States."

I didn't know what to say. I spent a long time listening to Matt as he talked about his life; the situations he had been in that first night. He went to places in his mind that were horrifying where only the stoical could go. Matt did not necessarily share those daunting flashbacks with me; instead he sat there on his stool looking vacant. I would sit there quietly sipping the watered down whisky he had bought me. He indicated that it was fine to buy me another one when the glass was empty. Matt knew the score. The drinks were bought time and time again so that the bar owners made money from the GIs' and the bar staff got a percentage. Sometimes when sitting in silence, I would slip away to serve another guy who then offered me a drink also, I always went back to finish my drink with Matt afterwards.

"You know you are the only person I feel I can really talk to," he'd say.

"What about your family?"

"My wife divorced me years ago and I have been on my own ever since."

"Has there been anyone else?"

"Occasionally there has been a liaison here or there but I can't commit myself anymore. I've seen too much and besides I can't settle in any one place. I have a lady in Nam that I write and send money to. Maybe I'll send for her and her boy when I get out of here, who knows."

"Are you planning on going back there?"

"Yeah I always volunteer to go back and next time

maybe I'll bring her back with me but I'm not one for making plans. If anything happens to me though I've seen her right! She understands me being in a war zone and all. Lost her husband and two other kids, she did. In the meantime those two ladies from Southampton and that Spanish lady from Chipiona, they treat me real nice and I sure get value for money!"

For as long as I was in Rota Matt was around. Sometimes he disappeared for a while and was very cagey when I asked him where he had been. I learnt not to ask him.

"Hey, Amanda, coming to the Blue Star tonight?" shouted Patricia from the other side of the bar, a few days after we arrived in Rota.

"Hey, Amanda, coming to the Blue Star tonight?" a group of GIs' shouted in chorus mimicking Patricia as they sat on bar stools.

"What's at the Blue Star?" I shouted back.

"What's at the Blue Star, why hell, all the latest disco music," the GIs' shouted back in merriment.

"Well, we've got some good disco sounds in London."

"London, in England."

"Yes."

"Are you from London, England?"

"Yes."

"Well, ain't that something and hey girl, keep talking, cos we sure like your accent."

"So what music are they playing over at the Blue Star?"

"They've play the latest Philadelphia sounds and they play James Brown, Curtis Mayfield; Marvin Gaye in fact the deejay plays all the latest sounds, that are just released States side. The music is real hot of the press."

"Well, I'll see you at the Blue Star, after the bar

closes then!"

"We'll wait for you lady, yeah we'll all escort you just like the Spanish ladies are chaperoned whenever they go out."

I discovered that the Blue Star was where everyone went to after the bars closed. The music was electrifying and everyone danced like there was no tomorrow and for some, it was as if there had been no yesterday either as they desperately tried to bloat out their time in Vietnam through music or often with drugs and alcohol.

"Let's go and ask the deejay for a sound," suggested Mary who had joined us.

We followed her to the sound system and I watched as she chatted to the deejay. The next day Manolo, the deejay came into the Pasopoga and asked me out. His father owned a sherry bodega in Jerez de la Frontier but Manolo was essentially a drop out and did not want to take over the family business.

"My father is a mulatto, like you, you know," Manolo revealed to me one night.

"Is he?"

"Si, my grandfather was black and was originally from Morocco and buenos, my grandmother was Spanish, from Ceuta, Spanish Morocco," Manolo informed me of this as he picked up the stylus from the stereo with the long fingernail of his little finger of his right hand. On this occasion he was changing the record to play Santana; he then picked up the book of poems he was reading by Federico Garcia Lorca.

It had not taken me long to find an apartment with Annabelle who was from South Africa.

"You are not going to move in with her, are you?" queried Jan who had by now one too many fights with Jose, so on the spur of the moment had hitched to Rota with an American woman who had been teaching

English in Granada. Jose had followed Jan to Rota with a friend despite his protestations about the presence of a US military base in his country.

"Annabelle left South Africa because of the apartheid system," I replied defensively.

"Oh really, she only left because the black South Africans are challenging the apartheid system now, what with the death of Steve Biko and Nelson Mandela's imprisonment, not to mention the international publicity that South Africa is getting now because of his stand against the racist system there."

"Well, if Annabelle does not like black people then why did she offer me a room to rent in her apartment?"

"To appease her conscious; no doubt and besides you are exotic which probably makes you more acceptable to her."

"That's not fair."

"What's fair, anyhow how come she's screwing some red neck Texan who looks like he's just stepped out of a Wells Fargo film with that Stetson he always wears: in fact this whole place is made out of cardboard, cardboard town that's what it should have been called. I cannot understand why the Spanish have allowed such a pretty fishing town to be destroyed by the US dollar."

"Rod's always polite to me."

"Yes, he probably has fantasies of black women."

"Jan, stop it."

"No, I won't stop it; you should read some of the feminist books which are coming out of the States because they are addressing some of these issues."

"Do white middle class women know what its like to be discriminated against on the grounds of race as well as sex?"

"Perhaps not, since white women are writing about issues of gender politics but Angela Davis is standing up for the black struggle. Anyway are you aware that Rod cannot stand the Spanish."

"How can he be racist against the Spanish, they are white!"

"Yes, but Rod sees the Spanish as backward and probably thinks that you have downgraded yourself by going out with a Spaniard rather than a GI."

"I've got nothing against GIs' but Manolo is who I want to be with."

"That may be so but a lot of GIs' want to go out with you including the white ones."

"Hmm," I said to myself wanting this conversation to end. I had to admit to myself that whilst Rod was always polite to me, he was often rude to Manolo when he came to the apartment or he totally ignored him."

"I don't want any Spanish person to step foot in this apartment anymore, do you hear," I heard Rod shouting at Annabelle a few days after my conversation with Jan. I packed my bags there and then got a taxi to work, put my bags behind the counter and negotiated with a Dutch woman who had a spare room in her apartment to move in and share the bills. I realised that Manolo had sensed the hostility and when I told him that I had move out of Annabelle's apartment, he just said "Bloody Americans, why don't they go back to their own country."

"Ha, but you like their money though, don't you?"

"No, I don't, my father is rich and has made his own money and does not need the US dollar."

Jan considered herself to be radically political and conscientious, and as a matter of principle she detested having to ask a GI for a drink, which she was expected to water down so that she could fleece a guy for more drinks. She never watered down the alcohol enough to prevent herself from becoming rather intoxicated by the end of her shift.

"It's bad enough having to put an ice cube in a Southern Comfort which I do, but to put water in the glass as well, to dilute the Southern Comfort even further is blasphemous. She gained tremendous respect from the GIs' for her alcohol principles however Jose was extremely frustrated by Jan's drinking binges. Jan spent a lot of time in the bar having political discussions with anyone who would listen, generally these debates proved to be educational at the best of times.

"I'm a Catholic too Amanda, in fact most of the women who have travelled over here to Spain are but I cannot imagine what it must have been like spending five years as a teenager in a Convent!"

"Yes, I assumed the whole world was Catholic when I left it so it was strange to realise that there were other religions in the world; for instance one of my teachers from primary school always sent me birthday and Christmas cards but when I told her that I had been offered a foster placement with a Jewish family, she told me unless I was offered a Catholic foster placement she would not write to me again."

"That must have been very disappointing for you."

"Yes, it was because I could not understand what the issue was, after all Jesus was Jewish and I visited the Holy Land when I was working at the Boulevard because I had been invited there by one of the waitress's who had lived all her life on a Kibbutz."

"There is no way I would ever go to Israel, anyhow I don't think they would let me in because I have travelled to Egypt and have an Egyptian stamp on my passport which suites me fine."

"Why would you not go to Israel?"

"Because of Zionism, the way the Palestinians are treated is appalling; they have a right to their land as well as Jewish people."

"When I was in Israel, Ziva my friend did not want to travel to Bethlehem so I took the bus to travelled there on my own, and when I arrived a young guy approached me and volunteered to show me around. He told me he was a Palestinian and that Bethlehem was where he had lived all his life. He mentioned that his people were discriminated against and were treated like second class citizens."

"Well, it's not acceptable to illegally occupy their land and then discriminate against a dispossessed people, anyway did you take up his offer?"

"Of course I did. Why not, why should I have been prejudiced against his goodwill and generosity of spirit, besides he was very knowledgeable."

About five months after Jose had followed Jan to Rota, he returned to Granada after one row too many with Jan. She met a Moroccan guy and they were together until his visa expired, he then had no choice but to go back to Fez. Every three months we foreigners travelled to Alcaziers to take the boat to Tangiers in order to renew our work permits. There was always a GI travelling to Morocco so arranging a lift was never difficult. Sometimes we spent a couple of days in Tangiers or Ceuta while many of the guys travelled further on to Marrakech, Casa Blanca and Fez. Jan often travelled to Morocco to visit Mohammed until he was offered a job in Germany. She then conceded and started dating one of the GI's. Rob was a fun guy who absolutely adored Jan. They never argued and enjoying drinking together. They were always travelling down to Morocco for short breaks away from Rota. One time when Rob and Jan were planning to travel to Morocco because it was nearing the time for Jan to get her passport stamp renewed, she changed her mind and decided instead to go to Portugal with a couple of friends, however they agreed that Rob should go to Morocco as planned. Besides, Rob had set his heart on buying a couple of Moroccan carpets which he planned to ship back to the United States and Jan had agreed to go with him on his next leave since she fancied spending time in New York. When Jan returned from Portugal several days later, she was told by some of Rob's mates that he had crashed his sports car into a lorry. It has taken the Spanish emergency services three days to get his remains out of the car. His ID was the only means of identification and the cause of the accident was determined as Rob fallen asleep at the wheel of his sports car. Jan was heartbroken and shortly afterwards she left for Madrid.

In the daytime a group of us spent the time on the beach and sometimes after a swim either sunbathing or sun shading, we drank rum and cokes, or mineral water in the beach bars. Manolo and I often drove to Chipiona in his old dilapidated car just to get away from Rota. We normally spent the time sitting outside a local bar listening to flamenco music. The smell of the sunflowers and orange trees consumed us so much so that for me those memorable times superseded my childhood demons, which momentarily drifted away.

"Manda, Manda, "Manolo was beside himself with excitement one night as he came up to me in the bar. "Guess what, there is another black woman in Rota and she is working at Mama san's bar.
    "Where is she from?" I asked.
    "She's from London like you."
    "What part of London?"
    "I don't know, I think she said Peckham."
    "OK, let's go and see her later."
    "She is very pretty."
    After my shift Manolo and I went off to the Tokyo

bar that was owned by Mama san. Sure enough there was another black woman working behind the bar but because the bar was crowded, it took us both sometime to get to where she was serving drinks. Eventually we managed to attract her attention.

"Hi, I'm Amanda."

"And I am Sheila."

"Aren't you from Peckham?"

"Yes that's right, do you know the area?"

"No, I have never been to Peckham, where is it?"

"South London, where are you from?"

I have lived in Kent, Middlesex and Lewisham."

"Peckham is very near Lewisham."

"I lived in a Convent in Lewisham but I was never allowed out much, only to work when I had a Saturday job, or once or twice to visit a friend in Lee Green."

"What part of the Caribbean are your parents from?"

"My parents are not from the Caribbean they were from Africa and Ireland."

"My parents are Jamaican, hang on my boyfriend is calling me."

Manolo and I looked towards the direction Sheila was walking towards and I was absolutely stunned when I saw who her boyfriend was. It was Rod.

So he does not like the Spanish but likes black women with English accents.

"Sorry about that but Rod wanted to know what restaurant I wanted to go and eat at after work."

"Don't you know that he is racist," I told Sheila.

"He's not racist well not towards me. In fact he treats me like a Queen even buys my sanitary towels for me from the shop at the Base, in fact there isn't a thing he wouldn't do for me, he even paints my toenails; he's such a pussycat," said Sheila sounding completely in control of the relationship.

"How long do you intend to stay here?"

"Not long, I'm off to the States."
"With Rod."
"With or without Rod."
"Nice to meet you and Good Luck."
"Same to you, goodbye."

One night about one o clock in the morning, I found myself stranded on the road leading to Chipiona. It was very dark despite the lights from the street lamps. All I could hear were the crickets, humming in the background, and mosquitoes could be seen by the light of the street lamps. The aromatic smell of the oranges trees gave out a sweet fragrance to the night air. Manolo had told me to get out of his car after a blazing row. I stood there on the road feeling helpless and abandoned. There was no taxi in sight and I had no idea how long I stood there but finally I could see car lights slowly heading my way as it swerved to avoid the pot holes in the road. The American Cadillac slowed down and stopped right in front of me.

"Hey, pretty girl, what are you doing all alone in the middle of the night, do you wanna a lift somewhere?"

"Yes, please, where you heading?"

"We are heading for Chipiona to a party, do ya wanna come?"

"Why not since my boyfriend has ditched me by the roadside."

"Oh, don't mind him, come and have some fun with us."

I looked in the car cautiously but I knew that with the Shore Patrol driving their vans around to make sure that if any GI's were getting themselves into trouble they would be carted back to the base, and what with the Civil Guard, chances of being mistreated by these guys seemed remote, especially since none of the GI's fancied being locked up in a Spanish jail. I climbed into the back seat and sat beside a guy who wore a

Moroccan gellaba. We greeted each other but I was immediately, disturbed by his face, because there were numerous lines and wrinkles etched on it and his eyes looked like he had lived a million dead weary years. I realised that he was on drugs and I also understood that whatever his nightmares where they had accompanied him from Vietnam and his drug taking was his means of tolerating them.

"You've just come back from Vietnam, haven't you?"

"Yeah."

"When?"

"About a week ago and I have been dropping acid and tripping ever since."

"Yes I can see that, you look burnt out." I said noticing that he looked like an old man yet I knew he was probably in his early thirties.

"Yeah, I'm burnt out man, so burnt out, that now I want to party."

We shortly arrived at the party. It was one of those intellectual parties where everyone sat around intellectualising the Vietnam War, the civil rights movement, the feminist movement and South Africa, while the rock music played on in the background. The guy I had spoken to in the backseat of the car, I observed, just sat and stared at the stars out on the veranda after dropping another LSD tablet. Instinctively, I knew that no matter how many drugs he had taken, the nightmares were hauntingly alive and closing in on him.

There were a few guys whom I bantered with and sometimes I would go dancing with after work particularly when Manolo and I had argued about something or other. Manolo was essentially a control freak and felt that his masculinity had to be proven by trying to control how I spent my time when I was not with him. The fact that there were more guys in Rota than women did not help the matter either, since women could pick and chose who they went out with and who they forged relationships with.

"You are some foxy lady."

"You are some foxy guy, Eddie."

"You know I only come into town to see how you're doing, otherwise I wouldn't bother."

"What about the Blue Star, don't you and your mates love dancing to the latest soul sounds there?"

"That's true but we've got a disco on the base and besides the drinks are a lot cheaper on base because they are subsidized. The guys only come out here because of the young ladies, they want to find themselves some girlfriends and have some female company."

"There are just too many guys here."

"That's for sure, hey when are you going to dump your old man and come out with me?"

"Well, you never know."

"Don't give me that, you and your old man are so hooked up with each other, that there's no chance your ever going to leave him."

"Like I said Eddie you never know, there may be one quarrel too many that may tip the scales."

"I'll be waiting!"

"I'll come with you to the Blue Star tonight, if you like!"

"Where's the old man?"

"He's gone to Jerez."

"OK, I' II come and pick you up later."

"Oh, Eddie, pop into the Dutch bar and tell Mary, I'll see her at the Blue Star about midnight and tell her I bought the things she wanted from Cordoba today."

"Sure."

The Blue Star was crowded when Eddie and I

entered. We sat at a corner table with three of Eddie's mates. Mary and Bobby her guy, joined us later.

"This is Marvin, JJ and Floyd. Floyd and Marvin are from Harlem and JJ's from the Bronx where I'm from."

"Hey guys."

"Are you from England?"

"Yes."

"A black woman from England, that's nice."

"Her old man's Spanish."

"Is that right, why don't you like your own?"

"I can choose to go out with who I like!"

"Let's dance, we've got to dance to James Brown," said Floyd pulling me up to dance.

We stayed until the Blue Star closed at three in the morning. Most people stayed until closing time because each night was party night since the music was funky and the atmosphere charged. We got cabs and were invited back to Floyd's villa for breakfast where we sat on Moroccan cushions eating hash browns, pancakes and offered coffee.

"Actually, have you got tea?" I asked.

"You English with your cups of tea, no I haven't got any, but I've got orange juice."

"That's fine."

"How you do like living in Rota while working at the base?" I asked Floyd.

"Wow, that's a loaded question; it's OK but the base gets claustrophobic at times and so does Rota. I like to travel further a field to Huelva, Cordoba and Seville, you know, to see other places in Spain while I am stationed over here."

"You're brave brother." said Bobby "some of those Spanish are sure racist."

"Yeah, that's true but you've got to know yourself and stand firm, just like the brothers who have taken up wearing black arm bands at the sports events back home and look at Mohammed Ali, he's refusing to fight in the Nam war," Floyd replied picking up the latest Curtis Mayfield album to play on the stereo.

"Yeah, but some of those Spanish are rude," Marvin declared joining in the conversation, "and naturally they like Eddie because of his blond hair, blue eyes and bronze skin. I always travel with him whenever we drive out of Rota."

"Yeah, they like our fancy cars," stated Eddie.

"Eddie, you can get yourself a nice signorita and take her back to the States, with you," teased Bobby.

"Naw, the only lady I want is a black lady."

"There are plenty of black foxy ladies at home, but not so many on the base." injected Floyd.

"There's Sharleen and Elaine."

"Yeah, but they are already vouched for."

"Well, I've got my baby back home and I'm arranging for her and my little boy to fly out here to see me next week," said JJ, who had just come into the room after coming from one of the bedrooms.

"Yeah and I am going back to Harlem in two months time to see my lady," said Floyd, "and I can't wait!"

"What's it like for blacks living in England?"

"It's Ok," I said not wanting to be an authority on the subject.

"We only enlisted in the Navy so that we could get an education afterwards," said Bobby.

"What do you mean?"

"In the States if you join the Navy when you get out, the Navy will fund

our college education, otherwise we could not afford the fees."

"In England we get a grant to go to college or university."

"You get a grant to go to college," the guys said all

at once.

"Yes."

"Hey man, that is unbelievable so when are you going to go to college?"

"I don't know."

"You, don't know, hey the lady does not know when she is going to go to college, man, that is something else, that sure it something else."

"What's it's like in Vietnam."

"Hmm, some of those white guys are just plain racist, it's like they think the States belongs to them only," stated Marvin.

"Too many brothers have been killed or maimed in Nam," concluded Floyd.

"Some of those white guys give Eddie a hard time, what with him associating with us mainly," declared JJ.

"I don't care a shit about those guys, their dickheads," retorted Eddie.

"A lot of the white women only go out with the Black GI's over here," I said.

"Yes," said Mary "but I don't know what my mother would say back home in Ireland, if she knew."

"That's why Mary is coming back with me to the States," announced Bobby.

"It's not just because you want a green card, is it?" enquired Eddie.

"You deserve a slap for saying that Eddie, how dare you, I can get a white guy to get me a green card if I want, anytime," said Mary pretending to slap Eddie.

"Some of the white guys don't like it though seeing all these English and Irish women shacking up with the Black GI's, in the States that wouldn't happen so much," said Marvin.

"You know Elliott was shipped back to Stateside last week with his baby girl." JJ informed us.

"Yeah, that's good news," affirmed Bobby.

"Why was he shipped home with his baby?" I asked curiously.

"Didn't you know, Kathy took their baby girl home to Ireland last year but her family wouldn't let her keep the baby because it wasn't white? They said either she gives the baby up for adoption or they would never speak to her again and she could never come home, ever," explained Mary "so she brought the baby back here and gave it to Elliott, when it was only two months old, before going back to Ireland, and he kept his little girl on the base after talking to his Commanding Officer. He hired a Spanish lady to look after his baby girl until he finished his duty every day," continued Eddie.

"It changed him, you know," said Bobby, "he's only twenty three but he stopped partying to look after his little girl."

"Yeah, he said that no one was going to adopt his child because no one could bring up his baby girl better than he could," continued Mary.

"And last month he heard that he could leave the Navy early due to special circumstances and his family have decorated a room for his baby girl, so he was more than ready, to take his baby home with him!"

"Yeah, he did what he said he would do, which was that he would take care of his little girl himself, and when he telephoned his family and told them about her, they told him to bring her home and they would help him look after her."

"Jane managed to finally get away from Joachim last month," said Mary speaking directly to me.

"How did she managed that, what with Joachim not allowing her out of the house and always assaulting her, even in front of their children," I said amazed to hear this news.

"Well, she had been plotting to get away from him

for over a year now; what she did was tell him that they should all go back to England to visit her parents because you know that he would not let her or the children travel abroad, and in Spain the father has the rights of the children, particularly if the couple are married and the kids did not have their own passports; anyway he finally agreed that they should all go to England because you know he could never find work here and Jane's parents offered to pay for the airfares."

"It's not surprising that he could not find work, he had no motivation, besides he has such a short fuse," I responded.

"She had been here for six years putting up with him battering her about, especially when he's drunk and the three children were also afraid of him," continued Mary.

"How did she get out though because I never ever imagined that she would do," I asked.

"Like I said, her parents began to visit her every three months and between them, they arranged passports for the children, whom they paid for of course, and the air fares since neither Jane nor Joaquin had any money, despite Jane doing all those cleaning jobs. Her parents said that he could get a good job in Manchester so her parents flew over and collected them all and took them back to Manchester; of course Joaquin couldn't settle or get a job and when he insisted that Jane and the children go back with him, naturally they refused and Jane's father stepped in and ordered him out of the house. He paid for his flight back to Spain and told him he never wanted to see him again because of the way he had treated his daughter and his grand children. He told him, "he was a disgrace.""

"I am so happy for her because she always looked so sad even though she tried to stand up to him," I said.

"He sounds like one crazy Spanish guy," said Bobby.

"He's not the only one," continued Mary" what about Helena's guy, you know Carl, he's always assaulting her and she is too scared to leave him."

"Oh, that crazy brother," proclaimed Floyd.

"Yeah, that crazy brother," agreed Bobby.

"Hey Floyd, what's it like when you go travelling outside of the base, to all those little Spanish towns with all the locals staring at you all the time, just because you are a black man," asked JJ laughing.

"I ignore them essentially however there are always exceptions,"

Floyd replied.

"What do you mean?" asked Bobby.

"I mean that sometimes when I travel and visit historical and cultural places of interest someone will smile at me or say Buenos dias, so that's always nice," answered Floyd.

"Not many though," confirmed Bobby.

"But some," replied Floyd.

"What with the Spanish history and all, they have nothing to be arrogant about, look at what they did in the West Indies and in South America, they were brutal to the slaves in the 15th century," declared Marvin.

"Indeed they were," replied Floyd.

The exact day the letter arrived from Sue informing me that she wanted to come over to Spain, is a day that I cannot vividly remember. I recall though feeling very excited as I told everyone who would listen at the Pasapoga that my sister wanted to come over to Spain to join me for a while. I decided to fly back to London and arrange for her to travel back with me. At the last minute we decided to hitch hike back to Spain after I told her what fun I had previously hitching across Southern Spain with friends. We disembarked at Bilboa where our ship docked and found the nearest motorway which headed south; and stuck our hands out. I recall Sue wearing a Biba hat and rolled up dark brown corduroy jeans and similarly I was wearing the latest London fashion. We looked striking in our fashionable clothes as we stood by the roadside in the late morning sunshine. In no time we were on our way travelling from the north west of Spain towards the South.

"What shall I say to him, I don't understand what he is saying to me?" said Sue anxiously when after saying *si* for the hundredth time to the driver she could not get any further with the conversation.

"Don't worry, I'll speak to him," I said trying to show off my basic inept Spanish while sitting next to the driver as we sped off towards Valladolid.

On the road from Madrid to Cordoba we were picked up by two rather gregarious looking Argentineans in the early morning despite my policy of only accepting a lift by one male driver. The two guys turned out to be a lot of fun and we spent most of the time laughing and joking with them. In the late evening we found a pension where Sue and I shared a room and the guys another. In the morning I discovered that I had lost my purse and despite my constant searches in my handbag the money was not there. Luckily the Argentineans gallantly paid for us. They dropped us off the following day in the late afternoon after wishing us good luck.

"Mandy how could you be so silly as to lose your purse, that was all the money we had, now what are we going to do?" asked Sue clearly annoyed by my irresponsibility.

"It must have fallen out of my bag," I replied feeling upset.

"At least the Argentineans bought us lunch and mineral water but when that runs out what will we do," said Sue.

"I just don't know," I replied anxiously.

"I wish I had kept the money now but you insisted on looking after it because you said that I would lose it," confirmed Sue as she reached into her bag for her mirror and comb.

"Mandy, what's this?" exclaimed Sue pulling out a wad of hundred peseta notes.

"The Argentineans," we both said at the same time.

We had been waiting around for a lift for quite sometime so I made the decision to take the lift offered to us by a lorry driver who was only going a short distance but was able to drop us off at a bar along the way. It was not unusual to discover that whenever we ordered drinks for ourselves when we requested our bill, we discovered that a group of men or indeed a single solitary man had already paid for them out of courtesy.

"Hey Mandy, look at the amount of rum the bar man is putting in my glass, I will be legless at this rate."

"You better not, we still have a long way to go," I warned my younger sister sounding rather worried because Sue seemed to have developed an over zealous taste for alcohol since I had last seen her.

"Let's have another one for the road," she said after downing a few more Cuba Libras.

"No way, let's go," I reacted, trying seemingly to drag her out of the bar.

"Hey, what are you staring at?" Sue shouted at the old ladies who were dressed in black as they stood staring at us whenever we were dropped off at a remote village.

"Oh, don't take any notice of them," I said becoming irritable by now.

"Haven't you seen black people before," Sue yelled

at them while ignoring me.

"Come on Sue, stop getting paranoid," I said trying to placate her.

"Hey, Americana's," shouted some of the Spanish children.

"We are not Americans, we are English," retorted Sue earnestly.

"English, you are not English, you Americana's," the children replied sounding very sure of themselves.

"Look they are obviously only going to associate black people with America," I said getting really fed up now.

"They are ignorant and all they do is stare, don't they know, that it's rude?" stated Sue.

"Come on Sue, don't start getting paranoid.

"I'm not getting paranoid, Mandy, they are just so ignorant," retorted Sue angrily. "And they can't even cook, look at all the grease they cook their food in; it reminds me of the Convent food."

"It's not grease, its olive oil," I corrected.

"It's still greasy; I want a Wimpy and chips right now. In fact I miss England and I don't like Spain, it's backwards and far too hot," Sue objected.

"Well, if you walk around with that long sleeve jumper on then I am not surprised that you are hot, take it off."

"No, I don't want to catch the sun and I can't understand why you have to, aren't you dark enough?"

"Oh for goodness sake, what do you look like and why are you putting that white powder on your face."

"It's foundation and it's to cover my spots, silly."

"If you didn't wear that muck on your face then you wouldn't have spots in the first place."

"Mandy, I know my own skin, thank you."

We stuck our hands out and a lorry pulled up. We climbed in.

"Seville, por favour."

"Malaga."

"OK, Malaga."

We had travelled for about forty minutes when Sue started to fidget and become uncomfortable. Prior to that she had been chatting to the driver and asking me every five minutes what he was saying to her as she sat beside him and I sat on the other side of her.

"Mandy, he's trying to touch me up," claimed Sue sounding annoyed again.

"Just slap his hands away and shake your hand at him and for goodness sake stop giggling."

"He won't stop it, why don't you sit in the middle instead of me?"

"OK, por favour hombre, stop the lorry, we want to get out!"

We were back on the roadside and a car stopped with two guys inside. I refused their offer. We waited for about an hour before another car stopped, it was a quiet road so we were relieved when the car had stopped with only one driver inside. I sat in the front and Sue in the back. We arrived in Malaga in no time and the driver invited us for lunch.

From Malaga we were offered a lift from another lorry driver and climbed in.

"Mandy, the driver is trying to touch my leg!"

"Tell him no, say no!"

"No!" said Sue firmly.

"No," repeated the driver, looking somewhat surprised.

"Franco, not like that," said Sue to the driver.

And so it went on through to the late evening. From Malaga bypassing Seville; to Jerez, the conversation consisted of:

"No!"

"Why, no?"

Franco, no like!"

"Don't speak of Franco!"

"Then keep your hands to yourself, or we will tell the Guardia Civil!"

"No, no por favour."

"Then keep both hands on the wheel."

"OK, please you are Moroccan girls,?"

"No, we are not Moroccan girls, we are from London, England

"No, No, you do not look like from England; you look like from Morocco, don't worry I like Moroccan girls!"

"We are *not* from Morocco,"

"You can tell the truth, its OK with me."

"We *are* telling the truth."

"You like fino"

"It's OK."

"You like a glass of fino when we get to Jerez."

"OK"

"I invite you for a glass of fino; Is she your sister?"

"Yes, she is my sister."

"Hmm, I thought so, she looks very much like you."

"Thank you."

"You like a small black coffee with your glass of fino?"

"Yes, thank you."

"De nada."

Sue got a job in the Tokyo bar working for Mama Sun who was in her mid forties. She wore a traditional kimono and never went out in the sun. Sue took to working in the bar like a duck takes to water. She loved all the attention the GIs gave her.

"Your sister is not like you is she?" announced Manolo one day.

"In what way?"

"Bueno, she does like to drink a lot!"

"She is only having a good time!"

"She is very funny when she is tipsy but sometimes she has to leave work earlier because she has had too many drinks, and sometimes she drinks herself into oblivion and some of the GI's have to carry her out of the bar and make sure that she gets back to her apartment safely. You need to watch her!"

"OK".

I always kept my weekly appointments at the hairdressers. In fact I was very impressed with the way the Spanish hairdressers did my hair. They would put a huge hair roller at the crown of my head and then pull my hair around it while the rest of my hair they wrapped around my head in order to straighten it. They always left some of the conditioner in my hair as they spent time combing through every strand of my hair and then finally blow drying it. This was a treatment that was never done in London until a few years later. Sometimes I persuaded a guy to buy me some hair straighter from the base. I then applied to my hair myself. The times when I did not apply a mild relaxer to my hair or sometimes after having my hair done at the hairdressers and it happened to rain which was a rare occasion in Rota, my hair gleefully frizzed up again; such was its organic preference. One day at the hairdressers, I was surprised to bump into my sister. Sue was there with one of the Irish girls having her hair done.

"Your sister has got one head of hair. It's as thick as Elizabeth Taylor's.

She is so lucky because my hair is so thin." commented Sue's friend.

I looked at Sue who was by now under the hair dryer. I failed to recognise her at first because her face was virtually white. I looked at her more closely and then I noticed that she had white foundation powder that was caked onto her face. My sister looked utterly ridiculous because her hands were a deep brown, which showed off the deepening colour of her skin due to the sun but she had not noticed. She looked rather like a theatrical character, grotesque because she looked unreal and clownish.

"Sue, take that powder off your face, you look ridiculous," I hissed at her when I sat down beside her, to take my place under the next vacant hairdryer which had been allocated to me.

"What, I can't hear you," she shouted.

"Yes you can, look at your hands, and then look at your face, you look shocking."

"Oh shut up, Mandy."

I left the hairdressers feeling embarrassed and wondering what to do about Sue. She would never go out in the sun only when it was absolutely necessary and she often told me that Mama Sun had told her that the sun was bad for the complexion anyway.

"You must take your sister home, she is drinking far too much and why does she put so much powder on her face, does she want to be white?" Manolo asked me one evening after he had met me from work.

"Yes, you are right I need to take her home. I don't know if she wants to be white though but something isn't right. It's ludicrous, that she is applying so much white foundation on her face especially here in Southern Spain, where everyone cannot get down to the beach fast enough because they are so obsessive about getting suntans and darkening their skins," I replied trying not to sound upset.

"It's a pity because she is nice and very pretty too, but I don't understand her," said Manolo staring into his San Miguel bottle.

"I will book some train tickets tomorrow," I said finally accepting that the situation was desperate.

"Sue, we are going back to London as soon as I can book seats on the train to Madrid. We will change there and get the train to France and then the ferry to Southampton."

"Great, I am ready to go. I am getting home sick and besides I can't wait to see Sister Charlotte in Southampton, she has written me so many letters since I have been away."

"Yes I'd like to see Sister Charlotte too, you were so lucky to spend some time with her after all your problems in London particularly after you left the Sacred Heart Convent. She was so different to the other nuns; in fact you are right she is like your best friend."

"Yes, I told you she was my best friend. She has even sent me money while I have been here."

"I feel quite envious."

"She has invited me over to Ireland to spend sometime with her family so when I return to England she will make the arrangements."

"I have never had the opportunity to visit Ireland yet."

"I am sure you will one day and by the way I've got some news for you. You will never guess what, Julie Morgan told me in her last letter that social services have shut down the Sacred Heart Convent!"

"What do you mean, shut down the Convent?"

"What I mean is that the nuns can no longer look after the children because social services have discovered that none of them has ever had any formal training or qualifications to look after children!"

"How on earth were they allowed to look after children from broken homes in the first place?"

"It seems that there was a Lord, who was known as the Lord of Lee Green who was a strict Catholic and when he died he gave his mansion to the Sacred Heart Order so that the nuns could use it as their Convent, as their home in other words. It also appears that they originally started to take in orphans and abandoned children after the 2nd World war and they just continued with this practise until social services discovered only recently, that this was the tradition."

"Did you say that you were planning on going back to London by train soon?" inquired Mary who had interrupted our conversation.

"Yes that's right," I replied.

"Can I come with you, I think I need a break," asked Mary.

"Sure."

That night Manolo and I went to the April disco, which was on the road to Jerez. It was much more upmarket than the Blue Star and the Jerez elite visited it regularly since to the dee jay had many connections with the business families of Jerez. Many of the GIs went dancing there although a strict dress code was implemented.

"When will you come back?" Manolo asked.

"As soon as I have settled Sue," I replied.

While Manolo got up to go to get his cigarettes from his car, Antonio, the deejay came over.

"I heard that you are going back to London shortly."

"Hopefully tomorrow or the following day, depending on what dates are available for the train journey."

"You know this life working in a bar is no good for you, you should see it as only temporary, besides it's not a proper job, you should do something more with your life."

"Like what?"

"Go to college" replied Antonio.

"Maybe."

"Anyway have a good journey."

"Thank you."

On Sue's return to England, her cycle of drinking did not stop, even when she was employed as a chambermaid in one of the plush West End hotels. My sister was either late for her shifts or would not turn up for work at all due to a hang over. Eventually Sue could not hold down a job for any length of time and the white mask of face powder she now wore permanently. In fact the face powder became her face, her mask. I cannot exactly pinpoint my sister's final dissent into alcoholism. No doubt Sue had become completely dependent on alcohol misuse while in Spain although the signs were there before then. It did not occur to me that Sue had a substance misuse problem or that she desperately required professional help and treatment. Sometimes I visited her in her flat after finishing my foundation course in education at Holborn College. We talked about all sorts of things and laughed until we cried at some of the antics we got up to particularly when we were younger because whatever we had endured; Sue had a wonderful sense of humour. We also commiserated with one another when we talked about the times that had been so entirely wretched and the struggles for our self preservation; when we were made wards of court and assigned to the care system. There were times when I went to visit Sue only to find that her front door to her council flat was ajar. One time I went in to discover that one of her drinking partners was trying to sexually seduce her while she was out cold due to one of her daily drinking binges. He made a hasty retreat but Sue always defended him whenever I challenged her about his motives. She was dependant on him for her alcohol purchases. He knew that and manipulated her vulnerability. She simply could not deal with her demons because of the abuse she had been subjected to in one form or another throughout her childhood. The lack of understanding, care and emotional support that had been denied her had taken its toll.

"Do you remember my friend in Southampton called Adobea," asked Sue suddenly on one of the occasions she was sober enough to engage in a meaningful conversation.

"Of course I do, do you know that I have met up with her a few times since she has moved to London."

"Yes, you poached her from me because she used to be one of my best friends," joked Sue.

"She wants to come to Spain with me but I told her that I don't want to go back to Rota, I would rather travel to other countries whenever I can take time off from work and college."

"She had a hard upbringing too you know and isn't it a coincidence that she spent time a Convent in North London, rather than the one in South London."

"Yes, she told me that she has two younger siblings and that her mother rejected them all when she met her new husband."

"She has had two other children from him."

"I'm going to Ghana next week."

"Why are you going there?" Sue asked me sounding surprised.

"I want to see the country our father originated from." I replied.

"Well, he's did nothing for me apart from give me an African name that nobody can pronounce correctly."

"Never mind."

"I don't know why you want to go there for but I know that you like to travel."

"Yes I do, and now I want to travel to Ghana."

"See you when you get back."

"Yes and lay off the drink and foundation powder."

I've got a singing audition next week".

I looked at my sister sadly because I knew that she

would arrive at her audition drunk as she had done so many times before. The pity of it all was that she had a wonderful voice, which could have given any one of the professional soul singers a run for their money.

Zagba and I flew to Ghana the following week and arrived at Accra late at night. We stayed in the capital for a week visiting some of his friends, then we travelled on to the coast stopping at Tema and then on to Kamasi. One night we were travelling back after celebrating the twenty fifth anniversary of Ghana's Independence Day where we had been dancing to some superb traditional highlight music played by one of the local bands. The fire flies were magically lightening up the midnight skies like little Christmas lights as we watched them in awe.

"Is this your first visit to Ghana?" asked Adjoa, Zagba's sister.

"Yes," I replied.

"You don't have a Ghanaian first name," noted Adjoa.

"No, but my sister Sue does," I replied

"What's her name?" asked Zagba.

"Sod, dye," I responded.

"How is it spell?"

I spent my sister's name out loud.

"Oh, you mean So dy ee, that's the way it's pronounced," corrected Adjoa .

"What part of Ghana was your father from?" she continued.

"I believe he was from Tema and from the Ashanti ethnic community."

"I noticed that in your passport, your surname states you family name as Mensan, but I think that you will find that your surname or family name is Mensah, not Mensan," stated Zagba.

"You are right, because I was told by a dentist

recently who also happened to be Ghanaian, that my surname might be Mensah. I subsequently made some enquiries and my sister Sue told me that my mother had disclosed to her that the registrar who registers and issues birth certificates mistook the h for an n".

"So how long have you used the surname Mensan," asked Zagba.

"For most of my life and up until this passport expires. I shall definitely ensure that Mensah is printed in my next passport."

"If I were you I would enquire about having the incorrect surname changed immediately when you return to London."

"It makes immediate sense, I know!"

"So, will you?"

"Yes, I will."

"Promise."

"Yes. I promise."

We hailed a taxi after the celebrations and continued our conversation.

"There was a very famous Ghanaian warrior Queen known as Yaa Ashantewa who was from the Ashanti ethnic community: she led an army to fight against the British colonialist rule in the late nineteenth century and she was an extraordinary woman as well as a very brave one!" remarked Adjoa.

"You need to visit the slave castle at Cape Coast before you return to England," insisted Zagba.

"Did you know that Ghana has more slave castles and fortresses than any other African Country?"

"And in Cape Coast a thousand slaves were kept in tiny rooms where gutters were built to evacuate their faeces and urine and the stench can still be smelt today."

"Many black people in the diaspora are moved to tears when they visit the slave castles."

"A political, social, cultural and economic void was left in Africa because of slavery, given the loss of the enormous human and mineral resources which were plagiarised to build up Europe and the United States."

"There are so many struggles in life to overcome."

"As long as the yellow head picathartes can still fly, there is always hope." commented Zagba.

"I guess there must always be faith in one's courage," affirmed Adjoa

"Hear, hear," agreed the taxi driver as we crawled slowly up the very steep hill admiring the fire flies.

I am now back in England and watching the rain as it begins to fall on Sue's grave while I stand in front of it and reflect once more on her life. She never stopped abusing alcohol and the foundation powder became a permanent fixture to the extent that her natural skin tone on her face was never visible again. Sue was reduced to masquerading her emotional wounds which emanated from the white face make up she wore; which invariably was symptomatic of her traumatic state. Sometimes, her make up was expertly applied while at other times her make up was scary because of her lack of finesse in applying it due to her alcohol intake at the time. As I stand at her grave, I ponder on her life a little bit longer wondering what my younger sister's life could have been, if her circumstances had been different. Sue never disclosed to me directly but often implied that she had been sexually abused before she was placed at Miss Breen's care home. At least we were both reconciled with our mother after we had left the care homes which was a huge relief to both of us. I knew that Sue had never been kissed or cuddled while in care and the only time I was embraced was the few times when I was placed at Mrs. Gregory's. No one ever told us that they loved us apart from our mother when she wrote in our birthday and Christmas cards that she loved and missed us. After a few more lingering moments, I take my leave as I move away from her graveside; to walk on; to meet, the rest of the day.

Lightning Source UK Ltd.
Milton Keynes UK
UKOW04f0333181213

223237UK00001B/4/P